A Widow's Curse

By Phillip DePoy

THE FEVER DEVILIN MYSTERIES

The Devil's Hearth
The Witch's Grave
A Minister's Ghost
A Widow's Curse

THE FLAP TUCKER MYSTERIES

Easy
Too Easy
Easy as One-Two-Three
Dancing Made Easy
Dead Easy

A Widow's Curse

PHILLIP DEPOY

ST. MARTIN'S MINOTAUR NEW YORK

This is a work of fiction. All of the characters, organizations, and events portrayed in this novel are either products of the author's imagination or are used fictitiously.

 For information, address St. Martin's Press, 175 Fifth Avenue, New York, N.Y. 10010.

www.minotaurbooks.com

Library of Congress Cataloging-in-Publication Data

DePoy, Phillip.
A widow's curse / Phillip DePoy. — 1st ed.
p. cm.
ISBN-13: 978-0-312-36202-7
ISBN-10: 0-312-36202-1
1. Devilin, Fever (Fictitious character)—Fiction. 2. Folklorists—Fiction. 3. Mountain life—Fiction. 4. Appalachian Region, Southern—Fiction. 5. Georgia—Fiction. 6. Family secrets—Fiction. 7. Talismans—Fiction. I. Title.

PS3554.E624W53 2007
813'.54—dc22

2007010866

First Edition: July 2007

10 9 8 7 6 5 4 3 2 1

This book is for Lee, who took me to Barnsley Gardens,
both real and imaginary; and for Kristin and Diana, whose perfectly
combined collection of dogs and paintings is a continuing inspiration.
All three were essential to the process of this book because
it takes three women to ward off any hint of
a true widow's curse.

A Widow's Curse

One

What was left of the Barnsley estate rose into view at the hilltop. A full moon made the mansion skeletal, something from a grotesque animal more than remains of an antebellum home: a vision to match the story of its curse. A razor of wind cut across my fingers and kicked up leaves; I thought they might have been footsteps following behind me.

Moonbeams revealed a dwarfed boxwood maze that seemed to guard the entrance walkway. Winding through a rose-framed garden knot, the path to the front door was deliberately designed to slow the pace of anyone coming to the house. A visitor was forced to take more time, appreciating the grandeur of the house. A resident would have a moment to assess the visitor from behind an upstairs curtain, or inside a hidden shadow.

That small garden attacked the senses, even in the September night. The air was filled with black crickets' bowing, the funereal scent of white gardenias, the red noise of cicadas, and the blood of roses. A moldering angel at the center, head bowed, seemed to be weeping rust tears. Tall cleome and shorter cockscomb shivered in each gust of cold wind.

I stood staring up at the house, one more visitor the ghosts could evaluate, wondering how I'd gotten to that very black moment. The process of collecting folk stories, my own psychoarchaeological exploration of the collective ancient mind, could never have prepared me for such a circumstance. I found I was having a very basic ontological dilemma: Was I actually the man standing in this dark garden?

I began to imagine myself, instead, standing in the upstairs window of the derelict mansion, looking down on myself standing in the cleome. How did the man down there, I thought, get from his perfectly comfortable life to that desperate garden, wanted by the police, pursued by a murderer?

The idea that a single phone call from a stranger had transported me there seemed insane.

The schizophrenia of that moment made me shiver.

And with each shiver, I found myself recalling, one by one, the doomed events of the Barnsley family curse.

The Barnsleys lived happily for centuries in Derbyshire, England. The first American Lord Barnsley was Godfrey, a cotton magnate who amassed a great fortune in Savannah. By the late 1830s, his wife, Julia, could no longer tolerate the heat and flies on the coast. Godfrey determined to come up from the sea to the cool, clear hills of Cass County. That decision sealed their thorny fate.

Lord and Lady Barnsley had the misfortune to arrive at the site of their home just after the Trail of Tears.

Cherokee people, who had lived happily for centuries in those hills, had been forcibly removed from their land. Men, women, and children were herded a thousand miles under the orders of astonishingly indifferent military men. Over four thousand died, compelling the remaining Cherokee families to name their sorrow *Nunna daul Tsuny*—literally, "the Trail Where They Cried." Each tear that hit the ground, one story said, became a binding curse, contaminating all the land around it.

Apparently, the feeling was palpable to anyone who set foot on the acorn-shaped hill near the holy springs where Barnsley would build his stuccoed Italianate mansion. So much so that he was warned many times not to build on the site. But Godfrey was a man who had been warned not to come to America, not to plant cotton, and not to marry young Julia Scarborough—all of which he had done to great success. So build he did.

He called his home The Woodland: twenty-four rooms constructed at ridiculous expense. Even in the nineteenth century, the mansion enjoyed hot and cold running water and flush toilets. A copper tank near the main chimney furnished hot water to bathrooms, and another tank in the bell tower provided cold water to house and gardens. The wine cellar was, reputedly, the most extensive in America. Doors and paneling were fashioned by London cabinetmakers. Marble mantels were brought from Italy.

And when it was done, the fortune of the entire Barnsley clan had been tempered in hell.

Godfrey's infant son died in an upstairs bedroom; his beloved Julia succumbed to tuberculosis; their second daughter, Adelaide, passed away in the front room of the house. The eldest son, Howard, was killed by no less than Chinese pirates while on a mission for his father to find "amusing shrubberies" that would complete the family garden.

The Civil War destroyed much of the house and grounds: Furnishings were burned and Italian statuary was smashed by Sherman's troops, who were hoping to find hidden gold. All the china was broken; all the wine was drunk.

When the war's end brought no relief, Godfrey moved, by himself, to New Orleans in the hope of re-creating his fortune. He left son-in-law Captain Baltzelle and daughter, also a Julia, to manage the estate, but Baltzelle was killed in 1868 by a falling tree—a bit of inescapable irony, in that his plan to recoup the family fortune lay in timber sales.

Godfrey died alone and penniless in New Orleans in 1873; his body was returned to Woodlands and buried there.

In 1906, a tornado robbed the house of its roof.

By the end of 1942, the house and gardens were entirely hidden under a green blanket of kudzu, forgotten by everyone save the many spirits who inhabited it.

That, alas, was only the beginning of the curse—or at least the start of my part in it.

Early in the twentieth century, Godfrey's granddaughter had two sons. One grew up to become the nationally known heavyweight boxer who called himself K. O. Dugan. Unfortunately, he killed his brother, Harry, and was sent to prison for the rest of his life. The family had nothing. When his mother, last of the Barnsleys, died in 1942, the estate and its few remaining furnishings were to be sold at auction.

My great-grandfather, Conner Devilin, was then reported to have been "strangely compelled" to travel from our home on Blue Mountain to the more western Cass County in order to bid on several items of the Barnsley estate that he said were of "immense personal value" to him. This made little sense to the rest of the family, as they had never heard of the Barnsley estate, or family.

Conner had been born in Wales and apprenticed in Ireland before coming to America under dire circumstances of his own. He had narrowly escaped conviction and imprisonment for murder. He was a strong-willed man, and once he set his mind to a thing, the best course of action was, everyone knew, to stand well clear of him while he went about his task.

So he traveled to the Barnsley auction, successfully bid on three items, returned home, locked the items in a trunk, and never spoke of them again. When he died at eighty-six, his possessions were sold, and some of the money was used to pay for my university education. Because of him, I was able to escape my home place at seventeen, gain my doctorate, and grow to an adult in an urban environment far from my own parents' bizarre lives.

Was it only a few days ago that I came to realize that the inheritance was the beginning of my part in the Barnsley curse? It seemed like a year.

And the curse was apparently in fine working order: I was shaken from my reverie by the certain sound of footsteps rustling the leaves not far behind me.

Someone was following me in the darkness.

Two

The events that brought me to the Barnsley mansion had begun only a few days earlier, the first Wednesday in September. It had been unseasonably hot; humid air that usually stayed in the lowlands had decided to vacation in the mountains. Perhaps it hoped to catch an early turning of the leaves. But true autumn was well over a month away; tourists were still in shorts and T-shirts.

I was moving stones in my yard, under the illusion that my arrangement would be more pleasing than God's. It was two o'clock in the afternoon; I was drenched in sweat; I had huge purple bruises on my left arm. When the phone rang, I considered it a reprieve. The boulder I'd been muscling toward two others went rolling, slowly away, back to where I'd gotten it, and I limped toward the house.

My living room was dark. The sun outside was stretched in white sheets, blinding, from certain parts of the sky through breaks in the canopy of pines. For a moment as I went through the front door, I was blind. In retrospect, it was a clear omen, but that kind of cold warning goes unheeded in unseasonable heat.

I managed my way to the kitchen phone. The man on the other end began speaking before I could say hello.

"Is that Dr. Devilin?"

"It is."

"My name is Carl Shultz." He waited. "Do you know me?"

I took in a slow breath. Often a former student or someone else I had known in Atlanta would call me, and I hardly ever wanted to have the rest of the conversation. A student might be looking for a job recommendation; someone from the university might be calling from the fund-raising campaign: "As a former faculty member, your donation would . . . ," which is about as far as they'd get before I'd say something like "*Your* university closed down my department and sent me home, so I'm not entirely disposed to any sort of donation, thanks."

And to make matters worse, the man on the phone had a Yankee accent.

"I don't think so," I said hesitantly.

"Oh well." He offered a philosophical sigh. "It was really too much to hope for."

"What was?"

"My father," he said, as if that answered my question, "same name, bought this *thing* from someone up there in the mountains, and it's old and sort of folky in the Joseph Campbell sense. Don't you just love Joseph Campbell? I saw him on that television show. Anyway, I called around, and apparently you're the man who knows. So I thought maybe you'd tell me the name of the person he bought it from, or, if not, at least, I mean, you'd know what the hell it is. And second, of course how much is it worth. You understand. Mostly for insurance purposes."

I took a second to piece together his jagged diction.

"You have a piece of folk art from Blue Mountain?"

"I think it's older than that. I mean, and it's not *art* as I would call it. It's a coin, really. Or a medallion. They said at the university that you were the guy—"

"What's it made of, do you know?"

"Silver. Old silver. It's not dated, but the guy at this jewelry store said it was pure and, as I was saying: old."

"And someone in Blue Mountain sold it to your father?"

Despite my best efforts, curiosity's ugly pate reared up.

"About fifteen or twenty years ago. I believe it was a woman. Who sold it."

I stared out the kitchen window. I could actually see waves of heat rising from the granite stone I'd let roll away in the yard.

The primary reason I was engaged in such a useless occupation was hard to admit: I was bored. If Lucinda had been in town, of course, I'd have been at her house. She might have had me moving stones in her garden, but it would have seemed a more valuable enterprise. Solitary endeavor will always seem less productive than work contrived by two. Under most circumstances in my life, in fact, I would never have admitted idle curiosity, but it was the first part of September: I was hot, a bit lonely, and intellectually dehydrated. What harm could possibly come from asking a few innocent questions?

"Can you describe the images on the coin?" I sighed.

"It's some guy," he ventured. "I guess he's an angel or a saint—he has one of those halos around his head that looks like he has a big dinner plate glued to the back of his skull. You know the kind?"

"Sort of. Is he standing, sitting?"

"He seems to be leaning over a . . . kind of a bubbling spring, or a well, maybe."

"And the other side."

"A very ornate letter *B*. Nothing else."

Who in my little town would have owned such a thing? It certainly wasn't a product of the Georgian Appalachians. In the first place, most of the people who had come to settle in the hills around my home had been dogged Protestants. And they would have had precious little silver of any kind.

I had a brief thrilling thought that Mr. Shultz might have something in his possession that one of our families had brought to America from the old country.

Settlement patterns in Colonial Georgia were fairly easy to trace: most well-born Englishmen settled on the coast or in the lowlands; Scots and the Irish—a few Welshmen, came to the hills.

There was a time when I might have been able to trace any family in Blue Mountain back to their medieval clans in, say, Scotland, generation by generation. And the families here would still have songs and stories and ideas that were almost as old as those roots. In the twenty-first century, alas, most evidence of that sort was gone, gone for good. Plywood spec houses stood empty and waiting where two-hundred-year-old log homes once sat. Pop music blared from car radios in place of ancient fiddle tunes on the air.

If Mr. Shultz had somehow acquired anything with a genuine history, it would certainly be worth my time to investigate. Maybe I could even get a nice article out of it.

"Well, this *might* be interesting, Mr. Shultz," I said slowly, "but of course I'd have to see it."

"Oh my God, I'm really relieved to hear you say that," he shot back quickly, then lowered his voice as if he were sharing a secret. "Some of the people at the university said you'd be too grouchy to help me. Did I tell you I called the university to ask them about this?"

"They used the word *grouchy*?"

"I'd rather not say the exact word that was used," he hastened on; "the point is that I was led to believe you wouldn't care to help me."

I looked out the window again. I thought about going back into that heat. I thought about the reasons I was rolling boulders around like Sisyphus. My fiancée, Lucinda—and I was still getting used to *that* terminology—was in California. She wouldn't be back until the end of the month. My best friend, Skidmore Needle, the town sheriff, was in Birmingham, engrossed in a computer seminar that would revolutionize the crime-fighting world, or so his postcard had told me. I had absolutely nothing to do, no one to talk with, and there I was, about to turn down the only conceivable bit of interesting activity for the foreseeable future.

Sometimes any activity at all is better than inertia.

I was suddenly painfully aware of how I can crust over if I'm not doing anything. I get an angst roughly the size of Canada tangled in my aura. I wake up at three in the morning with nameless dread and stay awake until first light, then complain to myself about how tired I am by two in the afternoon. I worry about everything, and have vague neck pains that are probably a harbinger of cancer. I eat terrible food, and my stomach declares war on what little well-being I have left. Nothing is right. I can't do anything well. I pore over past foibles endlessly, emphasizing foul deeds; no accomplishment seems significant, no merit justified. Then nothing is any fun: Food is tasteless, music lifeless; every joy is gone.

"Mr. Shultz?" I croaked into the phone. "Why don't you bring your coin up here. I can see it firsthand and you and I can make some inquiries together, see if we can't find you some answers."

"You can't come to Atlanta?"

"Your father got the coin from up here. Here's where the answers are. And, P.S., you called *me*—so you have to come up here, right?"

"Right," he mused. "But I don't know."

It sounded for a moment as if he were consulting someone else in the room, mumbling with his hand over the receiver.

"Do you want to send it to me through the mail?" I prodded.

"God no."

"Well, I have to see it somehow, if you want me to try and tell you what it is."

He gave out a terrifically heavy sigh. "I could take a long weekend."

"There you are. And to make things easier, I'll get in touch with a friend of mine in Atlanta and he'll drive you up. You'll both stay at my place, we'll have an adventure, and you'll be back in Atlanta before you can say 'I can't believe I wasted all that time in the mountains.' "

"Lovely," he sneered. "You realize that if *I* hadn't called *you,* I'd think this was a con."

"The person you'll be traveling with is a bona fide college professor with an English accent and everything," I assured him. "Check him out, ask around all you like."

"What's his name?"

"Dr. Andrews, at my university."

"He doesn't have to teach?"

"He's on a Tuesday/Thursday schedule. He'll take tomorrow off and make a long weekend out of it."

"I don't know." Shultz had taken his mouth away from the phone again, consulting the other person there with him.

"Well"—I yawned—"decide soon. This is a whim on my part, and if you call back tomorrow, I'll probably have changed my mind again. I may even deny that I invited you at all."

I really couldn't say why I had insisted on Shultz's visit, but part of the thinking, obviously, was that it gave me an excuse to call Andrews.

Dr. Winton Andrews, Shakespeare scholar at my ex-university, was the last remaining good friend I had from my academic life. In fact, we had only recently returned from being in London together. He had directed a strange new version of *The Winter's Tale,* and for some reason he'd hired me to help him with the music for the production. He'd wanted authentic reproductions of folk music from Shakespeare's time instead of courtly, composed music—though that would have been easier to come by. I'd spent weeks in research, tracing song types, mostly ballads, back as far as I could, then inferring the rest; deciding on the perfect period instruments for the job; jotting down the most feasible melodies. I'd done most of the work at home, only spent a week in London, but I was able to see the opening-night production. It was quite impressive, and, apparently, a hit. But Andrews, of course, had been preoccupied with his work and we really hadn't *seen* each other in almost a year, not to relax and catch up—or drink heavily. So having him squire Shultz up to my place in Blue Mountain seemed a perfect plan all around.

After Shultz agreed to the trip, I arranged for him to meet Andrews at the university. I called and explained the situation to Andrews in detail, and asked him to take the scenic route up to my little town—which was also the slower way by about two hours. I thought it would put Shultz in the right mood, get him used to the pace of the mountains.

I did my part, first doing a bit of cursory research so I would have something to say to Shultz when he arrived and then, the rest of the day, dusting and airing out the bedrooms upstairs in my home, a more haunted enterprise.

Growing up, the three of us in my family had lived out our lives in separate bedrooms. Mine was a corner room, always so crammed with books that my father, angrily, changed all four walls into floor-to-ceiling bookshelves one day when I was at school.

"Fill all *that* up!" he'd growled.

I had, in about a week. There was only room for a double bed, an antique secretary that had belonged to my great-grandfather Conner, and a huge overstuffed armchair in the corner between two windows. Best of all, I had my own small bathroom in the other corner, more a concession to my father's desire for privacy than a convenience for me, but a delight nevertheless.

The oak tree outside had made a perfect ladder when I was younger, and I'd left the house by window and tree more often than I had through the front door.

My father's room, where Andrews often stayed, was a bit more spacious: a double bed there, too, but less clutter. It was across the hall from mine, and made the opposite upstairs corner of the house. The windows faced east, and morning light poured in after the autumn leaves fell every year. Pictures of family members crowded the walls, but the only other stick of furniture in the room was a trunk the size of a casket: all the tricks from my father's magic show stuffed into a box. He had earned his living with the things in that trunk, enough to keep a wife and strange child above the poverty level, clothed and fed most of the time.

When I was young and he was gone, I would often open that trunk and try to figure out what trick he could get out of, say, a red bandanna, a hoop made of copper, and a tiny dagger. Those particular items were in a wooden box marked ESCAPADE. I never learned what trick they were used for. Some things were less fascinating to a boy of eleven: an old pair of shoes, a packet of musty letters from strangers, a locked pair of handcuffs without a key.

Nearly everything in the trunk was absolutely baffling—just like my father. He might let a person see what was inside the box, but when he did, it proved to be as much of a mystery as the closed box had been. He even explained his tricks sometimes, but in such a way as to make them more astounding, more impossible to comprehend.

I investigated those mysteries in my father for two decades before I gave up, surrendering to the possibility that there was no explanation—or maybe that there was nothing there at all.

My mother's room, on the same side of the hall as my father's, where Shultz would stay, was the most haunted of the three. A single wrought-iron bed stood in the exact center of the room. The walls were covered with strange tapestries she'd said were from her family in "the old country," though in my presence, she had never been specific about which country that had been. The tapestries were faded. Some were woodland scenes; some might have been Bible stories. By the time I was interested enough to look at them closely, they had mostly faded beyond deciphering.

My mother had often kept fresh flowers on the sill of her only window—a box seat. By that window there was a worn leather chair, a floor lamp, and a footstool. As far as I could tell, they had never been touched, the chair unoccupied, the lamp never turned on.

The wooden floor was nearly covered by a thick Oriental rug, mostly golds and greens. The room was always dark and quiet, and had never been in the kind of disarray found in my bedroom. This was not because my mother had been more fastidious than I. Her bedroom had always been clean because she'd rarely stayed there. She'd usually stayed in someone else's bedroom, in someone else's home—first one, then another. Unlike most ghostly rooms, that room was haunted more by her absence than by the presence of any spirit.

So cleaning up the spare bedrooms was a jolly affair, as usual.

Summer air made the whole house musty, and there didn't seem to be relief in sight. Though I had conceded to most modern conveniences over the years, my cabin did not have air conditioning. With fans and open windows, the house might be cooled to a bearable level in the evening. To ensure greater comfort for my guests, I drove all the way to Pine City for new window fans to put in each bedroom. The dust churned up by these fans actually made the air in the house look foggy, even when I opened the windows upstairs and down.

There was little need to clean or even straighten up the first floor of my little cabin in the sky. I always kept it neat as a pin, in the great southern tradition: As long as the living room is clean for unexpected company, it doesn't matter what the rest of the house looks like. Alas, for me, the living room and the dining room, as well as the parlor and the kitchen, were all basically one big room. Bronzed oak beams framed the room. A larger-than-normal galley kitchen lay to the right as you came in the front door. A cast-iron stove had been set into the stone hearth to the left by a large picture window when I was a boy. Quilts on the walls suggested a stained-glass brightness; the staircase in the far corner led up to the bedrooms.

I gave the downstairs a quick inspection, then spent the rest of the day in research, hoping to be prepared for what Shultz was bringing me.

Around sunset, shortly after I'd remembered to shower and get into a nice black T-shirt and jeans, I heard a car pull up in the front yard. Two men emerged, both talking nearly at the same time, and loudly.

"Pure shite!" Andrews bellowed. "In a bucket!"

"You can say that all you want," the other man, presumably Shultz, answered pleasantly, "but I read the book and you have to at least acknowledge that some people in the world agree with me. I mean, I didn't make up this crap, right?"

I threw open my screen door and attacked the front steps.

"This moron," Andrews moaned to me before I could say anything, "thinks that Bacon wrote Shakespeare because somewhere one of the sonnets secretly spells out the word *pyg*—with a *y*!"

Andrews was dressed in his customarily inappropriate mountain-visiting costume: cutoff shorts, loud Hawaiian shirt, and tennis shoes.

"*Pig* with a *y*?" I was completely in the dark.

"Because where do you get *bacon*?" Andrews shouted.

Light dawned.

"From a pig." I turned to Shultz. "And you think . . ."

"*I* don't think anything," replied Shultz, correcting me. "I was just telling Dr. Know-It-All that the theory was, in fact, advanced by the Bacon family, and massively researched."

"*Dr. Know-It-All*," I said calmly, "least loved of the James Bond movies."

"You were right," Shultz said to Andrews, warming. "He does look a little like an albino."

Shultz had decided on the more ordinary flannel shirt, chinos, and hiking boots, expecting it to be colder than it was. His red hair was desperately receded and he was a bit on the heavy side, in his midfifties.

"Except for the eyes," Andrews pointed out. "He doesn't have albino eyes."

"You have to be Dr. Devilin," Shultz said, extending his hand to me.

"I suppose I have to be. I offered my hand, as well.

"And I must be . . . going to the bathroom," Andrews said, breezing by me, blond hair flying backward. "Did you know that the so-called scenic route to your little blue heaven is neither scenic nor much of a route, and takes almost twice as long as the way I usually go? I have to pee like a pistol."

And he disappeared into my house, leaving Shultz and me to complete our hand-shaking moment in silence.

"So," I offered at last, "need help with your bags?"

"Nope. Only got the one." He reached into the car. "I discovered once, on a trip to Europe, actually, that you generally wear the same pair of pants for, like, a week before changing. Two or three shirts that work with one jacket, two pair of shoes, enough clean underwear and socks, and everything I need for a month's vacation fits into this one light item."

He held up a battered leather travel bag only about twice the size of an old-fashioned satchel briefcase. The presentation came with a smile.

"Come on in, then," I said, and turned toward the house.

"Nice place," he told me, his voice softer. "Nice view."

"I grew up here" was all I could say.

Shultz followed behind me up the porch steps. The living room was already dark, so I went around turning on all the lights while Shultz stood in the doorway, uncertain what to do. We could both hear Andrews knocking around upstairs.

"Let me show you your room," I said suddenly, finally realizing that Shultz was waiting for me. "It's up here." I indicated the steps with a nod of my head.

"After you," he said cheerily. "I don't know where I'm going."

"Right." I almost jumped to the steps. "This way, then."

We were up the steps before Andrews was out of the bathroom. I stood to one side of the doorway to my mother's room. Shultz walked through it into the room.

Which was his mythological mistake, in fact: When you have a choice, you should never cross a threshold into the other world.

"Wow." He set his suitcase down. "Spooky room."

"What makes you say that?" I asked quietly.

He turned my way.

"I'm just the tiniest little bit psychic." He grinned. "Or so I've been told."

"And?"

"This room belonged to a woman." He looked around. "A sad person. A nun maybe."

I almost choked.

"It was my mother's room," I hastened to tell him.

I omitted the rest of the story, that my mother had slept with half the available men in the county when I was a child—and possibly more than half of the unavailable ones.

"So I was right." Shultz nodded triumphantly. "A woman."

I looked around at the flowery bedspread, the ornate bed, the slope of the chair by the window. A seven-year-old might have guessed that the room had belonged to a woman.

"You and Andrews share a bath, I'm afraid," I went on. "Across the hall, just there." I pointed.

"Great." Shultz lowered his voice. "Now, Andrews mentioned

something about a certain apple brandy. Went on and on about it. That's just the sort of thing that can take the sting out of a long trail ride."

"Don't start without me!" Andrews called, coming out of the bathroom.

"We could have a tiny libation now, if you like," I admitted, "but it's better after dinner."

"You're not going to believe this brandy," Andrews gushed from the hall. "Food of the gods."

"So dinner, you say," Shultz said uneasily. "It's not some—sorry, but it's not, like, hog belly and rutabagas or something, is it?"

"We could have that if you prefer," I told him, turning to go downstairs, "but what I have prepared is a nice peach-glazed duck breast over grilled chipotle polenta. We'll start with morels in lemon cream sauce, of course, and then move on to roasted acorn squash soup, finishing with a very thin apple tart."

"Which goes perfectly with the aforementioned brandy," Andrews chimed in.

"Am I dead?" Shultz said immediately.

"What?" Andrews shot back.

"Do you have any idea how much I love morels in cream sauce? And duck? It's my favorite food. I never in my wildest—am I dead?"

"Blue Mountain isn't heaven," I assured him over my shoulder, going down the stairs.

Behind me I could hear Andrews tell Shultz, "Reserve judgment on that until after your third brandy."

By the time I poured the third brandy, we had discovered that among the three of us, we knew everything there was to know. We were very happy with ourselves concerning our scope of knowledge. The homemade apple brandy, a secret family recipe, was just that good.

We were sitting on the front porch. The air had cooled nicely. The moon was up, dusting powdery white through all the impossible breaks and cracks in the black branches above us. The moonlight was soft but visible, even through the buttery interference of the five oil lamps I'd lighted and set on the porch.

Shultz was slumped down in his rocking chair.

"Boys," he said grandly, lifting his glass in our general direction, "the only thing better than making great new friends is spending time with the old ones. Here's to my experience of the first tonight, and my hope for the second in the not-to-distant future."

"Absolutely," Andrews agreed.

Andrews was sitting on the steps, shoes off, enjoying being cold.

I set my brandy down on the floor of the porch.

"But now it's time," I said, sobering just a little, "for a first look at the reason for our little gathering."

"Huh?" Shultz said, genuinely confused.

"Let's have a look at the coin," I urged him.

"Oh yeah. God."

He fished in his pants pocket, produced a manila envelope the size of a business card.

"You don't know the name of the person from whom your father bought the coin?" Andrews sipped.

"Nope."

"Do you know how much he paid?" Andrews went on.

"I believe he paid five thousand dollars," Shultz bragged, "which, twenty years ago, was a hefty sum for a dinky coin."

"Especially to someone here in Blue Mountain," I said.

"You're sure it wasn't closer to five hundred?" Andrews squinted. "You know how time can exaggerate things like this."

"I *know,*" Shultz agreed heartily. "But the insurance company who, well, insures it? They have in their files or something that it was purchased for five thousand dollars. I mean, I guess the old man might have been trying to pull a fast one—it wouldn't be entirely out of character for the guy—but wouldn't somebody at the insurance company have actually looked at the thing? I mean, would they just take his word?"

"I don't know," I confessed. "But it does seem like quite a bit of money."

"Well"—he lowered his voice again—"a story goes with it."

Often that sentence makes the difference between an inconsequential find and a significant artifact.

"Tell us the story," I said steadily.

A sudden gust of wind shifted grass outside, shook leaves, and the sheen of white on the granite rocks seemed to shiver a moment, hover just above the surface. It was a phenomenon I had heard called "the ghost dance." I didn't know the origin of the phrase, but it meant an early autumn.

"Apparently, this woman," Shultz began, unaware of the climate demon in my yard, "the one who sold the gizmo to my father? She was desperate."

"In what way?"

"Her husband had just died, and she was in dire economic circumstances. Dad always said she had the look of a, you know, witchy woman, like the song?"

"I don't know what song you mean—" I sighed "—but did your father discuss this business often?"

"Why do you ask that?" He was only curious.

"The phrase 'Dad always said' would seem to indicate a certain frequency."

"Say, that's pretty good. You should be a detective."

"So the story . . . ," I encouraged.

"Right. Dad said the woman was distraught. Then she got out the coin thingy, and she said it was very old, and it would bring him good luck. She said it was a *talisman.* I mean, who uses that word?"

"Did it work?"

"What?"

"Did the coin bring your father good luck?" I was mostly asking just to vex the man. "Or not?"

"He thought it did," Shultz said, not the least bit disturbed. "And he wasn't a particularly superstitious man."

There was a long silence.

"Go on," I prompted after what seemed like five minutes.

"What 'go on'? That's it. I thought you were thinking."

"That's the story?" I didn't bother to keep the irritation out of my voice.

"Yes."

"No," Andrews corrected him. "A story is: 'And he always kept the coin in his pocket, and that was about the time he began to amass his great fortune.' Or: 'He was looking at the coin in a restaurant one day, not long after he bought it, and it attracted the eye of a strange woman. And today that woman is my mother.' That sort of thing."

"Yeah," Shultz admitted, "that kind of thing would be a great story. But Dad was already rich when he bought the coin. And my mother was no miracle, I can tell you that. I assume you're familiar with the term *gold digger.*"

"In a somewhat more historical context, possibly," I said, "but you rarely hear it in the twenty-first century."

I moved to the oil lamp that was set on the railing by the steps and took the coin out of the envelope Shultz had handed me. I happened to pull it out on the side that contained the ornate capital letter *B.* It was very intricate, almost like the first letter of an illuminated medieval manuscript. There was a tiny hole in the coin at the top of the *B,* worn and almost closed by time, as if someone had worn it as a necklace long ago.

It was about size of an old silver dollar; I rolled it over in my fingers. The other side did indeed show a man, presumably a saint, bending over a well. The well was bubbling up, and on the horizon you could dimly see scores of people traveling toward the well, some on crutches, some in bandages, others being carried. It wasn't just any well. I was almost certain I recognized the image.

"Oh my God," I whispered.

Shultz sat up. Andrews turned my way.

"I'll have to go back to one of the books I was looking at earlier today," I began, "and maybe look at this thing under a magnifying glass—but I think this is an image of Saint Elian."

"Who?" Andrews stood.

"Saint Elian," Shultz said absently, as if he were somehow my translator.

"He was Welsh," I told Andrews. "And the well in this image—it's based on an actual place, a real well, in Wales. Let me think."

"This is amazing," Shultz leaned forward. "You really *are* the guy. One look and you know."

"I don't *know,*" I insisted. "And, as I was saying, I did some research this afternoon, or I wouldn't have remembered this story at all. It's really something of a coincidence."

"But—," Shultz began.

"Shh," Andrews told Shultz. "Let him remember the Saint Elian story."

I took in a breath.

"I wouldn't know anything about this at all, really, except for my old mentor, Dr. Bishop. He was fanatical about Welsh stories."

"God, there's a story: Dr. Bishop," Andrews whispered to Shultz.

"Shh," Shultz said, his tone only a little mocking, "let him remember the Saint Elian story."

"I think it was in the fifth century," I began slowly, "that Saint Elian was traveling the hills of Wales, above the coast where Colwyn Bay is today. He was very tired, thirsty, but there were no settlements around. He was a man of great faith. He prayed to God for the barest of necessities: a warm night and some fresh water. As his prayer ascended to heaven, a pure spring bubbled up from the ground at his feet. Elian thanked God, and the night turned soft. The saint drank, spent the night there, and then moved on, but the well remained and soon became famous for its powers."

"Like Lourdes," Andrews interrupted.

Crickets, tree frogs, bats were all beginning to sing.

"Not exactly." I stared down at the coin. "The power of Elian's Well was used for darker purposes. Most people went to the well to make curses on someone who had offended them. It was a booming business, in fact, by the seventeenth century. People would pay large sums to the keeper of the well, a priest or a monk in charge of the water, to curse other people. Then, of course, the keeper of the well would let it be known to the curse victim that he had been done in, and he'd go to the well himself to ask the monk to remove the curse."

"Which he would happily do for a *larger* fee," Shultz guessed.

"Exactly," I confirmed.

"Maybe this coin was minted," Andrews said excitedly, "by some clever Welsh entrepreneur for people to use in curse payments or curse removals!"

"You said it was a real place," Shultz whispered. "Is this well still there, in Wales?"

"Sort of," I said, slowly remembering. "The well was filled in, or at least covered over, during the nineteenth century. Apparently, the cursing got out of hand."

"So this coin is, you think, Welsh?" Shultz asked, sipping more brandy.

"I couldn't say for certain," I told him, "but silver *was* the primary incentive for expanding the Welsh mining industry in the sixteenth and seventeenth centuries. I seem to remember something about the mines in Wales producing a significant amount."

"Of silver?" Shultz set down his glass.

"That's right." I flipped the coin over again and stared down at the *B.* Why did it seem to be telling me something?

Shultz stood up.

"This is great!" he said a little too loudly. "Scary mountain cabin, silver coin from Wales, magic curse water—and it's almost autumn. I got a valuable objet d'art, a cracking mystery, and two new friends. Am I the luckiest son of a bitch in the world or not?"

Shultz bent over to pick up his glass, immediately hit his elbow against the arm of the rocking chair, knocked it sideways. He dropped his glass, took an uncertain step backward, and tumbled down hard on his side.

Andrews exploded with laughter, and even Shultz himself saw the humor in the moment—to his enormous credit.

"I'm going to need *lots* more of that brandy." He grinned up at me, rubbing his sore elbow.

Looking back on things, of course, we were witnessing the dark beginning of something wicked coming our way.

You can cover a well if you want to, but the water doesn't disappear—it just goes somewhere else, underground.

Three

The next morning, with somewhat clearer heads, we began our investigation in earnest. We'd slept in. The sun was tall, higher than the pines. The kitchen was bright and the scent of fresh whole coffee beans filled the room. We all arose at around the same time. And when we did, we seemed to want to plunge into the riddle right away—but each in his own way, as if we were some sort of odd, circus-based research team.

I'd been the first up, setting the espresso machine and yawning. Andrews had come bounding down next, wanting to know when breakfast would be ready. Shultz was last up, brow wrinkled and wincing—apple brandy had obviously taken its toll on the man.

I was in black T-shirt and jeans once more; Andrews, barefoot, had donned a bowling shirt and baggy shorts; Shultz had dressed up: slacks, polo shirt, penny loafers.

I'd found a few slim books on Welsh folk motifs and stories in my bookcases. In one, we found the tale of Saint Elian, some pictures of the well as it existed in 1945, the publication date of the book. I had remembered most of the story correctly, though the book, called *Ruined Wales,* had strong anti-Catholic sentiments that clouded the tale for me.

For several hours, the three of us sat in my kitchen, strong slanting light pounding the wooden tabletop and darker wooden floor, reading silently, sipping espresso.

"Here's something," Andrews mumbled.

He had opted for a volume of Welsh history.

"It says here," Andrews went on sleepily, not looking up from his book, "that metal mining in what used to be the county of Cardiganshire dates to the Middle Bronze Age."

"How long ago is that?" Shultz asked me.

"About four thousand years," I said.

"It was copper first," Andrews droned on, "and archaeologists have discovered some mining evidence as far back as the Roman occupation."

"We're not really looking for a history of mining," I began.

" 'Silver,' " Andrews continued, reading from the book, " 'greatly expanded the mining industry in the seventeenth century. *So much so* that in 1637 a mint was established at Aberystwyth to coin locally mined silver and was active into the 1640s and the First English Civil War.' " He looked up. "Then it goes on about something called the 'Mines Royal Acts' and how the whole silver thing was over by the late 1800s."

I set down my book.

"A mint in Aberystwyth," I repeated. "Nice work, Andrews."

"You mean you think—," Shultz began.

"It just sets up the possibility that the coin was minted there," I interrupted. "I think there are probably collectors or museum people who could tell us right away if we're on the right path."

"I brought my laptop," Andrews yawned, closing his book. "I'll make inquiries."

"Don't be too specific," I said quickly.

"And don't say that you have this coin," Shultz added.

Andrews leaned forward, eyes clearer.

"I'm not an idiot," he intoned. "I just dress that way."

"I was just reading about the gold mines in Dahlonega," Shultz said, leaning back in his chair, holding up a brochure that had been stuck in one of my books. "Turns out there was a mint there between 1838 and 1861. They had all kinds of gold, which was the main reason the Cherokee were forced out. The name of the city comes from the Cherokee word *talonega*, which literally means 'golden.' "

"Could that be anything?" Andrews turned to me. "Maybe the coin isn't Welsh after all. Maybe it was minted there, and that's the reason someone in Blue Mountain would have it."

"No." Shultz consulted his pamphlet. "Says here they only minted gold coins, and only in four specific denominations. They closed the whole thing down after the Civil War, so apparently the coins are quite prized today."

"So where are we?" Andrews sniffed.

"Didn't someone mention breakfast awhile back?" Shultz prompted.

"Miss Etta's?" I suggested.

I had not completed the upward inflection of the question before Andrews was on his feet.

"You're not going to believe this place," he gushed to Shultz. "I could live there."

"You could die there if you eat the way Andrews does," I warned Shultz.

"What kind of food is it?" Shultz seemed a bit nervous. "Is *this* going to be a hog jowls and rutabagas place? I can't eat that stuff."

Andrews was already out the front door.

I glanced at my watch.

"Well, it won't be breakfast," I called after him. "Not at this hour."

Miss Etta's place was crowded when we arrived, only a little after 11:00 A.M. Few tourists had ventured near the place; every face inside was familiar to me. The storefront facade still had a hint here and there of the gold-leaf lettering that had once said HORTON'S PHARMACY—though Dr. Horton had died in 1927. Toward the end of the Great Depression in the Georgia mountains, Miss Etta, then a married girl in her early teens, opened up her eatery. A hand-painted sign still hung behind the cash register, once having informed the people in Blue Mountain that they could have GOOD FOOD FOR A NICKEL.

The price had gone up steadily since 1943, and Miss Etta's no-account husband had long since run off. She'd had the marriage annulled, kept the diner, and become as much of a fixture in our town as the ancient trees around the courthouse or the strange high rock outcropping called the Devil's Hearth, which you could barely see from her establishment in the winter months—and then only if you had a window seat and knew where to look.

Without trying at all, Miss Etta had become an old woman, and her food had been perfected over the course of six decades, fired in the culinary ovens of the gods, until miraculous alchemy had arrived in her linoleum kitchen. Simple boiled squash and onions had achieved a golden color, a sublime texture, and a flavor unmatched in the five-star temples of Paris. Fried okra had a crunch, a saltiness, and an independent character that ensured it would stand up to any conversation it might have with yellow squash. Catfish, always fresh-caught by local boys, was utterly without a hint of the oil in which it had been fried, tasting like sifted sunlight on transparent mountain streams. Each bite of every dish was so much more than food: It was an experience of pristine nature, the touch of an angel's hand, a hint of the original garden that fed us all before the fall from grace. And all for six dollars, including sales tax.

I opened the door and let Andrews and Shultz go ahead of me. Everyone in the place gave invading strangers the once-over, but when I stepped in behind them, most people nodded. Everything was all right: The strangers were with that odd Devilin boy.

The inside of the place was nothing special. A startlingly eclectic assemblage of tables and chairs cluttered the room; an old counter left over from the pharmacy's soda fountain lent a few extra spaces for sitting. Walls were covered, haphazardly, with sixty years' worth of taxidermied fish, children's drawings, and photos of smiling faces that now lived only in memories. The floor was worn, the lights were too bright, and the crowd was noisy. It was heaven.

"Now the trick here," Andrews explained to Shultz, "is to take the biggest plate you can find and get as much variety on your plate as possible."

Shultz was at sea.

"You have to get your own plate." I pointed to a stack of mismatched plates beside the cash register at the far end of the long yellow counter. "You take it back into the kitchen and dish up the food yourself from anything and everything on the stove. You can fill your plate as much as you want, balance the cornbread on top. It's one price for everything. You come back for the sweet tea, but you can't go back for seconds of anything."

Shultz nodded, eyes darting here and there, as if he were in a foreign country, struggling to assimilate the strange customs of the natives. He watched Andrews and copied him exactly.

Miss Etta was, as usual, dozing in a ladder-back rocking chair behind the cash register. Her perennial cardigan sweater and shin-length dress were customarily brown. Her hair was in a bun, but a good deal of the hair had come loose and made a sort of gray haze around her head—almost like a halo.

The kitchen was stifling, but the air was rich, flavored with cooked onions, sage, sweet roasting corn husks. The ceiling was barely six feet high, the walls were black with smoke; the floor actually had ruts in the wood where thousands and thousands had walked before.

Shultz put everything on his plate exactly as Andrews did, and the two of them had created a culinary sculpture, topped with a golden triangle of cornbread, that threatened to capsize with every step they took.

I took the road less traveled. With a conveniently placed oven mitt, I fetched an ear of corn from the oven. It had been roasted in its husk and was hot even through the mitt. I carefully peeled back the husk and tore away most of the corn silk, burning my fingers a little, and threw the husk into a paper bag already filled with a dozen others.

Next: greens. Miss Etta used a combination of greens, the exact description of which was a secret she would one day carry to her grave. She swore, when forced to talk about it at all, that most of the leaves were turnip greens, but some might be wild greens she gathered from the fields around her house. The result, whatever the ingredients, was a dish unlike anything anywhere else on earth. The flavors were a balance of sweet and salty, sharp and soft, rich and clean. I put them in a bowl, because the liquid in which they were cooked was to be soaked up with cornbread, which was, in fact, the reason God invented cornbread at all.

Finally, I turned to the catfish. Huge filets sat on a rack, crisp, dry, their color that of sunbeams in deep woods. Beside them, Miss Etta had made her concession to incessant public outcry: a white porcelain bowl filled with tartar sauce, another insulted by catsup. I eschewed both as a minister would a sinner, and made straight for the cornbread.

Andrews and Shultz had found a wobbly table in the corner and were already eating when I emerged from the kitchen. Andrews's fork was moving almost faster than the eye could see.

I made my way toward them, but I was momentarily stopped by a sudden crack of thunder. Everyone in the place jumped. The sky was still bright, the clouds were high and white, and the temperature was creeping toward the mideighties.

"What was *that*?" Shultz managed to say between bites when I sat down.

"Autumnal weather up here," I explained, setting down my plate, "can be unnerving, especially this time of year. I've been in this very diner before when the air went from a balmy eighty-one degrees to a sprinkling of snow in the time it took for me to eat my lunch."

"No." Shultz rejected my reportage. "You exaggerate."

"I do not," I insisted.

"It can happen." Andrews took a single breath to support me, then returned to his more noble work destroying mashed potatoes.

"It's going to snow?" Shultz peered out the window at the sky.

"Not necessarily," I told him, staring down at my catfish. "But something's going to happen."

We finished the rest of our meal in relative silence, each of us reluctant to spend valuable eating time in idle conversation.

By the time our plates were empty, the sky was black. Half the crowd had cleared out, most talking about the weather as they left.

Shultz had pushed his plate away from him on the table, the ancient ceremonial gesture of gustatory satisfaction, and was leaning back in his bentwood chair.

"Well, boys," he said grandly, "I have to tell you that I love this place."

"I told you the food was amazing." Andrews wiped his lips with the back of his hand.

"No, I don't mean just this diner." Shultz waved his hand in the direction of the street. "I mean the whole shebang. The cabin, the town, the hills—love it all."

"Don't hear the word *shebang* in these parts a lot," Andrews teased, amused. "You're not from around here."

"Look who's talking, Ivanhoe," Shultz countered.

"Ivanhoe? Seriously?" Andrews's eyes were bright. "That's what you went with?"

"It was the first Limey thing that came to mind. I hated reading it in high school." Shultz shrugged. "As it happens, I was born on a farm in Iowa. So while my accent may be a little different from the folks *in these parts*, the background is a whole lot more similar than you might think."

"Not many farmers get rich in Georgia," I said thinly. "You're clearly of a wealthy family."

"Well, you've got me there," he admitted. "Dad didn't make much money farming. But he was kind of a lucky man, as I think I've mentioned. He invented a sort of artificial pig testicle. And, as it turns out, there was actually a demand! Who knew?"

Andrews exploded.

"Artificial *pig testicles*?"

"I'd rather not talk about it right after lunch, if you don't mind," Shultz said, his voice lowered. "He was having trouble with one of his hogs, he got an idea, and we got rich; here we all are."

"No, no, no," Andrews insisted. "I need details, many details of this phenomenon. You're heir to a pig-testicle fortune."

"No details now." Shultz was stone. "Maybe later."

"At least you have to tell me how you got from Iowa to Atlanta," Andrews insisted.

"Dad invented the thing, we moved to Georgia because that's where he got the best manufacturing deal, and I ended up in Westminster by the time I was fourteen. Now I live more or less at my leisure. Except that I'm on, like, a hundred boards of directors and stuff."

"Westminster? Is that the chichi private school on the north side?" Andrews quizzed me.

"That's right," Shultz replied. "When I was there, we had to wear uniforms and everything. I don't know if they still do that."

"I *have* to hear more about the hogs," Andrews pressed.

"Maybe we'd better think about getting back to the cabin," Shultz said, tilting his head toward the street.

It was beginning to rain outside, and it was so dark, I couldn't see the far end of the block.

"Good call, I think." I stood. "Lunch is on me."

Before anyone could object, I strode to the cash register, opened it myself, and put in a twenty-dollar bill. Tipping wasn't customary, but I always left a little extra. I could never tell if Miss Etta even noticed.

She did come to life enough to smack her lips when I closed the register.

"Thanks, Dev," she said, eyes still closed. "Got company?"

"You might remember my friend Andrews," I said softly. "The other guy—"

"I don't need to know your business," she said, interrupting. "Just noticed, that's all. It'll turn cold tonight. Got you some wood for a fire?"

She pulled her cardigan around her neck, still not opening her eyes.

"Yes, ma'am," I assured her, smiling.

"All right, then." She shifted in her rocker and, I thought, went back to sleep.

Andrews and Shultz were standing at the door; the place was nearly empty. Outside, the sky was a swirl of charcoal and soot. Heavy rain began to blast the cars, the street, the window of the diner.

Shultz turned to Andrews.

" 'When shall we three meet again,' " he whispered. " 'In thunder, lightning, or in rain?' *Macbeth,* right?"

"Well, yeah." Andrews glared at Shultz as if he'd been insulted.

"I'm not stupid," he countered, "I'm just from Iowa."

"Okay," Andrews said quickly, "but you know it's bad luck to say the actual name of that play out loud."

"It is?" Shultz was genuinely baffled.

"I thought that was just if you were in a theatre," I objected, joining them at the door.

"Look," Andrews said, grinning, "this eating establishment is every bit as much a theatre as any auditorium or black box or grand stage. It is to me anyway."

" 'All the world's a stage,' " Shultz chimed in happily.

"Stop it," Andrews demanded, laughing.

"You're not the only guy who ever read Shakespeare," Shultz assured us. "You're not dealing with a jerk, you know."

"All right." Andrews shook his head. "But you'll have to go outside now, turn around three times, and spit."

"Not for a thousand dollars," Shultz replied, opening the door.

"Fine," Andrews warned, mock-serious. "But don't blame me when the worst happens."

We piled through the door and made a dash for my big old green truck. Low thunder rumbled from every corner of the sky, and the rain was falling so hard, it actually hurt when it hit my arms.

We crowded into the truck, soaked.

"You've been quieter than usual this luncheon, Dr. Devilin," Andrews teased me. "Something on your mind?"

"Something." I turned on the headlights. The wipers were going a mile a minute, and I still couldn't make out anything six feet in front of me.

The road ahead was impossible to see.

Four

Black asphalt seemed to color my mood. Rain's good for melancholy introspection, and the more I thought about Shultz's coin, the more I sank into dark thoughts. Andrews sensed it, and he didn't pursue his question further.

I tried to occupy my thoughts by considering, then discarding, more than a dozen people in Blue Mountain who might have owned our so-called Saint Elian's coin. It seemed unlikely, in all that rain, that anyone here could ever have acquired such an arcane artifact. Then I spent the rest of the drive home trying to put my finger on the psychology behind thinking that rain made the possibility more remote. I was actually startled when my headlights illuminated the front porch of the cabin.

"I'm dropping you two off," I said absently, pulling close to the front door. "I'd like to ask around about the coin, and I might as well get started. It's something I really have to do alone, Shultz. Andrews can tell you that everybody in Blue Mountain knows more than they will ever tell you, but they'll never talk around strangers."

"And even the simplest fact is guarded," Andrews affirmed. "I'm for a nap."

Shultz nodded. "Well, I'm counting this weekend as a vacation. So this is good to me. I'll sit in the cabin, watch a little television, take a nap myself; look at the rain."

"All right, then." I stopped the truck a foot from the front steps.

Shultz bounded out and onto the front porch.

"Hey," he called, "how do we get in?"

"The door's not locked," Andrews told him. "Can you imagine that?"

"Not locked?" Shultz glared at the front door as if Andrews had lied about it.

Andrews, his hand on the truck door, about to get out, lowered his voice.

"Seriously, are you all right, Fever? You seem—I don't know—moody. I mean, more so than normal, which, we'll admit, is going some."

"I don't know what's the matter with me. But you're right: I am having a moment."

"Is it about the coin?"

"Maybe. Something I can't put my finger on about this whole thing."

"Well." Andrews slid out of the truck. "You'll uncover it. If the unexamined life if not worth living, your life is worth a billion dollars. I don't know anybody who broods about himself as much as you do."

"I'm not good-looking enough to be described as *brooding,*" I informed him. "I am *introspective.*"

"Potato/potato," he replied, pronouncing both exactly the same.

He slammed the passenger door and was almost into my house before I got the truck in gear.

I headed for the home of June and Hezikiah Cotage. Surrogate parents, elder teachers, folk resources—there really wasn't a facet of my life in which they weren't involved. Half of the traditional songs I had collected in the old days had been from June. All of the historical accounting of sacred harp music in Appalachian Georgia had come from Hek, a minister in his own church. June had always helped me when, as a child, I had been in turmoil about my mother's public infidelities or my father's private strangeness. Hek continued to provoke in me a sense of wonder about the spiritual content of everything in the universe—a red leaf, a shed snakeskin, the placement of three smooth rocks in a riverbed.

Between them, they also represented the greatest single source of gossip in the state.

Whenever the phrase "I don't like to say this" occurred in a conversation with either of them, I knew that something juicy was soon to follow. If they knew anything about a desperate widow selling a strange coin to an Atlanta slicker, it would take only a bit of prying and subterfuge to get it out of them.

Although it was not a long drive to their place from mine, the rain made it take longer than usual. Andrews had prodded something in my psyche that wanted attention, so I was driving slower than usual, as well.

I had barely turned my mind's eye to the troubled spot when a monstrous self-doubt leapt out of it, black and scaly, eyes red, and landed like a hulking demon on the seat beside me. It stared at my profile while I tried to keep my eyes on the road.

It whispered all the things I didn't want to hear. It started by telling me I couldn't be very bright if I didn't know anything about the biggest folk artifact in my own hometown's history. If all I could think to do was to run to my substitute parents, I couldn't be very much of an adult, either. And anyway, they weren't my real parents. My real parents were dead, and even if they'd been alive, I couldn't have gone to them for help, because they had never exhibited the slightest desire to help me with anything. All I could do was guess and rely on other people's research. And I was interested only because I was bored. I wasn't really a folklorist at all: dismissed from a university, a crackpot in his own hometown, and unable to care much about anything or anyone.

It was, alas, a familiar downward spiral, and one that happened all too often, but I was dealing with a particularly vile species of the well-known poisonous creature that caused it.

The demon on the seat beside me took my hand and encouraged me to veer the truck off the road.

The road was a black scar on the rain-blurred landscape. On either side, a smudged verdance ran in the gray rain. The sky was coal smoke; the air had little teeth that bit away any light that pried its way through the clouds. And when the road curved left, I had a sudden impulse to veer right, onto the charcoal air, down into the vague green valley.

But just as the thought was filling my mind, a white streak of smoke cut the sky, a thin pillar from the Cotages' chimney. Even in the early-autumn heat, rain meant a fire to Hek and June. Their house was just around the bend.

The merest sight of that smoke made the demon vanish—not forever, but for the moment at least. I imagined that cleaning my parents' rooms had called it forth, the Parasite of Doubt. It was a monster I fed daily, of course, but family memories most often drew it from its cave.

I was, in short, tremendously glad to see Hek and June's front door. Their white house was set in black soil between three mountains. Anyone driving by could see it was better kept than the other homes along the same road. Everything about the place showed God's attention to detail, as Hek always said: the evergreen clematis vine that twined the front railing, the laurel whose tiny flowers filled the air with swooning perfume, the bloodred daylilies. The porch was always crowded with bees, but they never stung. They were too intoxicated. A few minutes on that porch were enough to have the same effect on a full-grown man.

June appeared in the doorway before I was up the steps to her porch. I was always surprised to find her hair gray: it was so auburn in my memory. I knew her, it seemed, in several times at once. I knew a woman without wrinkles, despite all the evidence to the contrary on the smiling face in the doorway. I saw, simultaneously, her gingham skirt, a navy blue suit, and the long gray dress she was wearing as she waved to me. I could see her move quickly, like a dancer, even though I knew her joints were less agile than that. It was a comforting sensation, seeing June in a temporal blur, a hazing of linear moments exactly matching the way rain obscured the sky. Our relationship did not exist so much in a progression of moments as in a collection of experiences that could happen in a single expanded *now.*

"What's the trouble?"

She held the door open for me. We did not embrace; there was no meaningful eye contact; her voice was not flooded with the compassion that I knew lay beneath the words.

In my family, my town, emotion is a deep well that is most often covered over with great rocks and dead leaves—and years of silence.

But we know it's there.

"I have a few questions for you," I told her, "things you might know about."

"I don't mean that." She closed the door. "Go on in the kitchen. I'm talking about the reason your face looks gray."

"Oh, that." I headed for the kitchen.

Junie's kitchen was one of the models that certain religions use to describe the afterlife. It was always bright and warm, the air filled with smells that provoked immediate joyous emotion. I had seen people burst into tears walking into her kitchen; I'd done it myself. Something about the absolute peace, the perfect comfort, the sense of care, the satisfaction of home—something about an all-encompassing love made her kitchen heaven. It was small, and the counters were Formica. The wooden floor had been covered over by a "modern" linoleum sometime in the late 1960s. Everything was obsessively clean. The chrome percolator was almost blinding and had to be over fifty years old. The things in her kitchen didn't matter. The room was made supernatural by the daily presence of June's spirit, the years of creating food that surpassed physical sustenance, the long hours of conversation and consolation that had transpired there.

And the little moments of perfection.

"You been thinking about your mama again." She brushed past me. "You need apple cake."

There it was: June's eerie grasp of my emotional interior. The fact that she could tell I'd been roiling my head in family recollection was surpassed only by the precisely accurate solution in the form of apple cake.

June's apple cake was made primarily, as far as I could determine, from some sort of edible gold and solar extract. Apples were also included. Beyond that, the precise formula was never revealed.

I sat at the kitchen table, in the exact middle of the room. She somehow produced a piece of cake, a cup of coffee, a fork, a linen napkin, and a glass of milk in one continuous movement. Then she sat with me.

"I have company," I managed around a mouthful of cake. "You remember Andrews."

"English boy," she acknowledged.

"He brought a Mr. Carl Shultz with him. From Atlanta."

I waited.

"I see." She blinked. "You had to get the rooms ready for company, and that put you in mind of your parents, and that made your face gray."

"In a nutshell."

"When are you going to let them go?" She folded her hands on the table in front of her. They were veined and the knuckles were prominent, the fingers a bit bent, but they were steady.

"Well, I think they're gone," I said, continuing to shovel bites of cake into my mouth, "but then something happens, and there they are again."

"The living surely do haunt the dead," she concluded. "Lots more than the other way around."

She was right, of course. My parents were gone. Their ghosts came around the house less and less as the months rolled on. They didn't visit me of their own volition. I called them.

I finished the last bite of cake and pushed the plate away from me.

"So the name Carl Shultz," I said, deliberately changing the subject, "doesn't mean anything to you."

"No."

"Well, his father, same name, bought a silver coin from someone here in Blue Mountain about twenty years ago. She's described as a 'desperate widow,' which only makes this whole scenario more improbable. But I've seen the coin; it has a picture, I think, of Saint Elian, a Welsh saint, on it. It's quite valuable."

I had intended to continue telling her all the details, but her face had changed so much that I stopped talking.

She withdrew her hands, put them in her lap, hidden under the table. She looked out the kitchen window at the rain and began to rock back and forth ever so slightly.

"Hek." The volume of her voice startled me.

"Hek's home?"

"He was taking a nap. Good weather for it. But I believe he'll want to hear this mess."

"What is it?" The old man was not entirely awake.

"Fever's here. Come on in the kitchen."

"Fever?" The cocoon of sleep had not yet given way.

"Come in this kitchen!" June's voice was uncharacteristically impatient.

Hek knew, better than I, what it meant. He appeared in the door frame seconds later. White hair exploded in every direction from his head and his white shirt was a crumpled piece of paper. His work pants were clean; so were his socks.

"Sorry." He gave me a curt nod. "I was napping."

"Fever's got a question for us." June wouldn't look at anything but the glistening top of her kitchen table.

"You don't ever come by just to visit?" Hek creaked his way to the percolator.

"I wouldn't want to interrupt your nap time unless it was important." I did my best to keep the corners of my mouth from turning upward.

"I get up at four in the morning," Hek announced, grabbing a coffee mug, his back to me, "work the fields, tend the garden, do the chores, and preach on the constancy of sin, *all* before breakfast! I only came inside when it started raining."

I nodded. In the first place, I knew what he said was true, and in the second place, Hek took a nap every day at about one o'clock in the afternoon, though he always denied it with great vehemence, because he thought it gave an impression of sloth.

"Fever's asking about a piece of silver, a coin that some widow woman sold up around these parts," June interjected.

"Huh?" Hek was still fighting off the notion that he took naps.

"About twenty years ago, some woman had a valuable silver coin that she sold." June pronounced each word with supernatural clarity. The sound was sharp enough to cut hard wood.

Hek froze—only for a moment, but it was enough to tell me he understood what was beneath the actual words that June had said.

"Oh." He sighed, poured coffee, and did not turn my way.

I knew better than to press them at that moment. They were reluctant to reveal something; trying to decide how much to tell me, how much to hide. Any attempt to coax them would only make the process more difficult, could render it impossible. When I was younger, I had tried everything I could think of. But like trying to entice a turtle to show its head or a shy child to answer any question, nothing could budge the immovable—not anger, or pleading, not even a gentle bribing that passed for reasoning.

The only key to a locked secret was silence, and a patience I had barely acquired over the course of agonizing years.

So I sat, staring at Hek's back, counting each exhaled breath. The rain drummed on the tin roof and the eaves dripped. Distant thunder whispered over the hills. I could hear the clock on the mantel in the parlor clicking away seconds as intensely as the blood thumped my temples.

"Well," Hek said suddenly, turning my way, "some things you bury, forget, and you think they're gone. I haven't thought about that night in a good long while."

"I don't believe it would ever come to my mind at all," June agreed, "if Fever didn't dig it up."

"*That night*?" I heard myself say.

"I made a promise, boy," Hek growled. "I can't say a thing about it. Sorry."

I fought an impulse to rip the table in half, *mostly* because I knew he wasn't finished. Maybe he'd tell me right then, or maybe he wouldn't, but he had much more to say on the subject.

"A promise is a promise." He sipped his coffee, leaning back against the countertop.

"You know we'd tell you if we could," June added.

Even after a lifetime of running into stone walls exactly like this one, I still wanted to take a sledgehammer to the kitchen. I loved June and Hek, and I would have helped them rebuild the room once I'd demolished it, but the satisfaction would have been well worth the trouble.

"You know something about this coin." I pressed my lips together.

"We do." June sniffed.

"You know who sold it."

"Did I hear you say something about a Welsh saint?" Hek cleared his throat, still sleepy.

So he hadn't been entirely asleep when I'd been talking to June. He'd overheard at least part of my conversation.

"Saint Elian." Maybe I could lead them down some sort of alternate path that would at least parallel the story they wouldn't tell me.

"That's interesting, don't you think?" Hek looked me directly in the eye.

That was a hint. I just didn't know what it was supposed to mean. I stared back at him.

June distracted herself by clearing away my plate. The clatter of it seemed loud compared to the drip and splatter at the window nearby. She turned on the water in the sink and began to wash the plate. She spoke with her back still to me, her voice rising over the noise she was making.

"He means your great-grandpa being Welsh and all."

I actually twitched, as if someone had kicked the leg of my chair. "Damn." I said it before I could think.

June's head shot around, face scowling.

Hek was awake instantly.

"Boy, you better know you can't talk like that in *my* kitchen!"

"Sorry." I held up both hands. "Really. I just—sometimes I can't believe how slow I am."

June's expression softened immediately.

"Honey, you know you're better at seeing things that aren't so close to you." She even managed a smile.

She was right. I suffered from a malady familiar to most children of odd families: a kind of emotional farsightedness. I could pierce the veil of a stranger's psychology with three well-chosen sentences, but I couldn't see the foibles of my own troubled mind even if they were silver and shiny and handed to me on my own front porch.

"This coin has something to do with Conner."

June went back to her washing; Hek sipped coffee and looked at the rain.

My great-grandfather, Conner Devilin, had been born in Wales but had been apprenticed to a silversmith in Ireland, where he was accused of murder. He narrowly escaped prison and came to America. When he died at the age of eighty-six, most of his things were sold at auction and brought a sizable bit of money, some of which came to me for my university education.

One of the few things that hadn't been sold was a silver lily he had made in Ireland. Maybe he had also pressed the odd coin, though how or why that would be was certainly unfathomable to me at that moment.

"Strange family," Hek mused, still staring out the window, "the ones over there."

"In Wales," I prompted.

"Uh-huh."

"Strange in what way?"

"Mean. Crazy." He set down his coffee cup. "I remember your father got a phone call when Conner died."

June laughed, drying the plate.

"That Conner was a pretty ornery old pistol all by himself."

"He was that," Hek agreed. "Did I ever tell you that he killed—now I'm going back fifty years or more—he killed a bear. . . ."

"A small bear," June amended.

"Killed a bear," Hek went on, as if June hadn't spoken, "by hitting it in the head with a rock. That's the truth. The old bear, standing on his hind legs, come up on Conner while he was walking down the mountain to town. Your great-granddad shoveled up a rock about the size of his hand and brought it down once right between that bear's eyes. Right between. Old bear hit the ground like a chimney falling. Dead before it was down. Used to have the skin as a rug in your house until your mama got rid of it."

"And we know this story," I said, fingers intertwined, "how?"

"If you set one foot on that rug," June piped up, "Conner would growl like a bear and then hit the thing in the head with his cane, like it was come back to life."

"And he'd tell the story, word for word the same every time, about how he killed it." Hek was grinning.

"He told you all this?" I leaned forward. "Conner told you?"

"Well, no," Hek admitted. "We got it from your dad."

"When you visited our house," I said, pressing him.

They had not visited my house once in the several years I'd been back home, living there. I couldn't remember their ever coming over when I was a boy, either.

"Well, no," June continued. "We got this mostly from your dad's show."

My parents were itinerant entertainers, carnival performers. My father was a magician of some dexterity; Mother was his lovely assistant. They worked for the fabled Ten Show, a touring enterprise that featured the most bizarre combination of odd string-band music, startling freaks, and genuine magic ever assembled on the planet—at least according to the banners they always set up around the towns where they traveled. No one who saw the show went home unaffected, least of all me.

But I'd been twisted more, of course, by the perennial absence of my parents than by their cold professional occupation. My father dazzled onstage, told great intricate stories—mostly to distract the audience while he worked his tricks. My mother employed her sexual energies with the abandon of a flapper or the more liberated of the Pre-Raphaelite models, which is to say that her performances were as quaint as they were erotic: smoldering, enticing, and somehow from another time.

Together, my parents were mesmerizing on the boards.

But they were different people when they came backstage. Hidden, private souls came back to our house. My father barely spoke, and his eyes, though very kind, seemed never to see what was in front of them, but something in his mind instead. My mother was a libertine of epic proportions, and once, greatly drunk, undertook to describe to me the details of every back door in the county—because she knew every one by heart. It took all night. I was seven.

As much as the people of Blue Mountain loved the Ten Show and went to see it almost every time they could, they hated my mother and feared my father, though I could never put my finger on exactly why that was the case. Other men in our town were certainly strange, and my mother wasn't the only woman who had ever indulged in an affair.

"I see," I told Hek and June after too long a silence. "Did my dad have other stories about Conner's kin in Wales? You said something about a phone call."

"Surely did." Hek finished his coffee and took a seat at the table. "When Conner died, your dad sent a letter to the family in the old country."

"Hek told him to," June whispered, as if it were a secret. She took her seat, as well.

"Sent a letter," Hek repeated, "and got a phone call back. The kin over there wanted to know if it was money to be had."

"If Conner had left them anything in his will," June explained. "There was this one man who was a college professor, like you, and he—"

"I can tell you," Hek interrupted June the way he always did, "that it made your daddy plenty mad, the way those people carried on after Conner's death."

"According to what your father always said after that," June explained, "the Welsh are no-account. To a man. They work in coal mines and all they want is a free handout."

"They are a strange lot." Hek nodded slowly.

I considered how likely it was that everyone in the world thought of their own home as the norm and the rest of the world as at least a bit off-kilter. There was no doubt that the residents of Blue Mountain felt they were the model of humanity; the rest of the population would be well served by the realization of that fact. I was also secure in the suspicion that people in any small town in Wales felt exactly the same about themselves. An inability to see past that basic myopia was, I had always thought, the primary reason for 98 percent of the misery in the world.

"I'll tell you what's strange," I countered. "The fact that someone calls me out of the blue about this artifact, and it turns out I may have an intimate connection with it."

"That is quite a coincidence," Hek agreed.

"You say his name was Shultz," June said. "The man who called you."

"Right."

"And how much do you know about him?" Hek finally made eye contact.

"What?" I was a little taken aback, looking right into his eyes. It didn't happen that often.

"Seems to me, Fever," he said, as if I were an idiot, "that Mr. Shultz could have already known the coin had something to do with your great-grandfather, and that he called you for a completely different reason than you think."

Five

All the way home, I tried to imagine Shultz as a devious criminal with some great crime in the offing, but it didn't quite pan out. Hek, like most in Blue Mountain, operated out of the "never trust a stranger" motif. It was part of the general attitude of suspicion about most of the world.

And it was clear to me that neither Hek nor June would reveal the rest of what they knew about the coin. Even if I *had* destroyed their kitchen with a sledgehammer. Once a secret's locked in the rib cage of anyone I know in my little town, it's there for good.

So it was a quick good-bye and a dark road home for me, worrying about the things I *hadn't* been told.

Rain made things worse. It fell in silver stems, less translucent than water should be. All color was obviated. A dynasty of gray conquered the horizon. The buzz and hum of it on the roof and road conquered every other sound: Anything too soft could never be heard; anything too loud would be kin to the clatter. Thunder's will was dispersed; no bird would call across the indefinable sky. Each raindrop blasted the ground, an explosion of wet earth. Each shaken, blinding stab of lightning accomplished that same destruction in the air.

Finally, it came to me why rain had made it seem unlikely that anyone in Blue Mountain could have known about Shultz's coin.

Rain is a perfect curtain. It hides sound and sight, and when it's done, it draws aside, allows the sunlight back. But rain does the same thing to the mind that it does to the sky. It obscures; it fogs. It robs the color and distracts the eye until nothing seems plausible, nothing seems clear.

But the rain had subsided to a drizzle by the time I pulled my truck up to the house.

Andrews appeared on the porch, holding a notepad, before I'd turned off the engine.

"About time," he called.

I climbed out of the truck and stepped quickly to the porch.

"While you've been out uselessly doing whatever it is you so uselessly do," he told me, "Dr. Shultz and I have been finding out everything you need to know."

"Everything I need to know," I repeated, voice dry. "Then the notepad you so vigorously hold is, we assume, only an outline."

"What?" He looked up. " 'Outline'?"

"Turn to the page that explains quantum mechanics, then. I've been needing to know about that for quite a while."

"About the *thing.*" He grimaced. "You really can take the fun out of helping you."

"You've found out something about the coin."

"We've found out *everything* about the coin. Mission accomplished. Fait accompli."

"Is Shultz packing, then?"

"Packing? No. I mean we just found out, you know, where this thing came from, not how it got here or who sold it. Damn it, you really can take the fun—"

"Shultz is still in there, then?" I headed for the front door.

"Of course." His voice dropped all of its remaining joviality.

"Shultz," I called, "have you got a second?"

"What is it?" Andrews followed me into the darkened living room.

"Wait." Shultz floundered on the sofa, shoes off, where he had fallen asleep. "Who's that?"

"Why did you call me?" I asked.

"What did he say?" Shultz glared at Andrews, who stood just behind me, still flourishing his notepad.

"He said—"

"I mean," Shultz interrupted. "I know what he said, but why did he say it? What does it mean?"

"How did you come to call me about your coin?"

"I told you," he said, a bit of irritation creeping into his voice. "I got in touch with the university and they gave me your name."

I turned to Andrews.

"If you had a valuable coin, or one you thought might be worth something, where would you go?"

"Me?" Andrews scowled. "I guess I'd find some antique-coin guy."

"Right," I agreed. "If you were looking for a pompous opinion about something that didn't matter, you'd call a university. If you wanted information you could actually use in what we would laughingly refer to as 'the real world,' you'd call some *guy*."

"I did." Shultz managed his way to a sitting position. "Remember I told you I talked to a silver collector? I mean, Jesus! I even made long-distance calls, overseas, because the jewelry guy said it was European. But everybody I talked to, they just told me the facts. Had no idea what the *story* was. It's the story that makes a doodad really mean something, don't you think?"

I exhaled.

"He did tell me that he took it to a guy at a jewelry store," I told Andrews over my shoulder.

"And the story is, in fact, what makes a doodad interesting," Andrews replied. "You've always said so yourself."

"What's going on?" Shultz finally had his stocking feet on the floor, rubbing his eyes.

I exhaled.

"Nothing." I gave him a bit of a raised eyebrow. "My friends are suspicious of you. But they're suspicious of everyone, so I'm—"

"You're uncomfortable that you invited me into your house." Shultz sniffed.

"Probably right," Andrews chimed in. "It's completely uncharacteristic of him to do it.

"And I suppose it could seem strange of me to accept." Shultz sat back on the sofa. "But that's the kind of person I am: jump at a free trip to the mountains."

"So. What did you two find out?" I was trying to change the subject. "Andrews said you'd made progress."

"Oh, well, *there's* something." Shultz was back to being unbelievably affable. "This thing, the coin, was almost certainly minted in Aberystwyth, or however you pronounce it, in Wales. There was a place, during the 1630s, solely for the purpose of coining locally mined silver. It was owned by a family called Briarwood, who were also owners of the most profitable silver mine in Wales at the time."

"I was right." Andrews beamed. "I found out about the mint in a book, I did a bit of the old Internet research, and I got the real stuff. Case closed."

" 'The real stuff'?" I stared.

"What the hell do you think is on the back of the coin, Dr. Igmo?" Andrews shook his head.

"The giant *B*," Shultz answered, leaning forward on the sofa, barely able to contain himself. "For Briarwood!"

"Yes. Why does that name sound familiar to me?" Andrews returned my stare.

"Well," I began cautiously, "that's just the thing."

To my dismay, I found myself thinking exactly what Hek and June must have thought when they were talking to me: How much should I reveal, and how much should I hide?

Andrews, somewhat unfortunately, read my face.

"Hang on," he mumbled, obviously scanning his brain.

I realized I was grinding my teeth; my jaw hurt.

"Don't break anything, Andrews." I sighed. "I'll tell you why you know the name Briarwood."

How much to show, how much to shadow? I tried to read Shultz's eyes, but they only seemed eager and innocent.

"Sit down, I think," I instructed Andrews.

He took a seat on the sofa beside Shultz; I dropped into the ancient leather chair perpendicular to it.

"My great-grandfather, Conner," I began.

"Oh my *God*!" Andrews had remembered.

"What is it?" Shultz was a fascinated adolescent.

"It's his *family*!" Andrews blurted out.

"*What's* his family?" Shultz shot a glance from Andrews to me and back.

"Conner was born in Wales," I explained. "As a young man, he left his family, whom he always claimed were a cold lot, and traveled to Ireland. There he apprenticed himself to a silversmith named Jamison. Soon after, Conner had the misfortune of falling in love with a serving girl in the Jamison household. The girl, Molly, promised to marry Conner, but a short while later, she got a better offer from a rich lord. Conner happened on Molly and this other man and thought the man was taking advantage of Molly. He killed the man in a sword fight and was arrested for murder. Only technical flaws in his indictment—and a particularly observant judge who blamed Molly as much as Conner for the murder—set my great-grandfather free temporarily. Before the lawyers could revise the legal papers, Conner jumped a boat to America and settled here. To escape any trouble that might pursue him, he changed his last name to Devilin when he got here."

"Something about, I kid you not, having the devil in him," Andrews revealed.

"Wait." Shultz leaned my way. "He changed his name to Devilin? What was it before?"

The questions seemed genuine. Shultz did not appear to know my original family name.

Andrews jumped in, unable to contain himself—or to wait for me to respond.

"It was Briarwood!"

The rain had stopped and the wind had come up. The temperature outside had dropped twenty degrees since morning.

Andrews had insisted on espresso before I told any of my Conner

Briarwood stories. We were all on our third cup, sitting down in the darkened living room, when I began.

"A *bwbach,*" I told them, "is a goblin with a relatively sweet spirit, often responsible for good deeds in exchange for strong drink. A *bwbach* generally disapproves of abstinence in any fashion and enjoys nothing more than good ale, a clay pipe, and a seat close to the fire."

"Here we go." Shultz clapped his hands, delighted as a child.

"Don't encourage this," Andrews warned, mock disdain dripping from his words.

"Conner always told a story of his departure from Wales," I went on, ignoring them both, "that included a *bwbach.* He said he was walking across a field toward a waterfall for a drink when something tapped him on his shoulder. He turned around and saw himself: A man his mirror image stared back at him. The man grinned and said, 'Have a cup!' and handed Conner a bit of ale. Conner declined because he was a Calvinist and would not touch alcohol. 'Then have you a pipe!' the doppelganger charged Conner. But Conner did not care for tobacco, even as a young man. 'Well at least you can shake my hand!' the man demanded. Conner offered his hand; the thing took it but then let it go immediately. 'Cold as ice!' it pronounced. 'I must ask you to get out of my country. You're no fit Welshman!' At that, the man returned to his natural form, a grinning wraith with barely human features. Conner nodded and left his native land at sunrise on the very next day."

"Did he really?" Shultz asked Andrews, voice hushed.

"He did," I answered. "Though his exodus probably had more to do with the fact that his mother was dead and his father had little use for him."

"But that's the story he told?" Andrews wanted to know.

"Always. And when I began to study folk stories as an adult, I came to realize just how significant a bit of psychology it was that Conner faced himself—the form of a spirit that looked like him—in order to leave home. He seemed to be telling himself that if he stayed in Wales, he'd become nothing more than a hot-blooded drunk, sit around the fire smoking, and never amount to anything."

"That's what that story means?" Shultz sat back on the couch.

"So he went to Ireland and killed a man instead." Andrews's arch voice insulted the air. "Then fled to America."

"This just gets better and better." Shultz was completely awake now and clearly overtaken by the turn of events.

His hair was a mess, his eyes sparkled; a grin seemed to defy the constraints of his facial muscles. In that instant, I couldn't imagine why I had ever suspected him of anything more than overeating.

"This is all new to you," I said to him softly.

"As a two-day pup," he shot back happily.

I wasn't completely ready to give over to him, but I wasn't going to be calling the police about him, either.

Andrews slumped down, and his voice warmed.

"I begin to see why you're acting so strangely. It's quite a coincidence that a man you'd never heard of called you about a coin minted by your great-grandfather."

"It wasn't minted by my great-grandfather," I said patiently. "He didn't stay in Wales, he didn't take up the family business, and he was born sometime in the late 1800s. The coin's much older than that, I believe."

"Based on what?" Andrews asked.

"Doesn't anybody believe me that I went to a jeweler in Atlanta?" Shultz shook his head. "The guy said it was old—took a guess at three hundred years."

"And when were you going to tell us that?" Andrews scowled.

"I thought I did." Shultz shrugged.

"The point is that the coin probably belonged to my great-grandfather. But it wasn't among his things, as far as I know, when he died." I glanced at the kitchen window. The rain was starting up again.

"Do you have any other family around here?" Shultz asked. "Someone we could—"

"No. All dead."

Andrews looked as if he might object to that statement, but Shultz went on.

"Would it be worth a call or something to Wales? Are there still Briarwoods there?"

"There are." I nodded. "I don't know any of them, not remotely. But Hek and June told me they called my father when Conner died."

"Heck and who?" Shultz's grin got bigger.

"Hezekiah and June Cotage," I told him. "A couple of my primary folk informants."

"And his spiritual parents," Andrews added, teasing.

"Not quite that," I objected. "But I am close to them. I've just come from their home."

"Should have known that's where you'd go first." Andrews nodded sagely.

"And they told you . . . ," Shultz said slowly.

"That as of the mid-1970s, the family in Wales still wanted to know about Conner's death. Or about his will, actually."

"His will?" Andrews growled. "After they hadn't seen him for—what, fifty years?"

"More."

"What would he have had that they would want?" Andrews went on. "He wasn't going to leave them any of the land he had here in the mountains. And he didn't really have a fabulous bank account, did he?"

"Well," I said, "he did have a sizable savings, and, you'll remember I told you, enough money to set aside for my university education. All of it. And a bit of money to live on while I was studying."

"You're kidding," Shultz chimed in. "This old guy left you money to get your degrees?"

"Left it to my father, actually," I corrected, "who was his favorite grandson. My father held on to the money, even when we needed it for food and the basics."

"So Conner didn't really know you," Shultz said softly.

"I barely remember him at all," I confessed. "I've learned more about him from a few personal things of his that were kept here in the house than I have from any experience of him. Mainly some of his writings."

"They're over there in that trunk." Andrews nodded in the direction of a back corner of the room. "I remember."

"Something he wrote is in that trunk?" Shultz stared, wide-eyed.

"He was in love with this woman, Molly." I stared at the trunk. "Even though she caused him to kill a man, even though she testified against him at his trial, even though he moved to America, got married, had children and grandchildren, and grew old without her. In that trunk, yellow and moldering, are literally scores of stories, all nearly identical, retelling that part of his life over and over again, as if he were trying—and failing—to exorcise a demon. That told me more about him than any ten or one hundred conversations ever could."

"Jeez." Shultz shot a look at Andrews. "You were right: This *is* the Addams Family on Walton's Mountain."

"So you think," Andrews said to me, ignoring Shultz altogether, "that the coin is some sort of family item or heirloom that Conner took with him to Ireland and then brought to America. Maybe a good-luck charm."

"The actual place in Wales that's called Saint Elian's Well is on Briarwood property, or was. And, of course, the ornate *B* on the back of the coin could certainly stand for Briarwood."

"But you still sound skeptical." Andrews sat back, trying to read my face. "It all seems so obvious."

"I just don't want to rush into anything. The coincidence makes me uncomfortable."

"It involves your family. You're always uncomfortable about that." Andrews pulled at his earlobe, a certain sign he was deep in thought. "And on second thought, given the history of the fabled well, maybe it wasn't a good-luck charm at all."

"Maybe it was a curse coin!" Shultz finished Andrews's thought. "You said that by the seventeenth century, people would pay large sums of money to curse one another."

"*I* said that maybe the coin was produced by some clever Welsh entrepreneur for people to use in curse payments!" Andrews seemed quite pleased with his previous observation. "Your family history makes it difficult for you to see, because you'd rather not think about them at all, but it's all pretty clear."

I took in both faces. They were quite satisfied with themselves: mystery solved.

"In the first place," I began slowly, "my belief—and years of research and experience have supported this contention—is that nothing is ever that simple or easy. One of my chief complaints about the twenty-first century is that no one gets past the surface of most questions."

"It's the Internet," Shultz interrupted sagely. "You have all this knowledge at your fingertips, but it's nothing but quick, easy answers."

"You're saying this coin thing is *not* something to do with your ancestral family?" Andrews groused.

"I'm saying," I answered him, "that your explanation is the best we have so far, but even if it is the truth, we're only scratching the surface, and there's much more to this issue."

"Maybe for you and your psychiatrist," Andrews sneered. "But for young Dr. Shultz here, I think the mystery is solved. He's got answers and he's got a couple of pretty nice stories."

"Not really," I countered. "I mean, just to start with, there's the question of who actually sold this valuable family treasure, if it is that, and why. If it's worth so much, both in economic terms and with regard to sentiment, who in my family would have let it go? Maybe it was stolen and sold illegally. Maybe Shultz's father stole it and lied about how he acquired it. No offense meant. I'm just—"

"No, no, no," Shultz interrupted cheerily. "It's really quite possible that the old man could have held up some poor widow at gunpoint to get something he fancied. No offense taken whatsoever."

"I'm only saying," I went on, "I've been told hundreds of times by folk informants that they don't sing, or don't have any stories, or don't make anything by hand. I change the subject, I talk about the weather, and after a while, something emerges. If I look it in the eye, it goes away. If I chase it, it recedes. It's elusive."

"What is? I'm lost," Shultz confessed, looking to Andrews for help.

"By 'it,'" Andrews answered wearily, "he actually means the great mysteries of life. He imagines that his work uncovers the truth of the ages. In a clay jug. Or the sound of a poorly played violin."

"He does?" Shultz seemed more confused.

"Most of the things we take for granted in this century—television, computers, instant news—got their start in human culture barely a hundred years ago. If we consider that civilization began, let's say conservatively, ten thousand years ago, we have to admit spending a lot more time telling one another stories than watching CNN. We can't ignore the way things have been done for most of human endeavor in favor of the immediate moment, no matter how compelling the wonders of that immediate moment might be. If we lose touch with mythology, with ancient stories and songs and ways of doing things, we lose our humanity. We become as superficial as an Internet search or a television comedy. We'll end up looking back on our past with as little comprehension as most people today have of Egyptian hieroglyphics, or the meaning of Stonehenge."

"Say *amen* very quickly," Andrews muttered to Shultz, "or this could go on for another couple of hours."

"No," Shultz protested, "I actually agree with him. The good old ways are the best."

"That's not remotely what I mean." I closed my eyes. "I'm saying this: You hear the story of Saint Elian's Well or of Conner's encounter with a fairy and you think it's a quaint story for children. I'm telling you that these are actual phenomena. They happen all the time."

"Your great-grandfather saw a spirit disguised as himself in a field in Wales." Shultz gave me a withering eye.

"A supernatural event is only an occurrence that some idiot can't properly explain."

"Hang on," Andrews protested. "I thought you always said these stories served primarily as metaphor."

"Their significance is metaphorical; their action is actual."

"Could we stick to the part where I'm primarily right about everything?" Andrews reclined. "We have a silver coin with a big *B* on the back and a family named Briarwood who minted silver coins."

"Those are facts," I agreed. "But I could assemble them a hundred different ways. The *B* stands for Britain; the well isn't Saint Elian's at all, but something, say, in the Lake District, or on the way to Canterbury. Saints walked all over the place around there."

"The *B* stands for Breton." Shultz beamed. "It's a *French* saint, and it's not a well at all; it's the grave of, you know, Jesus or something. This is fun."

"When you're a first-year medical student," Andrews began wearily, "you're told that the most obvious answer is nearly always the correct one. If someone in Kansas is describing a four-legged mammal with hooves and a mane, it's more likely to be a horse than a zebra."

"You know this from your years in medical school." I sighed.

"As it happens, my roommate in graduate school was on his way to being a surgeon, and he made me study with him because I made him run lines with me when I was in plays."

"Aside from the very distracting image of you onstage," I told him, "I probably have to admit at least a modicum of agreement with your premise."

"Yes, you have to admit that—fond as you are of Occam's razor."

"Who's what?" Shultz barged in. "Is that another folktale or something?"

"It's a philosophical concept of which I am fond," I explained. "The precise statement is: 'Universal essences should not be unnecessarily multiplied.' The useful extrapolation is generally given as 'The simplest answer is the best.' "

"KISS rule." Shultz nodded slowly.

"Kiss what?" Andrews's eyes widened.

"K-I-S-S," Shultz spelled. " 'Keep it simple, stupid.' Plain good advice, in my book."

"I used to think it was just you," Andrews told me, "but now I realize that *all* Americans are irritating."

"And proud of it." Shultz grinned. "So where are we on the subject of my doodad?"

"At the frustrating, somewhat embarrassing admission on my part"—I sighed—"that my great-grandfather might have had something to do with it."

"Why would that be so bad?"

"You have no idea how many ghosts are in this man's head," Andrews said simply, nodding in my direction.

I stared out my kitchen window. Charcoal rain clouds shadowed the pines, and each individual drop of water on the pane seemed to magnify those shadows, a hundred black prisms dividing the color of night into spectra of darkness.

"I don't know why this story just occurred to me," I said softly. "Maybe it's because it also involves a well in Wales, or maybe it's an omen—ghosts, indeed. On Glasfryn Lake, in the parish of Llangybi, is a place called Grace's Well, speaking of wells. In the days before history, it was a fairy well, guarded by Grace, a fairy who had taken human form because she fell in love with a man. She was a tall woman with large, bright eyes, dressed all in white silk. She waited by the water every night for her love to come walking. Her only fairy duty was to cover the well when it wasn't in use. One night, she was distracted by the beauty of swans on the lake, watching them glide over the black water, and did not realize that her love had drawn from the well to bring her a drink. Grace and the man walked along the lake's edge while water poured out of the well. Next morning, the man was gone and the well had flooded the fairies' dancing ring. When Grace saw the destruction her neglect had caused, she was overcome with guilt and paced back and forth, weeping and moaning. The fairies punished her by changing her into a swan. Every night after that, for many months, her love would come to the lake and call her name. Every night, the man was approached by a pale swan with large, bright eyes, but he looked away, longing for Grace—never realizing she was the swan. Eventually, the man ceased his visits. Grace lived as a swan on that lake for a hundred years before she was allowed to resume human form. When she became a woman again, she was forbidden to enter the fairy kingdom. She went looking for her love, but all she found were his great-grandchildren, so she went back to the lake and lived on as a swan. But on certain nights of the year, a tall woman with large, bright eyes, dressed all in white silk, may be seen wandering up and down the high ground around the lake, weeping."

"She's crying because of the family that might have been hers." Shultz's voice was hushed.

"She's weeping because she lost the man she loved," Andrews corrected.

"People in the area, to this day, tell stories about seeing her," I said. "They call her the White Widow or sometimes the Widow of the Swans."

"Why?" Shultz's face screwed up.

"She's an immortal," I answered. "She outlived the man she loved, she outlived all the swans she knew—in time, she'll outlive everything. She's the world's widow."

"Jesus." Shultz shivered a bit. "I could never figure out why some people want to live on and on forever. Thank God you can't really do *that.*"

"But I'm afraid you can do just that." I turned my eyes his way. "You can be the world's widower, Mr. Shultz. What do you think a family *is* but a succession of people outliving their loved ones? Any two people who get married *know* one of them will end up widowed."

"Not to mention the legacy of family guilt that trails along behind us like a vapor," Andrews added, "whether we're completely aware of it or not."

I was momentarily silenced by Andrews's melancholy, his own family's curse.

"*Jesus,*" Shultz repeated, standing. "You two are giving me the grand willies. I believe that's the medical term I'm looking for."

"From the Latin, *willikus maximus,*" Andrews said immediately.

"I don't believe I've given anyone the willies since—when was it?" I looked to Andrews.

"Well, I did, in fact, have a case of them the last time I was up here," he reported. "But it's hard to say if I actually got them from you or if they were just going around."

"And P. S., Dr. Shultz?" I tried to sound as serious as I could. "It's a ghost story. It's supposed to have that effect."

"Yeah, well, mission accomplished. Tell me a joke, or turn on the television or something. I don't know why, but I got a chill."

"Like someone was walking on your grave," Andrews intoned in his best Karloff.

"Stop." But Shultz grinned.

He didn't see the sudden flash of white out the window behind him. It was a burst of sunlight though the clouds, but it looked very much like a giant swan in the pine trees.

Six

"So let's get this straight." Andrews attempted to recover a smug tone. "You're willing to admit that the thing, this coin, may have belonged to your family."

He didn't really know what a difficult admission it was for me. Though we'd discussed my family many times, I'd never actually revealed to him anything but the surface of the matter: the entertaining oddities, the freakish stories, things that would entertain more than inform.

To start with, if the coin had belonged to the Briarwood family, it must surely have been cursed. It had found its way back to me through the strangest series of coincidences. Someone had wanted to rid us of it, but it had returned. It was a ghost coin.

More troubling to me was the inescapable ubiquity of my family's darkness. Everywhere I looked in the house, I could see molecules of my mother trailing in the air like dust motes; I could hear my father's thundering silences.

Leave the house and walk through the town, they were there, and their parents before them: This one planted the chestnut in front of the courthouse; that one pounded the nails in the bench underneath the tree.

Blue Mountain was no moving stream. Everywhere I stepped was a place a family member had walked. Invisible footprints padded the sidewalks, bent each blade of grass, shuffled the gravel in the roads;

their skin was on door handles and windowsills, the bark of the trees and the crest of the rim—no place was untouched by my kith and kin.

This man Shultz had brought me more evidence, and the implication was terrifying: No place in the world was entirely safe from their taint. Go to Atlanta, and there was the coin. Go to Ireland, and there was the grave of a man my kin had killed. Retreat to Wales, and there they were, leering from the ancient wells, over the wind-blasted hills, and rounding the swan-filled lakes.

"Is he stalling?" Shultz peered at me as if I were in a trance.

"Fever?" Andrews had at least dropped his air of self-satisfaction.

"I'm just trying to scrub out the notion," I began, "that my family members are everywhere, and that they secretly run the world."

"*The* world," Shultz rejoined, "or *your* world?"

"Point taken." I tried to shake off a bit of the gloom that had shrouded me.

"So what's next?" Shultz's voice had returned to its more characteristic boyish tones.

"I have no idea." I rubbed my face.

The other two sat waiting, as if I were simply trying to gather my thoughts, but I could not shake the feeling that I would never rid myself of the family curse—if pathological loneliness could be elevated to such a mythic proportion.

When the silence moved from anticipatory to uncomfortable, Andrews roused himself.

"Well," he began hazily, "Shultz, didn't you say something about your father insuring this coin?"

"Dad? Yes. For five thousand big ones. That's what he told me. Remember I said we should check insurance records?"

"Right, Fever, what about checking records around here to see if Grandpa Conner did the same thing. Maybe we'll find something. Then we'd know for certain if he'd ever owned it or not, and we'd know how to proceed—at least a bit better than we know now."

"Good point." I nodded. "I know that the money he left was in some kind of trust or legal protection. I was too young to care about the particulars when I left home, and I really haven't thought about it since I've come back. Maybe the lawyer who handled that also took care of other business. Maybe records were kept."

"Sounds kind of half-baked." Shultz shook his head slowly.

"Do you remember the lawyer's name?"

"No." I stood. "But Conner kept everything of importance in this trunk, and papers of that sort would certainly be no exception."

"You wouldn't have seen them already," Shultz asked, "after all this time?"

"As I was saying"—I sighed—"I wasn't that interested in anything other than his stories when I was young, and since I've been back home, I really haven't thought about anything like this."

I moved to the far right corner of the room. Though it was framed by two windows, it was still a darker part of the house. Its sole occupant was an antique trunk. In that trunk were the tortured writings my great-grandfather had left behind, and packets of other papers, long unopened.

The lid creaked like a coffin top. Dust rose up like dead spirits. I sorted through heartbreaking manuscripts, unintelligible notes, and packets of unread letters before I saw several thick legal envelopes and gathered them up. One was printed with a return address: *Brinsley Taylor, Esq. Pine City, GA.*

"Here we go," I said, a bit too weakly to qualify as *triumphant.* "This might be something, then."

I only glanced at the first page of the long missive, but it was indeed quite something.

A single phone call to Taylor and Taylor, Attorneys at Law, listed in the Pine City phone book, had confirmed that their founder, now deceased, had, in fact, been Brinsley Taylor.

Alas, the phone call did nothing to assure us one way or another that any sort of helpful information could be had there. Only the secretary was in the office, and she could only tell us that everyone had gone but might be back later. I said I wanted to come in anyway, and she told me she'd be in the office until five o'clock. I thought a personal appearance was in order—I can be very persuasive in person—but Shultz didn't remotely believe that the trip was worth the effort. He elected not to bother his vacation with such nonsense. He was a bit reticent to let me take the coin with me, but when I told him where to find the apple brandy, things seemed to change.

He didn't even bid Andrews and me *good luck* or *happy hunting* or any other such well-wishing. His last words were, "It's a wild-goose chase, boys. You're wasting your time. I'm staying here where it's safe and dry."

So it was odd, in retrospect, that he waved good-bye.

The road to Pine City had been repaved since the last time I'd driven it, and the recent rain had made it a black mirror, glazed and glowing.

The drive was tedious to me, but Andrews seemed to enjoy the scenery. Twice, he almost made me stop the truck so he could take advantage of a so-called scenic overlook. I persuaded him that the vista had not significantly changed in quite some time from that vantage point and was likely to be available to him at some other juncture when time was not of the essence.

We pulled into the driveway of a palatial Victorian-era mansion just before 4:30. The somewhat weathered sign said TAYLOR AND TAYLOR MEANS BUSINESS.

"They have their office in their home," Andrews mused, "or did they buy this place because it makes an impression?"

The place was a fortress of southern aristocracy clichés: painted Confederate gray and bloodred, American flag flying at a forty-five-degree angle from a white column in the front porch, and situated right next door to the Episcopal church.

"Let's ask." I climbed out of the truck.

Andrews bounded out the passenger side and was up on the steps in a flash.

We made a pair, I suppose. Andrews had not been convinced to change, so his wrinkled Hawaiian shirt seemed to wrestle the American flag for attention in the breeze. I was in black, a funeral mourner or some rebellious priest in jeans, sans collar.

Andrews shoved through the front door of the place as if he were entering a shop on the town square.

"Hi," he trumpeted before I could even get to the door. "We called."

I hurried in behind him. The reception area was huge: a wide wooden stairway to the right, a dozen overstuffed chairs to the left, and tall potted palms, perfect for the place, in three corners. The ceilings seemed fourteen feet high, with a pounded tin pattern and framed by thick crown molding. The area had been artfully arranged as a reception area and waiting room.

The person behind the reception desk had, as I feared, been frightened. The nameplate on her desk read BECKY MEADOWS.

"I'm Dr. Devilin." I shot out my hand. "This is Dr. Andrews. We'd like to speak to one of the Taylors, if anyone's come back yet."

"Oh." Becky blinked three times, her tongue between her lips, then took my hand for a split second. "Doctor . . . yes. You called."

"I said that." Andrews looked at me.

"Shh." I smiled. "I did call. Is anyone available?"

Becky was a short brunette, not long out of high school. My guess was that her father knew the Taylors—hunted quail with them or was an old fraternity brother. Her charcoal suit coat was a bit tight over a frilly white blouse; her skirt was a tad short. I decided that Becky's father had gotten her the job to "straighten her out"—and I was a little uncomfortable by what he might have meant by that phrase. I assumed he wanted to make his daughter into a good churchgoing wife and mother, but Becky's eyes betrayed at least a restless, if not a wild, heart.

"Mr. Taylor?" she called suddenly. "It's him."

"Oh?" The voice came from the hallway behind Becky's desk. "Well, send him back."

"He's got someone with him," she sang out.

"Then send them both back, Becky." The voice betrayed strained patience.

She smiled quickly up at us both.

"You can go on back," she whispered, as if it were somehow a secret.

"We can go back," Andrews whispered to me.

"Behave, or wait in the truck." I smiled at Becky and navigated around her desk.

"First on the left." Becky was still whispering.

"Thanks," Andrews told her, his voice barely audible.

The first room on the left had been, I thought, the formal dining room of the house. It was huge, oval-shaped, not rectangular. A brilliant chandelier, perhaps twenty lights and hundreds of crystal bobs, hung in the air, exactly centered in the room, and spotlessly clean. Beneath it lay a round rug, royal blue and antique gold. In the epicenter of the rug was an oak desk that looked presidential. Behind that desk sat a man with the best haircut I had seen in three years. He was in his fifties, wore a starched French-cuffed shirt with infinitesimally thin blue vertical stripes. His tie was silk, of the palest blue, and matched his cuff links perfectly. He did not stand.

"Gentlemen." He stared.

He did not offer us a seat, and there were no chairs in front of his desk. Andrews took care of the dilemma in characteristic manner. He sat down on a corner of the man's desk.

"I'm Dr. Andrews," he began in dead earnest, "and this is Dr. Devilin. I'm afraid we have a bit of bad news. Your chandelier? It violates what we call the *Phantom of the Opera* law: It intimidates the rest of the room and threatens to overshadow the main plot action. It'll have to come down."

Mr. Taylor only exhibited the slightest pause.

"It is quite something." His voice was dulcet and calm. "Original to the house."

His accent stuck pins in my forehead, right between my eyes. His were the tones of noblesse oblige, of deigning to respond, of season opera tickets purchased but rarely used and hidden back-room conversations that signed whims into laws. His voice was the equal balance, on the rich end of the cultural spectrum, for the screaming, red-faced, out-of-work mechanic who terrorized his wife and attended Klan meetings.

I hated judging him by his few words. It was a reflex conditioned by years of painful experience in a South I kept forgetting was not quite gone, not yet. I hoped I was wrong about him.

"My great-grandfather, Conner Devilin, had, I believe, some business with Brinsley Taylor, who was the founder of this firm."

"He was." Taylor sat back in his chair. It did not squeak, did not make a sound. "He and your great-grandfather were—well, not friends, exactly, but they were acquainted."

"In what way?" I clasped my hands behind my back, reminded myself to stand up straight, and peered down at Taylor.

"They were both Masons."

That made sense. No one in Blue Mountain would ever discuss Masonic affiliations, but Conner had certainly been a brother, and would have taken it seriously. In small mountain towns, that sort of bond was significant, and often formed the basis of all manner of relationships. Conner had doubtless become a silver Mason in Ireland, though it was harder to determine the exact nature of Brinsley Taylor's craft.

"Is this your family's home?" Andrews allowed his eyes to roam the room. "We were wondering."

"It was not. My father purchased it in the 1950s, when it was about to be condemned and torn down. He had a passion for architecture as well as the law. Of course, owning an old home is tantamount to a good marriage: It takes daily care and a good bit of money just to keep up appearances."

He smiled with his mouth but not his eyes.

"So," Andrews concluded, "business must be pretty good."

"You called," Taylor said to me, ignoring Andrews, "and drove here for a reason."

I locked eyes with him and drew an envelope from my hip pocket.

"I have a letter from Brinsley Taylor to my great-grandfather. Shall I read it to you? It is the proximate cause of our visit."

Taylor sipped the slightest breath.

"You would prefer to read it to me rather than let me see it for myself?"

I held the envelope before me.

"It says that Conner Devilin helped to establish this firm of yours, in that he was its first big client. It goes on to say that if he or any of his heirs ever has a legal question concerning the Devilin family that we will have immediate pro bono counseling and swift action. I believe most of those phrases are exact quotes. But, of course, you can see it for yourself."

I tossed the envelope onto the desk; it landed exactly in front of Taylor. He didn't look at it or move to take it. He kept his eyes on me.

"Then I assume you're here about your trust." He didn't blink.

I kept my face stony, though my mind seesawed. *My trust.*

"Along those lines." I didn't want to give him any more information than that if I didn't have to.

After another long moment of lid-itching eye lock, he leaned forward.

"Remarkably, we still have all those old files. I mean the real files, not on the computer. If you give me a hint as to what it is you're looking for, I might even steer you to the exact folder."

"Looking for anything that would establish legal ownership of a certain valuable item, perhaps insurance records or some document transferring title of something . . ." My voice trailed off.

"Ah." There was the joyless smile again. "Then it does have to do with the trust. Which item?"

Andrews gave us away. He shot a look at me like a bullet before he could contain himself.

Taylor sighed heavily, clearly irritated, I thought, by our reticence to share with him.

"Becky!" His voice was so sudden and so loud that Andrews jumped off Taylor's desk.

"Yes, sir?" Becky sounded terrified.

"Would you bring in those files I asked you to pull, please, ma'am?"

She was in the doorway, holding manila folders, before he had even finished his sentence.

"If you'll follow her," Taylor said, suddenly quiet again, "she'll take you to a conference room where you can look over those documents. I believe you'll find what you're looking for, but of course I can't be certain, since you won't *tell* me what you're looking for. And would you please keep in mind that we're at the end of our business day. I'll stay until you're done, of course, in case you have any questions, but Becky will be leaving soon."

"I can stay," she ventured.

"Absolutely not, Ms. Meadows," Andrews insisted. "We're a nuisance, and you've already been inconvenienced."

"It's *Miss,*" she insisted.

"Even more so," Andrews concluded, somewhat inexplicably.

She turned to Taylor.

"You know I can stay, Mr. Taylor."

"Coffee, gentlemen?" Taylor asked.

"Love some," Andrews said immediately. "Lots of cream."

I shook my head. The brown liquid that surely had been warming in a Mr. Coffee in the "break room" since 8:30 that morning did not legally qualify as *coffee* to me, not remotely.

"And then you may leave, Becky."

"You won't need me any more tonight? You had me place those long-distance—"

"Good night, Becky!" Taylor interrupted impatiently.

"Good night, Mr. Taylor." Becky motioned with her eyes in the direction we were to go.

We followed her out of Taylor's office and down the hall.

The conference room was a cozy affair. A long oak table, perhaps two hundred years old, filled most of the room, but there was a fireplace at one end and a small buffet at the other. A French press and a coffee service for at least ten sat waiting on the latter. The wainscoting had at one time been painted, but it had recently been sanded, left natural and oiled, so that it brightened rather than darkened the room. Another chandelier hung over the oak table, but this one, at least, was somewhat proportionately agreeable with the rest of the room.

Becky laid three manila folders at the head of the table.

"Sure you won't have some coffee, Dr. Devilin? It's real good. It's a French press, they call it. And I grind the beans right here. On the spot."

"I see," I told her, delighted. "Well, you've talked me into it."

"Great, then." She smiled, bright as a penny, pleased with her powers of persuasion.

She busied herself with the appointed task; Andrews and I sat at the table—neither of us presuming to take the head seat—and each took a file at random.

Andrews took the one entitled "C.D."

Mine was labeled "Correspondence." In it I found papers indicating that the man named Jamison, to whom Conner had apprenticed in Ireland, had left Conner a bit of land in that country. Some of the letters were over a hundred years old. Fascinated, I began to read, but Andrews interrupted.

"Here we go," he said slowly. "This is something. In 1942, your great-grandfather 'acquired at auction three items of value'—I'm quoting—'best insured at top assessment,' whatever that means."

I set my folder aside.

"Does it say what the items of value were?"

He leafed through several pages, then looked up.

"This is exciting." He was a child.

"Isn't it." I was deadpan.

"I love research."

"Could we . . . ," I encouraged.

"Right." He filed though the pages until he came to something that interested him. "Right."

"And?"

"Jesus."

"Andrews."

"It says here, again," he began slowly, "that the items were recently acquired—that is, in 1942—and they were as follows, and I quote: 'a silver coin or medallion; an Indian artifact, possibly Cherokee; a portrait apparently by Cotman.' "

"Wait." I reached for the pages. " 'Recently acquired.' Then they weren't exactly Briarwood family heirlooms, including the coin."

"That means I was wrong." Andrews couldn't believe what he was saying.

"Well, you were right about the idea that the coin might have belonged to my great-grandfather, but this is why I always say it's best not to rush to judgment. Let me see here." I read over the papers. "Oh."

I could feel the blood drain from my face.

"Fever?"

Becky glanced my way, then whispered to Andrews.

"Is he all right?"

"He gets this way all the time," Andrews assured her. "He's sickly. His first name is *Fever*, for God's sake—what can we expect?"

"*Fever*?" She didn't seem to believe it. "Really?"

"You know that I just told Shultz," I said slowly to Andrews, "how I was afraid my family ran the world? And he said, '*the* world, or *your* world?' "

"Yes." Andrews had no idea where I was leading him.

"I meant to say that whenever you find out something about your life, it applies to the entire world; and, conversely, anything you find out about the world has direct, exact relevance to your life. Everything in life is metaphorical."

"I don't—," Andrews began.

"When I discover some new variant of a folktale, for example, it speaks directly to me, it tells me something about myself, even though I know its intent is more universal. And when I encounter some new insight about myself, I believe it opens a door to understanding the entire human condition, because I am everything, and everything is me."

"All right, but I still don't—"

"The variant with which I'm dealing at the moment—I mean, I have it in my head that if I can discover why my great-grandfather bought these things at auction somewhere, and what he did with them, I can also discover why and how Shultz's father bought the coin, and what he thought he was going to do with it. It's all tied up together."

"Right." Andrews still didn't follow me.

"If I can find out about this—all of this business with fathers and sons—then I might be able to help Shultz."

"Help him *what*?"

"Understand his father."

Andrews started to speak, then sat back in his chair instead. He pulled on his earlobe and nodded slowly, blowing out a soft sigh.

"And the more you find out about other people," he began, looking down at the tabletop, "the more you understand your own—"

I interrupted before he could finish his thought out loud. "For example, the thing you just read, the part about the painting by this man Cotman?"

"Yes."

"Did you look at the value attached to the painting, and the rest of the page?"

"Not yet."

I turned the papers so he could see them.

"It was valued at two hundred and fifty thousand dollars. In 1942."

"Jesus." Andrews leaned in to examine the document.

"Apparently, it was the basis of my—what do I call it?—inheritance?"

"The funds that paid to get you out of Blue Mountain and into your university were all gleaned from—"

"It seems," I picked up, "that it was all financed by the sale of this painting—something that my great-grandfather went to buy at some auction. On a whim."

"Why couldn't it have been any one of the three items that you're talking about?"

"Look at the asterisk," I told him.

He squinted, saw the asterisk, and went to the bottom of the page, where it said, "Sold/money held in trust for Fever Devilin/see attached."

He shuffled through the rest of the papers in the folder.

"The painting is the only thing that was sold?" He kept looking. "So where's the piece of paper that says what happened to the coin?"

"Right."

We spent the next twenty minutes in silence, raking through yellowing evidence, pages that had been amended, erased, altered with white-out, torn, folded, and stapled. It was hard to make anything out of them. At least two generations of small-town father and son lawyers had seen fit to correct or update almost everything on the original page, when it seemed to me that a more ordinary practice might have been to keep the old pages intact and create new documents for new situations. But, of course, I had no law degree. The system that had been used by the people who *had* attained such degrees rendered the documents impossible to understand clearly. Perhaps that was their aim. Or perhaps such is always the case when a son tries to rectify the mistakes of the father; when the sins of the father are visited upon the son.

Becky brought us coffee and left silently. She even tiptoed out. I assumed she went home. I heard the phone ring once, then the sound of Taylor's voice on the telephone, but it was impossible to hear what he was saying. I tried harder to focus on the folders.

The third file, marked "Misc.," offered almost nothing in the way of useful information. It did have several typed pages describing the coin Conner had purchased: "Saint on one side, capital *B* on the other," but otherwise it was filled with petty receipts and inconsequential notes.

My "Correspondence" file yielded little better, offering tantalizing new mysteries. There was a letter from an art dealer that said, fairly plainly, "John Sell Cotman was, of course, a landscape artist and rendered no portraits." Another letter from a rare coin collector reported that the coin in question was not a coin at all, but a medallion and, in fact, a fake.

Nowhere could we find a document or even a notation that indicated any sale of the coin, nor was it insured or given a monetary value in any folder.

Andrews looked up at last.

"The painting was the only thing sold, it seems, and maybe that was a fake, too."

"Little mention of the coin, and less of the so-called Cherokee artifact."

"Any idea what *that* might have been?"

"The Cherokee thing? None. Not really my field."

He pushed the file away from himself.

"Did any of this tell us what we wanted to know," he asked, "or do I have to chalk this up to just another of your many and much-needed psychological breakthroughs? I mean about your father—"

"Well." I folded my hands. "In no particular order: We can be relatively certain the coin Shultz's father bought had once belonged to my great-grandfather; we know that neither he nor my father sold it to Shultz's father, and so we know that the sale may well have been illegal. We hear from an alleged expert that the coin is fake, though I believe that assessment to be incorrect. I discovered just enough about the Cotman painting to want to know more about it, and him—the painter himself. In fact, we learned many things from these files—not the least of which is the certainty that lawyer Taylor is hiding something from us."

"What?" Andrews sat up at that.

"Take a look at the outside of the folders. Line them up: 'C.D.' first, then 'Correspondence,' then 'Misc.' Lay them out side by side in that order."

"I'll bite."

He arranged the files in alphabetical order from left to right in front of him.

"Now look at the front of each folder."

He did.

It took him a moment, but he finally saw what I had already noticed.

"They don't—how would I say this?" He stared down at them. "They don't line up."

"Right."

The front of each of the old manila folders was faded and indented in the exact shape of the folder that had been in front of it, and the tab part of each folder was located at a slightly different place than on the other folders, so they could be placed in a cabinet in such a way as to have no tab hidden by any other tab.

Andrews had realized, after his brief examination of the three folders in front of him, that there had been at least one other folder, maybe more—something between "Correspondence" and "Misc." It was obvious.

"I thought you just meant that the information in the folders was shoddy on purpose, to hide something," Andrews said, still wondering at the clear evidence in front of him on the table. "Because they certainly are a mess. But it looks very much like they're keeping another folder from us. What the *hell*?"

I could hear irritation growing in his voice.

I waxed somewhat more philosophical.

"I often have this problem in my folk research," I told him. "You think you've asked the perfect question and all you need to complete your work is that one answer. But one answer, even a great one, can lead to a dozen more questions, issues that confuse the path beyond all recognition, and the work has just begun, because I often also discover that the person I'm talking with is hiding something—sometimes deliberately; just as often without their even realizing it. Maybe the missing file has nothing to do with Conner Devilin; maybe the files got shuffled—it could be an innocent mistake. You haven't learned an important academic axiom: 'Never impart malice to what is more likely incompetence'?"

"I don't know." He pulled on his earlobe.

The short musing silence that followed our comments was blasted quite suddenly.

"Gentlemen!"

Andrews and I both jumped.

Taylor stood in the doorway of the meeting room, a mask of gloom clouding his face.

"I'm afraid I have a bit of odd news." Taylor took a step into the room. "Something has occurred at your home, Dr. Devilin, in your absence."

I stood.

"What's happened?"

"You've just had a phone call." Taylor paused. "Something about bringing a coin back home. Are you entertaining houseguests?"

Seven

The drive home was a tense affair. Shultz had called the law offices in something of a panic, according to Taylor. Apparently, a man had broken into my house or gotten in somehow; Shultz had fallen asleep on the sofa, and so the intruder startled him. After a moment, Shultz determined that the man must be an acquaintance of mine. He seemed quite distraught; said he urgently needed to speak with me, even more desperately wanted to see the coin. So Shultz called.

The problem was, when I went to the phone in Taylor's office, it was dead. When I called Shultz back, no one answered.

The road home seemed longer than it had ever been.

"And Shultz didn't say who it was." Andrews kept going over the minuscule information we had, mumbling to himself. "Only that the man—"

"You can repeat what Taylor told us a hundred times, but you won't wring anything out of it. Just have a little patience and all will be revealed in a minute—when we get home."

"Can't this heap drive any faster?" He rocked back and forth a little, unconsciously, I thought.

"The roads are still slick, it's almost dark, and I'm going as fast as I can."

"Damn." He said it to himself.

"Is there a more impatient man on the planet than you?"

"No." He rocked faster. "But there's something more to my immediate discomfort than that. I have a stupid premonition. I know it's ridiculous, but I'm thinking about Shultz's saying the name of the Scottish play."

"You can't be serious." I gave him a sideways glance that I hoped would demonstrate my derision. "You're afraid something's happened because he said *Macbeth* in a diner?"

"And now *you're* saying it!" he exploded. "Drive faster."

The last of the light that had kindled itself after the rain had gone was raging at the western horizon. Burnt red went to rococo pink and was eventually overtaken by a Parrish blue canopy that was settling over the nighttime sky. It was bruised sky, an autumn sky. September may have taken on summer's disguise for a while, but the costume was wearing thin.

Night always falls hard in Blue Mountain, and the dirt road up to my house was pitch-black by the time we got to it. No lights were on at my place, not even the front porch sconces, as we climbed out of my truck.

"Is he just sitting there in the dark?" Andrews wondered as we pulled up into my yard.

"He could be watching television. You like the lights off when you watch horror movies."

"But I don't see the—thing, the flicker or whatever you call it. It doesn't look like the set's on."

And the house was silent as a tomb. Windows open as they were, we should have heard something.

I slammed the door to the truck and took three steps before I froze.

"Wait!" I held up my arm.

Andrews looked around wildly.

"What?"

"Shh. The front door's open."

He looked.

The door to my house was ajar by inches.

"This can't be good." Andrews's voice had taken on a hushed tremor.

I stood for a moment, wondering what to do. It wouldn't have been the first time my house had been left open, or the first time anyone had gotten in. I rarely locked the door. But where was Shultz?

I took a slow breath.

"Shultz!"

Andrews jumped.

"Jesus, what the hell are you doing?"

"I'm *helloing* the house."

"You're scaring the peanuts out of my M&M's."

"What?"

"Never mind." Andrews sighed, then called out, "Shultz, come on!"

Nothing.

"He went off with the intruder?" I ventured.

"Right." Andrews didn't move.

I bit my upper lip, then headed for the door.

"Wait." Andrews couldn't believe I was on the march.

"Only one way to find out what's in a dark house is to go inside and turn on the lights."

"Oh," he called after me, mocking my insight. "I understand *that* metaphor all right. Well, *you* venture into your 'dark house of the soul.' I'll wait for the paperback to come out."

"Honestly." I hit the front steps. "Shultz?"

"God." Andrews followed me, stomping.

I opened the door and hit the switch that turned on the kitchen lights to my right, the closest inside switch. They were enough to reveal the nightmare image.

Shultz lay on the living room floor, facedown in front of the sofa, dead as a coffin nail. The back of his head was sunken in with a hole the size of a rotten plum, oozing.

Outside, the night was black by the time Deputy Mathews's squad car roared into the front yard: no moon, no stars, only the glare of the headlights.

Inside, Andrews and I had turned on every light in the house, even upstairs, and had sat silently in the kitchen, trying to think of what to say to each other—not wanting to think about Carl Shultz. I'd seen dead bodies; I'd even witnessed murder. Nothing compared to sitting in my own house with a corpse ten feet away.

I couldn't stop wishing Skidmore were in town. When we were younger, we'd been inseparable. When I left Blue Mountain, he was the only one to say good-bye. When I came back, he was the first to welcome me home. Now that he was sheriff, we spent a little less time together, but it would have been nice to have that sort of a friend nearby—under the circumstances.

Deputy Melissa Mathews was young, but Skidmore had complete confidence in her, so I did, too.

"Dr. Devilin!" she called from the front porch.

I stood slowly.

"Hello." I didn't know what else to say.

She moved carefully through the front door and saw the body immediately.

"Okay," she hollered over her shoulder, "come on."

Several men and one gray-haired woman were coming up the porch steps by the time I got to the door to shake Melissa's hand.

"Thank you for coming so quickly," I told her, feeling foolish—it was something you'd say to a plumber if your water was running.

She held on to my hand.

"Are you all right, Doctor?" She searched my eyes, genuinely concerned.

"I—I'm a little shaken, actually. And my friend Dr. Andrews—have you met him?" I looked into the kitchen.

Andrews looked paler than usual. He held up one hand to wave weakly in the direction of the deputy.

"I don't believe we've had the pleasure," she said, all business. "Excuse me."

She held the door open and let the others in.

"This is Chester from over in Pine City," she told me, patting one of the men on the shoulder as he passed. "He gets fingerprints. And you remember Mrs. Tomlinson."

The grandmother nodded to me. She was carrying a Polaroid camera and had another, more serious one around her neck.

It took me a moment to remember where I had seen her. She was the wedding photographer in town.

"She's going to document the crime scene." Melissa pointed her in the right direction. "She's done this sort of work for us before."

Mrs. Tomlinson started snapping Polaroids immediately, and Chester had already popped on latex gloves and a surgeon's face mask.

I thought I recognized the other man, a deputy, though I could not recall his name. He began to search the living room.

Even for a million dollars, I could not have described any one of them the next day, except for Melissa, whom I knew. She'd been Skidmore's deputy for over a year, and many people in town had suspected their relationship, but Skidmore was married to Girlinda, one of the finest human beings on the planet, and he knew it. Besides, it would never even occur to Skidmore that Melissa was attractive—and never would.

Andrews, on the other hand, noticed right away.

Melissa's chestnut hair was pulled back in a braid that ran halfway down her back. Her expression was shy, but her stride was bold, and her mouth always seemed on the verge of a smile. She was still in her early twenties, and dozens had asked her out. She always refused.

"Could we step into the kitchen, Doctor," she said gently. "I'd like to ask you a few questions."

"Of course."

Andrews stood when she came into the room and offered his hand. She took it and gave him what appeared to be a firm, masculine handshake.

"Dr. Andrews, is it?"

"It is." He even managed a smile.

"And you both found the body?"

"I was first in." I stood by the sink. "Do you want some coffee or something?"

"No, thank you. Please have a seat."

Andrews and I sat at the kitchen table. She produced a small spiral notebook and a mechanical pencil and took a chair opposite us. For the next forty minutes, she took down the details of Shultz's visit, information about the coin, even a paragraph or two about related folktales, an indulgence to me, I thought. We finished with our trip to the Taylor law firm and what we had discovered there.

"All right." She closed her notebook. "I think that's enough for the moment. We'll save the rest until the people from Atlanta get here."

"What?" I thought I'd heard her incorrectly.

"I have to call Atlanta to notify the next of kin." She sat back in her chair. "And I believe they may send someone up here to take a look at things."

"You mean I have to wait up—"

"You can go on to bed if you want," she interrupted. "We'll be here."

"You mean I have to try to go to bed," I said without missing a beat, "with the dead body of a very nice man lying on my living room rug?"

She leaned forward.

"I called Skid," she whispered. "He told me to do it."

"You called him?" I was surprised at how relieved that made me—not because I didn't trust Melissa, but because I wanted my old friend to be there. "What did he say?"

"He said to try and keep you from doing anything until he got here. He left Alabama when he hung up the phone. He drives real fast. He might be here in a couple of hours, really."

I nodded, doing my best to rally.

"Did he give you any advice concerning just how you might keep me from doing anything?" I lowered my lids.

"You know those tranquilizer darts that we use on the rabid dogs?" She managed to keep a straight face, but her eyes were bright.

"You brought more than one, I assume. I'm fairly riled up."

"Got a whole case out in the car."

"Well"—I stood up—"go ahead and hit me with at least one. I'd like to get a good night's sleep."

"That's a good one." She finally gave in to her smile. It had exactly the opposite effect of a tranquilizer dart. "You surely are a mess, Dr. Devilin."

"Amen to that," Andrews chimed in.

He wasn't looking at me; he was staring into Melissa's eyes—or trying to. She looked away. I marveled at Andrews's ability to pursue her in light of the circumstances. My own courtship with Lucinda had progressed at a glacial pace, and there had been nothing of what could be called "flirtation."

"I'm going upstairs to try and sleep," I announced.

Melissa nodded. Andrews ignored me in favor of her.

I tried not to look into the living room on my way up the stairs.

I was awakened by loud voices.

I didn't know if I had slept a minute or a day. I couldn't tell what the voices were saying, exactly, but there was an air of disagreement that filled the whole house.

I dragged myself out of bed fully clothed. I'd only taken off my shoes. I tried to get them back on, but gravity had somehow increased its angry control over my body, and nothing was easy.

As I made it to my door, I thought that one of the voices might be Skidmore's. That eased gravity a bit and propelled me through the hall and down the stairs.

Before I hit the bottom step, I could hear the argument coming to a boil.

"I don't care who you *think* he is, Sheriff. I don't care if he's the mother of your *children.* He's our suspect!"

The man yelling was dressed in a cheap black suit and standing in my living room with his finger in Skidmore's face. His face was like a Halloween mask, contorted and vaguely ashen. Another man, older, stood behind him, looking down at his own shoes. Skidmore had his back to me.

"One more sentence," Skidmore warned between welded teeth, "and you're in my jailhouse."

"What?" the man exploded.

"Let's see. Assaulting a police officer, I think." Skidmore looked toward the kitchen. "Deputy Mathews, did you see this man assault me?"

"Yes, sir, I did," she called back immediately.

I cleared my throat.

"Excuse me, Sheriff. I heard the whole thing." I smiled at the faces suddenly turned my way. "It's a clear case of mistaken identity. I am *not,* in point of fact, the mother of your children, and I have the medical records to prove it."

Skid's face relaxed as he looked up at me.

"Hey, Fever." His voice was soft.

I was dismayed to see, over Skid's shoulder, that the body of Carl Shultz was still there.

"And as I explained to the very capable Deputy Mathews," I continued, entering the room, "Dr. Andrews and I were in Pine City at a lawyer's office when our friend here was killed."

"The time of death has not quite been determined," Melissa told me, wincing as she said it.

"You must be Dr. Devilin." The man in the cheap suit gave me what is sometimes called, in lesser fiction, "the once-over."

"This is Detective Huyne from Atlanta." Skidmore sighed. "Mr. Shultz's family, apparently, exerts some influence there."

"Bite my ass twice," Huyne growled.

"In my house," I said tersely, coming to stand just a little too close to the man, "I prefer better language. I'm not against profanity, exactly. I just think that any person with the intelligence required to become a police detective can probably think of ten or twelve better words to use, words that are more expressive and infinitely clearer. Now, if you have the idea that that you can bully my friends and me with an urban attitude and a few low-IQ insults, then I stand corrected in the matter of prerequisite brainpower for your job. Your bad manners, however, are only going to make it more difficult for you to accomplish anything on this mountain. So let me make things easy for you: I didn't kill Shultz, I have a witness who was with me all day, I have a witness in Pine City who is a pillar of that community, and anyone you'll ever talk to in Blue Mountain or in Atlanta will tell you I'm not capable of murder because I have too much guilt and psychological trauma as it is. I'm guessing that you haven't found a murder weapon, and if you ever do, it won't have a trace of me on it—this is assuming that he died from having the back of his head caved in. And on top of it all, my alibi in Pine City spoke to the deceased, who told him that a man had just broken into my house and was demanding to see me. It's the reason we hurried home from the lawyer's office—did I happen to mention that we were in a lawyer's office? So, obviously, the man who broke in killed our friend here. Any questions so far, or should I continue?"

"He did die from what they call a *blunt trauma* to the head," Melissa assured me at a whisper, her attempt to ease the tension. "It was stove in like a mush melon. His head."

Huyne tilted his head sideways at me like a hunting dog.

"You don't talk like the rest of these locals much, do you?"

Andrews appeared from the kitchen. I knew the expression he was wearing: rugby-ready for kicking the vital organs out of anything that crossed his path.

"On the other hand," Andrews said to me, voice knife-edged, "I was just thinking how your diction is much less pompous than it used to be. I think you're kind of settling in here at home."

"I've only been home for a couple of years." I smiled at Huyne. "I was gone from Blue Mountain a long while—teaching at a university in Atlanta."

"We'll check out your alibi in—" He turned to his cohort. "Where was it?"

"Pine City." The man didn't consult any notes; didn't look up.

He was a little older than Huyne and didn't bother to hide his exhaustion. It seemed a fatigue built into his bones and sinews over years of dull dangers and sharp knives.

"But it doesn't mean much to me either way." Huyne nailed his eyes to mine. "Time of death is close enough to indicate the possibility that you were in Pine City, motored home, killed Shultz, and called the local law enforcement. We get this sort of thing more than you know: The killer calls the cops, thinking we'll never suspect him if he's the one who reports the crime. 'Why would I call you if I did it, Officer?' "

"What about the man who broke in and threatened Shultz?" Andrews wasn't very good at disguising incredulity.

"Oh, jeez," Huyne's voice mocked with every letter he pronounced. "The murderer was a mysterious stranger. We've never heard *that* one before."

"And my companion/witness?" I indicated Andrews with my hand, as if I were asking him to take a bow. "The one who was with me all day and saw me *not* do it?"

"He's in on it." Huyne never took his eyes from mine.

"Okay." I couldn't prevent a slight smile from brightening my stare. "You've invented the opportunity. What's my motive?"

"A silver coin." He tried to pierce my eyes through to the back of my skull with his gaze. "You don't know where it is, do you?"

I returned his stare with equal electricity.

"It wasn't in Mr. Shultz's pocket? Could we suppose that the murderer got it?"

Huyne turned to his assistant.

"Frisk him."

The man moved instantly. Skid moved faster, coming between me and the man headed my way.

"Not in my jurisdiction," Skid hissed. "Nobody gets a frisking tonight. Are we clear?"

Skid had his back to me, but I could recognize the threat in his voice.

Huyne's assistant looked out the kitchen window.

"What's so important about this coin?" Skidmore asked Huyne.

"It's valued at half a million dollars. Sounds like a motive for murder to me."

Andrews and I sat in my kitchen with Melissa Mathews, trying to keep our voices down while Skid conferred, at a low boil, with the policemen from Atlanta.

"Where did he get that 'half a million dollars' business?" Andrews leaned into the table, almost hovering over it, his voice hushed, face drained of color.

"How did he even know about the coin?" My arms were folded in front of my chest. I realized I was rocking back and forth just a little, and stopped myself.

The air had chilled considerably after the rain; it was in the lower fifties outside. The sky was made of slate, an ancient blackboard with dots of chalk for stars, not made of air at all—or light.

"That Detective Huyne man?" Melissa's clear tones were bells compared to my grumbling fog. "Or however you say his name—I believe he came into this house already believing you killed the man, the dead man."

"What makes you say that?" I asked her.

"Demeanor." She nodded once. "And another thing. I didn't ever reach any of Mr. Shultz's relatives or anything, just left an urgent message, you know, on the phone machine. And that man showed up, out for blood."

"Well." I shivered. "We've got to find out a whole lot more—"

But one of the local deputies, a man who had come in with Melissa, interrupted my sentence.

"Mel?" he said to Deputy Mathews. He sounded nervous, looked twelve.

"Dr. Devilin, you know Crawdad, right?" She didn't seem to think there was anything out of the ordinary about the boy's name.

His hand shot out before I could say anything.

"It's a honor." He made the word *honor* sound holy.

"I'm happy to meet you." I took his hand; his grip was solid.

"My mama? She told a story into your tape machine once, and you put it in a book. We got the book. It's open in the living room so everybody can see." He looked at Melissa. "They say that story's in the Library of Congress. In Washington, D.C."

"Your mother is . . ." I'd collected so many stories over the years, it was impossible to remember them all.

"Dolly Pritchett. She was a Mathews, like Melissa. We're related some kind of way, but dang if I can suss it out." He grinned.

"*You're* Crawdad Pritchett?"

"Yes, sir." He seemed a bit nervous at my suddenly aggressive tone.

"I can't believe it. I haven't seen you in years." I turned to Andrews. "This young man, when he was seven or eight, won a very important state fiddling contest. He used to jump up and down while he was playing, as if he were on a pogo stick. Great musician." I turned back to Crawdad. "Are you still playing?"

He shrugged. "I was in a rock and roll band for a while, but the deputy work, it's hard and I'm kindly tired when I get home."

Kindly, I thought, marking his mispronunciation. If he's anything like the rest of his family, that's probably the way he would do anything: kindly.

"Too bad." I smiled. "How's your mother?"

"She passed." He cleared his throat.

"I'm sorry to hear that."

"It was the lung cancer. Took awhile. We said our good-bye."

"You came in here for a reason," Melissa said softly to Crawdad.

"Oh. Right. Look: That beat-up old trunk in the back corner over there?" He shifted his eyes in the direction of Conner's trunk, then lowered his voice considerably. "I believe it's been tampered with. It's the only thing in the house we can find that seems, you know, out of the ordinary. I ain't told nobody else yet. I mean, it's *your* trunk."

"This is why I brought old Crawdad with me," Melissa said, voice hushed to match his, a smile crinkling her lips. "He's better than anyone I know at figuring out what's 'out of the ordinary.' Got a real sixth sense about it—eerie. *That's* his genius. And he's using it to help you out."

I understood. She was telling me not to bother him about his fiddle playing. He wasn't called to music; he was called to this unusual ability at police work, somehow. I accepted her evaluation.

"What's strange about the way the trunk looks?" I tried not to look in the direction of it.

"I got it figured like this: You had some things in that trunk, but they were things that nobody hadn't looked at in a while—until today. The dust patterns on the top and inside that trunk are different from any other ones in the whole house. They look just the littlest bit frantic, the patterns do. Like someone was looking for something in there. That's what I found strange."

"Why?" Melissa was watching the men in the living room.

"Because there was all that activity in there recently," Crawdad explained softly, "and there's nothing inside of that trunk. It's empty."

By midnight, the detectives from Atlanta had created as much ill will as they were going to for one night's work. Huyne had insulted everything about Melissa's enterprise: the fingerprint expert from Pine City, the Polaroid snapshots of the scene, and her management of the first moments at the crime scene. He stopped short when Skid renewed an interest in arresting him and carting him off to a small-town jail on trumped-up charges that would keep him in hell for months. The rest of us knew Skid was bluffing, but Huyne seemed nervous enough about the prospect to shut down his worst ire.

After what Crawdad had told us, it was all I could do to keep myself from looking in my great-grandfather's trunk. The fact that it was empty did nothing to subdue my great desire to peer inside and see.

I was almost happy when Huyne made a point of saying goodbye to us in the kitchen.

"Dr. Devilin?" He stood in the archway between the kitchen and the living room, glaring down at me. "You don't leave town. You don't mess with anything. You don't look cross-eyed at anybody. And if I find out you have that silver coin, I'll beat you hard with a tire iron. I can see that you have friends here, people who prevent me from doing what I ought to do. That won't last. I'll be back, and you'll be screwed."

"There's that language issue again." I stood. "I'm letting it go because I've determined you actually *can't* think of anything better to say. As to where I go and what I do with my time, you have less chance of keeping me in one place than does Deputy Mathews. *She* has a tranquilizer dart."

She looked up at Huyne.

"It's true." She smiled sweetly. "Out in the squad car."

Huyne looked at his nameless companion.

"I can't tell if they're really like this," he said, throat dry, "or they're putting me on."

The man nodded, avoiding all eye contact.

"Where are we staying?" he asked the man.

"Mountain Vista Hotel," the man answered, "in Pine City."

"I'm making calls," Huyne assured me.

I had no idea what he meant.

Without another word, Huyne vanished into the night.

Or at least he made it out my front door before stumbling down the front steps, offering us his loudest, most vile curse yet, plunging into his car, and tearing up the gravel in the road as he tore away.

"I thought he'd *never* leave." Andrews yawned. "I'm checking your trunk."

Skid ambled into the kitchen.

"Don't bother. Crawdad told me about it; I looked. Everything's gone. Sorry, Fever—all those stories and papers about your great-grandfather."

Skidmore had seen me at that trunk a dozen times; heard me tell stories about Conner for most of my life. Andrews accepted Skid's assessment of the situation and kept his seat at the kitchen table.

"Why would the killer take that stuff, those dusty old stories?" Andrews looked at Skidmore. "And nothing else in the house?"

"I'm afraid that's what Fever is going to try and find out." Skidmore sighed.

He was too tired to say more on the subject. He knew it was useless to talk me out of doing anything, and that knowledge, apparently, took a lot of wind out of his sails.

"Well." I stood. "Do you want some coffee?"

"Not the crankcase oil you make in that thing." He glared at my espresso machine, then sat.

"No hard caffeine for the sheriff." I went to the cupboard and fetched the French press. "How about this?"

"Okay, I guess."

"How was Alabama?"

"Hot. Look, Fever, we have to get some things straight here. My investigation will assume that the intruder is the murderer. That's what we'll pursue. But this guy Huyne? He's not going away. He thinks you killed a man, and he's really hammering me. He's letting me handle the investigation for the time being because he *has* to. It's my jurisdiction. Only, I predict that Huyne will be trouble. For both of us."

"What exactly is his damage?" Andrews rubbed his eyes.

"He told me that Mr. Shultz's father," Skid began, failing to prevent his distaste for the subject from filling his words, "is a very wealthy man in Atlanta. He knows people who know people, and he's set Huyne on this like a pit bull on a rabbit. Huyne resents doing it, so he's taking it out on everyone else. Mostly you, but also me. He wants me to arrest you, hold you as a suspect until the evidence can be examined by someone he trusts, which would *not* be Chester and Mrs. Tomlinson. He sent them home."

"Fine by me." I wrestled with the cord to the coffee-bean grinder. "The so-called evidence is on my side."

"Not really." Skid let go a sigh made entirely of lead.

"What?" I stopped what I was doing.

"Huyne also told me that the Shultz family really has valued this coin thing at half a million dollars—very recently. And of course we know that the victim brought the coin to you."

"I said that—"

"I'm not finished." Skidmore looked out the kitchen window at the moonlight. "At the moment, I'm not going to ask you where the coin is, or if you have it here, because I don't want to know. But if it comes to be important, I'll have to hear what you have to say about it. Am I clear on this?

"What would be my reason—"

"Huyne knows that the coin used to belong to your family."

"What?" I froze. "How could he possibly—"

"I have no idea." Skid interrupted a third time, "but this Detective Huyne has no difficulty believing you're guilty—seems to have some kind of *Deliverance* nightmare playing in their heads: mountain-folk revenge and greed rampant—"

"Inbred flesh-eating hillbillies," Andrews interrupted sagely, barely able to keep his head up. "I can understand that."

I wasn't the only one glaring at Andrews, just the only one who spoke to him.

"What's the *matter* with you sometimes?" I shook my head. "You know these people up here, what they're really like."

"I need sleep." He yawned again. "There's a dead body in the next room—of a guy I was actually getting to like. And worst of all, Deputy Mathews won't give me the time of day. Jesus!"

Suspicion of murder and proximity to a corpse, it seemed, had done nothing to quell the mighty libido of Dr. Winton Andrews. There would always be an England.

Eight

The next morning was blinding—sky scrubbed, air glass-clear.

Of course, the beauty of such a morning was lost on me. I couldn't sit in my own living room, I'd been up since 6:30, and my brain was a rabid simian: branch to branch, chattering senselessly, trying to quell a mighty panic. The previous night seemed more a hallucination than an experience. Little about it was coherent, even upon ardent reflection.

How could the Shultz family have known that the coin belonged to my family? How was it possible that they'd valued it at half a million dollars? Clearly, the man who had disturbed Shultz's sleep was the murderer. And Shultz seemed to think it was someone I knew. Why had the man taken everything in Conner's trunk? Who was he?

And as my mind sailed from branch to branch on the Tree of Distraction, I knew I was avoiding the darkest shadows, the places where the sun couldn't reach, even on so bright a day. Part of the dexterity in my mental gymnastics was an ardent attempt to avoid thinking about Shultz, or facing the fact that a very nice man had been killed in my home. But it was always there, the image of the corpse, an oozing heap, just at the corner of my eye.

Skid and the rest of the local constabulary had stayed long enough to make certain that the dead body was properly removed by the Deveroe Brothers Funeral Parlor not long after midnight. That had been a strange affair: silent, slow; I'd stayed out on the porch for most of it.

Before he left, Skid reminded me that, legally, I was a suspect in a murder investigation and that, *technically,* I ought not to leave the house.

By my fifth espresso that morning, I was holding the keys to my truck in my hand, waiting for Andrews to wake up.

Jangling the keys in my hand, I kept thinking, over and over, Why did I ask Shultz to come up here?

It wasn't like me to have company. What had compelled me to do it? Lucinda's absence couldn't completely explain it. She'd been gone before. We'd been separated for years, in fact, before I'd come back to Blue Mountain.

Extraordinary heat in September—that was a better answer.

But the truth was that my own ennui had brought me to my state: a bizarre lack of direction, an aimless emptiness that wouldn't fix itself and was immune to hard work, mental distraction, or the promises of domestic joy.

That thought only made it harder for me to focus on any one of the dozens of bursting paranormal aneurysms that were exploding in my skull. But it did make the necessity for clarity paramount if I wanted to do the work I had to do.

And that work seemed fraught with psychological dangers. I had helped Skidmore investigate murders. I'd even gone looking for killers. This was different: It involved my family, my heritage—my home—more deeply than any enterprise before it.

I almost leapt out of my chair when I heard Andrews at the top of the stairs.

"God, how could you sleep like that?" I tried not to sound like a lunatic, but that didn't work out.

"What?" Andrews was holding on to the banister for dear life, barely able to make out the sound of my voice.

"I'm jumping out of my skin." I shook the keys in my hand. "I have to go."

"Where?" Andrews was managing his way down the steps with a pace and care generally given to brides headed toward an altar.

But he did have a point. *Where* indeed?

"I have to do something."

"I know." He achieved the last step. "Just let me—" He couldn't seem to remember the next words in his sentence.

"Espresso." I shot to the machine.

He leaned on the door frame.

"How many shots have *you* had?"

"We have to find out about the three items that Conner insured." I ignored his question. "That's the starting place."

"Possibly." He scratched the back of his head. "But have you tried to figure out why everything in that old trunk of yours was taken—and nothing else is missing from the whole house?"

"That's correct." I got out a cup for Andrews. "My assumption is, obviously, that the intruder came here for the coin, somehow knew that Shultz had brought it here. Shultz said he didn't have it. The intruder asked him where it was. Shultz said it was with me. The intruder asked where I was. Shultz couldn't remember the name of the lawyer but said I'd found his name in the trunk. The intruder looked in the trunk, found all sorts of things about Conner, and *by* Conner, and tried to go through them because Conner was connected with the coin, as we now know. Shultz objected. Maybe there was a struggle. The intruder killed Shultz. Then, realizing he had to get out, the killer gathered up everything in the trunk without looking at it, imagining that there would be valuable information somewhere in all those papers. He was wrong, of course, but he had no way of knowing."

Andrews stared.

"Jesus." He shook his head. "No more espresso for you, and I mean it."

"I have to *do* something. Any action is better than inaction."

"Well." Andrews sat. "Let's start with your basic premise: The killer was after the coin. Who knew about the coin?"

"God, that doesn't help. Anyone could have known: insurance

agents, office workers, anyone who overheard something or saw some kind of paperwork—"

"Also Hek and June," Andrews interrupted. "Therefore, all manner of local people hereabouts, and, we must assume, lawyer Taylor. Not to mention the fact that Shultz, bless him, was not exactly tight-lipped on the subject. So, I agree: That doesn't help. Serves me right for trying to think before coffee."

"The more I consider this question," I concurred, "the larger the number grows of people who might have an interest in the coin."

"You still have it with you, I presume." Andrews deliberately avoided looking at me. "The coin."

My hand shot to the left pocket of my jeans. They were the same ones I'd worn the day before. I'd slept in them.

The coin was there, a mocking imitation of the moon.

I took it out and showed it to him.

"Interesting how you didn't tell Detective Huyne that you had it."

I put it back in my pocket, then instantly began thinking where I could hide it.

"I didn't deny that I had it."

"No." Andrews didn't sound himself.

"What is it?" I glowered at him. "Why is your voice like that?"

"I'm just wondering." He finally looked at me. "If I didn't know you better, I'd think that you were feeling a sense of entitlement where this coin is concerned—that it belongs to you."

I let a number of angry responses pass through my mind without giving them voice, because it also occurred to me that he might, in some small way, be correct. Perhaps something in the murkier parts of my subconscious *did* make me think I had a right to the thing.

When my throat finally did let several syllables go, they were fairly innocuous.

"Single or double? Your espresso."

Andrews smiled.

"Don't you have any bigger cup than that?" It was clear he had nothing but absolute, righteous disdain for the demitasse I held in my hand.

I reached up into the open cabinet and retrieved a mug, held it out for his approval.

"I suppose it will do—if you fill it to the brim."

"With this espresso."

"Absolutely," he confirmed. "I had a bad night."

"You had a bad night? Let me tell you what an *actual* bad night looks like. Start with an inability to sleep. Make that inability a door that opens out onto a landscape of your worst, most personal demons and terrors. Step across that threshold and find yourself wandering aimlessly in a world of shadowy Jungian swill that occasionally and without warning vomits out the worst monsters of your id: grotesque, deformed images of your parents and a tangle of brambles that wrap around your ankles and keep you from moving toward a peaceful horizon. And then, when you can't move, you have the slow realization that in some way you're actually wanted for murder in a world more real than your little hometown. And worse, the true murderer is wandering around in that same hellish landscape, looking for you, because he hasn't found what he wants, and you have it in your pocket. Then—"

"Christ, I get the picture." Andrews rubbed one eye with an open palm. "I should know never to go head-to-head with you in the Festival of Angst."

I realized my fingers were shaking just a bit.

"Well." I exhaled, deliberately calming myself. "When you're the one who invented the game, you always have a pretty good chance of winning."

"If I don't get caffeine in three seconds, I swear to God—"

I shoved the mug under the espresso machine's spout and pushed the button. The whoosh of the steam was, at that moment, the most comforting sound in the known universe.

Andrews decided to have the rest of his espresso on the front porch. I sat with him, impatient, biting the inside of my cheek. The morning was still chilly, but it was a welcome relief from previous weeks of stifling heat and unusual humidity.

Something had broken open the hard shell of autumn, and the crack of blue sky, the thrill of cold fingers, the contrast of warm sun and bracing wind—all were a healing tonic for those last, sick days of summer.

He set his mug down on the floor of the porch and sat back in his rocking chair. Dressed in sweatpants and a flannel shirt, hair dangerously exploded from his head, Andrews was still a man on vacation, however horribly it had gone wrong.

I, on the other hand, was ready for battle: black jeans, work boots, light leather jacket over black T-shirt—perfect for a man who expected to be walking in shadows most of the time.

"So what now?" Andrews stared out at the mountainside directly across from my porch.

"Well, from what we saw yesterday—which seems a hundred years ago—I mean at the lawyer's office: Conner acquired three items at the same time, and those three items are related to me. They turned out to be things that were used in order to fund my college education. Now one of those three items is the center of a very bad sequence of events, and we have no idea where the other two are. I believe we have to find out as much as we can about all three of these things, including, especially, who has been interested in them recently. As in: Has someone else contacted lawyer Taylor? Or did someone else contact Shultz's father not long ago?"

"Sorry, your diction's falling apart a bit. Why would you say that last one?"

"What made Shultz's father change the insured value of the coin from five thousand to half a million and not tell Shultz?"

"Oh." Andrews sat forward in his rocker. "We have to find out more about those three items."

"Brilliant. I knew you'd think of something."

"It hasn't occurred to you that the sale of the coin might have been what put you through college?"

"For five thousand dollars? It was more than that *a year.*"

"Okay." He hesitated. "But didn't the police tell you not to leave home?"

"All this world," I pronounced, "is my native home."

"Then why are we sitting here on this porch?"

Clearly, his large dose of espresso had kicked in nicely, and Dr. Andrews was ready to move.

"We're waiting for you to change clothes, I think." I eyed his flannel shirt.

"It's your funeral." He stood immediately. "I won't be a moment."

And he was off.

"I'll follow you up," I called after him. "I have to do something in my mother's room."

I clutched the coin in my pocket. Andrews was already in the shower.

Andrews had dressed in his own kind of armor: rugby shirt, baggy shorts, tennis shoes with no socks. The day was attempting an early autumn, a crack in the air, sky as blue as Blind Willie McTell's soul. I was standing in the yard, looking into the woods.

"Okay, cappie." Andrews clamored down the steps. "Where are we going?"

"*Cappie*?" I shook my head. "That's what you're calling me?"

"It's short for 'Captain, my Captain—' "

"Shut up, would you mind?" I headed for the truck.

"Understood. No *cappie.* Fine. But where are we going? Seriously." He followed.

"We want to find out more about the three items that Conner got sometime in 1942. He bought them at an auction. We could try to find out something about the auction, but it seems to me we ought to find out something more about the items themselves." I opened the driver's door to the truck.

"We already know a good bit about the coin." He climbed into the passenger seat. "You mean we should find out about the other two things. I'm not certain how that helps us find the guy—"

But Andrews couldn't quite make himself say the rest of the sentence.

"The *guy,*" I said quickly, "was looking for the coin, we presume.

Or at least that's what the police are presuming. What they don't know is that the coin and the other two things are tied together somehow. And when the *guy* broke into my house, he didn't say 'Give me the coin"; he said, 'Where's Devilin?' or something like that. Isn't that what lawyer Taylor told us?"

"I think so." Andrews pulled on his earlobe. "Maybe we should talk to Taylor again, find out exactly what Shultz said."

"Agreed." I started the truck. "But also there's a pretty good library in Pine City, and computer access to Galileo, the—"

"The Georgia Public Library Service—the state's virtual library," he said, interrupting me. "Access to multiple information resources: scholarly journals, books, encyclopedias. I'm familiar. I'm a real academic and I teach classes and everything."

"I always forget that." I shoved into first gear.

"So what about the library?"

"Yes. How about if you go and try to find out more about the painting while I deal with Taylor."

"The portrait by Cotman. You know I could access Galileo on my own computer."

"In the first place, a library has actual books and a less superficial exploration of most topics than any Internet search," I growled, "and in the second place, do you really want to stay alone in my house while I'm gone right now?"

"I love a good library," he said without missing a beat.

And if our venture seemed a bit half-baked, or even more than a little desperate to either of us, we kept silent and did not share our doubts with each other.

Any action is better than inaction.

Nine

I dropped Andrews off at the Pine City Library. It was the best in the county, the product of an older generation's noblesse oblige to the poor mountain community that had spawned them. Railroad money had made some men in Pine City wealthy. Those who had prospered gave back to the community in the form of a hospital, a library, and a civic garden.

The library had been a fine modern design when it was built in 1954. My opinion of architecture from that era is that it reflects the sentiments of the age perfectly: It's square, unimaginative, determined to be boring—and proud of it.

This library was a sterling example of the genre: a low one-story L-shaped redbrick building with absolutely no distinguishing detail of any sort. The windows were eight or ten feet high and two feet wide, framed in white concrete. Landscaping in the form of militantly manicured boxwoods gave the look of the whole its final yawn. To make matters worse, the brick had gone to moss and grunge. It gave the whole place an appearance of never being used at all. Andrews looked so forlorn standing on the cracking entrance path that I almost told him to get back into the truck and go to Taylor's with me.

But he waved, a bit of cool wind tousled his air, and he was gone, disappearing into the shadows at the door.

The morning had opened up nicely: cooling breeze, warming sun, blazing sky. I headed to the offices of Taylor and Taylor, Attorneys at Law.

When I pulled my truck into the driveway, I couldn't see any other cars parked around the house. I got out of the truck and stomped onto the front porch, hoping to alert anyone inside that a large man who meant business was on his way in. My performance, alas, was in vain. The door was locked; the place seemed deserted.

Nevertheless, I pounded on the door like a man with a mission. Instantly, I heard noises within: a chair scraping across the floor, footsteps.

The door opened, and Becky Meadows was smiling up at me. She was wearing a pale blue spring dress and a white cashmere button sweater.

"I just knew it was you." She lowered her voice. "I believe I might be just a little bit psychic. They say lots of southern girls are."

"They do say that." I smiled back.

"Mr. Taylor is in court—or, really, what they call 'in chambers' with a judge. He won't be back until after lunch, he said."

"May I come in?"

She sighed, did not move.

"I'm not supposed to let anyone in. I mean, he said, Mr. Taylor? He said not to let anyone in while he was gone." Becky pursed her lips. "He said it was because he's worried about my personal safety, but I believe he might actually have doubts about my intelligence level, you know?

"I *do* know. And I'm not *anyone.* I'm a client—sort of."

"Oh, you're a client all right," she assured me.

"And you know why I'm here. Because there were several files missing from the group you showed me yesterday. And you know I know that—not only because you're a little bit psychic but also because your intelligence level is higher than you let on, and certainly higher than Mr. Taylor or your father can imagine."

It was all conjecture, but a third of all the information I had ever collected from reluctant folk informants had been the result of what I thought of as "the flattering guess."

Her eyes widened so dangerously that I thought they might actually pop out of their sockets. My technique had worked.

"How do you know all that?" Her voice was barely above a whisper.

I matched her tone. "I might be a little bit psychic, too." Alas, that was the best I could do in the way of *charm.*

"Especially about those files." She was amazed and wanted me to know it. "Everybody says you're a really smart man, but damn."

"So . . ." I made as to take a step in through the door.

She stood aside.

The office was dark even on such a bright day, partly because the house itself had been designed in an era when dark rooms were the fashion and partly because all the curtains were closed and the lights were off everywhere except over Becky's desk.

"Or course I'd like to see any files pertaining to my family that I did not see yesterday. I think there were two of them missing from the group, but there may be more."

"There are only two I know about." She looked down. "I mean, there's more, you know, that pertains to your whole family as a whole—but I know the two you want. I'm supposed to say, if you ever asked, that I misfiled them—you know, because of all the correspondence sent overseas was in the name of Briarwood, not Devilin. It is confusing, but I didn't misfile any damn thing. Mr. Taylor told me to put them in another drawer and not to tell you about them. That's a lawyer's version of honesty: never lie, but always hide the truth and don't mention it, you know?"

She looked out the door for a brief second, as if we were both cheating spouses, then closed it and went immediately to the bank of file cabinets behind her desk.

"I'm not going to ask you why he did this." I followed behind her. "I'd rather believe that you don't know."

I had decided to let go of whatever other files she had concerning my "whole family as a whole," at least for the moment.

"Believe away." She waved her hand over her shoulder without looking back at me. "You could write a book on what I don't know around here."

She made straight for a cabinet in the corner, pulled open the second drawer from the top, and fished out two manila folders.

"Here they are." She turned back to me. Her face was grim. "How long you reckon you might be—looking at these things, I mean?"

"Two hours?"

"If you get close to lunchtime, I'll have to take them back. I can't let Mr. Taylor see—"

"Understood," I interrupted. "Shall I just nip on back to the conference room where we were yesterday?"

"Uh-huh." She held her breath for a second.

I could see she had something more to say.

"Yes?" I wanted to give her the opportunity.

"That'n you were with yesterday? The English accent man? Is he as old as you? I don't mean to be rude."

I failed to keep a brief smile from lighting my face.

"You're not the least bit rude. Dr. Andrews is only a year younger than I, but he looks, I realize, closer to your age than mine. That's the boyish, ruddy complexion of an English heritage working overtime."

"I'm not entirely sure what that means, but he *is* cute."

"He is that." Why not make a bit of a match? I thought. "And I'm certain he felt the same about you."

"Doubt it." She blushed and looked toward the filing cabinet as if she'd forgotten something.

"I'll go and have a look at these files now."

She nodded without looking at me.

I headed down the dark hall, flipped on the light in the conference room, took a chair across the table, facing the door, and got to work.

I'd sorted through ten or twelve long legal documents in one of the folders, marked "C. Devilin, Instructions, Various," before I'd come across the first one that chilled me.

It was a detailed list of what should be sent to "one Molly O'Shea, without her knowledge of the sender." Attached to the list was a letter dated May 3, 1919:

Dearest Conner,

You should hear that Molly's died these three years past. Mr. Jamison let her go after your trial and she found work, we heard, at a good Dublin inn. There was an epidemic of influenza that came around that awful winter three years ago, and she succumbed. As she lay dying, she told another girl that she wished to send something to Adenton. When it arrived, we scarcely knew what to do with it, so Mr. Jamison kept it with his other things. Now he's gone, too, and I thought you should have this. It's the same silver lily you made for Molly when you thought her heart was true. Mr. Jamison always said you had the devil in you. Maybe this can help you find peace.

And may God rest all the souls of our dear dead and departed.

Mrs. A. Jamison
Adenton, Ireland

I knew that Molly was the woman for whom Conner had killed a man. I knew about the silver lily, and its importance. What I found fascinating was the list attached to the letter: items that were all, apparently, fair game for selling to convert to cash, which Conner had instructed was to be sent to Molly O'Shea. They included, among other things, a deed to a silver mine in Wales.

At the bottom of the list there was a forlorn little note: "Void, see attached letter." It was stamped with the date September 7, 1919, and after the stamp there was another handwritten note that said, "Ref. Silver Mine, doc. #31."

I shuffled through the folder and, surely enough, found a single piece of paper with the number 31 in the upper right-hand corner. That page outlined the details of a sale of the deed to a silver mine in Aberystwyth, Wales. The proceeds were invested, and then the entire account based on those moneys was closed in 1942, when Conner, quite abruptly, took the money out and bought "3 items at auction. See doc. 42."

"Doc. 42," as it happened, was in the other folder marked "Proposed Disbursements." It was a bill of sale for the portrait by Cotman. Attached to it were several other pages. One was a long letter from my father to Conner, the upshot of which was that my father had done as he'd been told; the portrait had been sold in order to pay for my university education. There was an entire paragraph imploring Conner to explain why the portrait was so important—obviously it had been the object of some argument.

That letter was dated 1975, which was, if I remembered correctly, the year Conner died.

But as I read further, I encountered my second chill.

My father wanted to know what to do with the rest of the proceeds. The painting had sold for $250,000.

Apparently, no one had realized that the painting would be so valuable, with the possible exception of Conner, who, it was beginning to seem, possessed as much brilliance as he did stubbornness—a mighty accomplishment.

Another one of the documents attached to that same swath was a letter from the Ashton Gallery in London attesting to the authenticity of the painting: ". . . rare, perhaps one-of-a-kind portrait by Cotman, of Lady Eloise Barnsley, circa 1804." The letter went on to say, however, that it was impossible to assess its value properly because there was no way to compare it with any of Cotman's other works, and that Cotman was a "negligible artist." Their explanation was: "Cotman often used a gray underpainting and thickly brushed color, which dull his paintings rather than let the light shine through. This muddy style is grim; not to the tastes of our London collectors."

So why, my father concluded in his letter to Conner, had it sold for such an astonishing price in 1975?

I set the papers down and took a breath.

What struck me most about all of this information was how a strange series of events had transpired in order to reach into my life and change it profoundly: a false love, a murder, a silver mine, a whim, an auction, a portrait: my ticket out of town.

And, with a pinch at the back of the jaw, I wondered, too, at the odd path a silver coin had taken from a mint in Wales to a rich man's son, who gave it to me just before he became a corpse.

The astonishing connection between seemingly random events was nearly overwhelming to me at that moment. It all seemed to confirm, as most things in my life did, my deep belief in folklore, in mining the past for the real treasure: my own desperate, mysterious attempt to prove an interconnectedness between all events and all human beings.

It was an attempt that had always failed, to my great disappointment.

Still, it was, I knew, the reason for the work I did—among the greatest reasons for doing anything on the planet: proving faith.

When you're looking at a dusty, yellowing piece of paper, you could actually be looking at the root of your tree.

When you listen to an old man tell a long, boring story about how things used to be, you're actually listening to the beginnings of human culture.

When you hear a tinny song cautioning young women in eighteenth-century Dublin not to be "easy and free," you're genuinely hearing a life-and-death warning, today, from your wisest ancestors.

If you don't know your roots, you'll never know your path. If you ignore the beautiful past, you're in for an ugly future. These stories and songs comprise precious information about the past and make the greatest mirror devised by the human will, because in it we can see ourselves. If you know the song "Johnny Has Gone for a Soldier," then you know the privation of all war. If you know the story of your grandmother's courtship, then you know the enduring, cyclical nature of all love. If you really listen to the sound of a fiddle scraping silver notes in a moonless night as they pierce like a dagger into the darkness, then you know all there is to know of life.

But just as my self-congratulatory silent sermon rose to a nearly anthemic pitch in my brain, it was interrupted by Becky Meadows, in a panic.

"He's in the driveway!" She was already shuffling papers and gathering folders. "He's back early, and he blocked your truck in, so you can't get out!"

"Easy," I told her, standing. "We'll tell him whatever he wants to hear."

"Like hell," she shot back. "He *wants* to hear that you didn't come by today, but he's not likely to believe that now, is he?"

"I can be pretty convincing." I smiled, I believed, wanly.

She was in no mood.

"What *are* you going to say, Dr. Devilin, no kidding?"

"Have you ever heard the saying, The best defense is a good offense?"

"No."

I handed her the last few papers just as we both heard the front door open.

"Watch and learn." I took a deep breath. "Taylor! Is that you?"

I stormed out of the conference room, motioning for Becky to stay put.

"Dr. Devilin?" His voice was a coiled cobra. "I thought that was your truck."

"Do you want my family's business or not?" I appeared in the hallway.

"What?" He paused in front of the door to his office.

"I wonder if other members of the Georgia Bar would be interested in the shoddy way you handle an account like ours." I lumbered in his direction.

"I don't know what you're—"

"You don't *know* that your secretary, Betty, misfiled important documents pertaining to my trust?" I thought calling Becky by the wrong name had just the right touch of boorishness. "Not to mention that *all* the files are a mess. Completely shoddy organizational work."

"Oh." He wasn't able to hide the fact that he was relieved at the nature of my complaint.

"I came here with a few questions about the phone call you received yesterday from my houseguest, and I just happened to ask your girl here if I had seen all the files concerning my great-grandfather. When she hesitated, I made her check. She found two in the wrong drawer!"

Taylor paused.

Before he could think of what to say, Becky appeared behind me.

"I'm *so* sorry, Mr. Taylor," she said as she passed by me in the hall. "I don't know how I could have put these in the wrong place."

"I'll speak with you later, *Becky.*" He was lizard-cool. "Now, Dr. Devilin, won't you have a moment in my office?"

He indicated with the palm of his hand that I was to precede him into his lair.

"I must apologize for my secretary." Oil—or was it venom—dripped from the syllables. "She's the daughter of a big client, you understand."

Not only do I understand, I thought triumphantly, but I already guessed something like that before I was told. I might actually have something of a talent for prescience.

"Now, in the matter of this . . . I'm not certain what you're referring to," he stammered, "when you say something about a phone call."

"The telephone call you received yesterday from my houseguest," I said patiently, "who was in such a panic that we left immediately after his call."

Taylor made his way to the desk at a deliberately glacial pace. He was dressed in a charcoal suit of raw silk—seemed Italian in design. The shirt was blinding-white and starched; the tie was the color of dark blood.

"No." He gave the appearance of trying to think. "A *desperate* phone call? I think I'd remember something like that."

"You came to get us out of the conference room." I stood directly in front of his desk, under the ominous chandelier. "When I got to the phone, it was dead."

"Dr. Devilin." He sat. "I have no idea what you're talking about."

As I stood trying to fathom his reasons for denying the event, I felt the ice of an empty cave in my stomach.

He was going to tell the police that I was lying about Shultz's call.

What felt like five minutes passed in silence.

My mind was racing from one supposition to another. In a flash of desperation, I took a sip of breath and called out.

"Becky?" I glanced at Taylor. "That's her name?"

"It is." He had pasted an amused smile across his lips.

I heard Becky appear in the doorway behind me and turned to look her in the eye.

"When Dr. Andrews, the cute one with the English accent, and I were in the conference room yesterday, didn't Mr. Taylor here interrupt our calm examination of the documents with an emergency phone call?"

Her face flushed so suddenly that I thought she might be having some sort of attack, and her eyes shot to Taylor.

"Not that I recall." She sounded like a tiny doll. She wouldn't look me in the eye.

"I see." I turned back to Taylor. "Well, we both know the truth of the matter. All I have to do is find out why you're lying, tell the right people what you've done, and then decide whether to tear down this house or turn it into a nice little bed-and-breakfast."

Taylor adjusted some papers in front of him so that they would line up exactly perpendicular to the back edge of his desk.

"I'd be careful about taking on a small-town lawyer with a hundred years' worth of community ties. Sometimes a man like that can be surprisingly—what's the word I want?—vengeful."

"You don't know the first thing about revenge," I snarled. "So I'll give you a short lesson. You come from English stock, a group of men and women who found financial gain and religious independence in a new world. I come from Scots-Irish heraldry. Most of us came to these mountains to escape execution for murder. I'm sure your hypothetical small-town lawyer, the one with an inadequate education and an unconscious death wish, would understand the difference."

As I had hoped, Taylor was momentarily at a loss. I was almost certain I could read in his face what I had suspected: He knew

Conner's history; understood the reference I had made. It was enough to keep him stymied just long enough for me to turn back to Becky.

She wouldn't look up from the floor.

"It's all right, Becky." I didn't know what else to say.

She nodded for a second, then vanished with almost supernatural speed.

"As it happens," I said calmly, returning my attention to Taylor, "the sheriff of my little hamlet is a friend of mine—in fact, my best friend. His primary case at the moment concerns the murder of a man at my house yesterday—although I feel you already know that, somehow. But I'm absolutely certain he'll be looking into your affairs, strictly in the line of duty, you understand. If every single little thing in your world isn't as perfectly straight as the papers on your desk, you'll need a lawyer of your own. And if you find yourself in a snarl with my family business, you may want an undertaker handy."

He coughed up what passed for a laugh.

"I'm sure that kind of talk intimidates the feebleminded in your tiny world, but *as it happens,* I was just in the courthouse this morning, where I ate a small-town sheriff for breakfast. With grits and gravy. Now are we done here? I have actual work to do."

Good. Arrogance was the perfect foible for Mr. Taylor. It's easy to erode and it produces a very satisfying loud crash.

Out on the front porch of Taylor's offices, trying to figure out how I was going to get my truck out of the driveway if he didn't move his black BMW, I wrestled with a more pertinent psychological issue. Why, exactly, had I threatened Mr. Taylor in such an uncharacteristically lowbrow fashion?

It was true enough that Taylor's kind had played a large hand in ruining the mountains where I lived. Shady real estate developments and systematically abusive contortions of the local judiciary had made his family rich. A sociopathic lack of responsibility or anything remotely resembling a conscience had kept them that way. But why had I displayed such a visceral response, coming as close to threatening his life as I could without being arrested?

Before an iota of light could be shed on the question, I heard the front door open behind me.

Becky breezed past me without a word before I could even turn to see her coming across the porch. She all but sprinted to Taylor's car, keys jangling like a sleigh harness in her right hand, and got into the BMW with lightning speed.

She started it up and backed it out into the street with a single jolt, then sat there, idling.

I realized after a second that she was waiting for me to get into my truck and leave.

I took my time, hoping that Taylor was listening or even peering through the curtains out the window. I wanted him to see how calm I was.

I made it to the truck, fired it, and pulled out slowly. I tried to catch Becky's eye, but she was looking at her feet, her face ashen.

Luck made me take a last glance at the house before I took off, and I saw the curtains in the window next to the front door snap shut.

Taylor had been watching me from his waiting room.

Ten

I was hoping to see Andrews standing in front of the library, maybe pacing impatiently, but he was nowhere in sight. I pulled the truck into the parking lot, still scanning for him. Mine was the only vehicle in the lot.

I was still in something of a muddle as I got out of the truck and made my way along the boring boxwood hedge toward the front door.

What was Taylor doing? What could possibly motivate him even to bother with me, let alone direct such aggressive malice in my direction?

The glass door to the library was cool to the touch, sighed open. The library seemed dark compared to the light outside. It was also quiet as a tomb and nearly as empty. The lone librarian, a young man who appeared to be in his teens, kept his eyes glued to a computer screen, took no notice of my entrance.

The place wasn't huge, but it took me several minutes of wandering, examining cubicles, before I found Andrews by himself at a long table in a back corner of the library.

"Well." I presented myself.

"Uh-huh." He didn't even look up.

He had at least twelve books spread out around him, and his hand was moving so fast taking notes on a tiny pad that the motion was actually a little blurred.

"How close are you to being finished?" I leaned against the table. "I'm anxious to leave Pine City; we might be wanted by the police."

He looked up slowly.

"I told you we shouldn't have left your house this morning," he told me, heavy-lidded.

I shook my head.

"It's not that. Our problem is going to be that Taylor says he doesn't remember getting Shultz's phone call yesterday."

"Doesn't remember . . ." It only took another second for Andrews to realize the implications of that single concept.

"Feel like a bite of lunch?" I shoved my hands into my jacket pockets.

"I guess I'm done here." Andrews stood, closed up his pad, tossed the pencil onto the table with the open books, and headed for the door.

I followed behind, eyeing the librarian. He didn't look up from his computer.

Andrews shoved through the glass door and into the light.

"What do you think is Taylor's game?" He saw my truck and made his way toward it without looking back at me.

"I'm worrying about that," I admitted. "But I'm also concerned about my reaction to him. I might have threatened his life, just a little."

Andrews stopped in his tracks, spun around.

"You *what*?" He seemed more amused that I would have thought, less incredulous.

"It was all very carefully worded." I stopped, too.

"That goes without saying—it's the way you talk."

"But I might have implied mayhem."

"Why did you do it?"

"That's what I'm saying." I fished the keys to the truck out of my pocket and started moving again. "I don't know what I was thinking. I don't know why I had that reaction."

"Well, it's not *that* hard to suss out. Taylor's clearly a bastard. I knew that the second I walked into his office."

Andrews fell in beside me.

"Still, I regret doing it." I sighed. "I don't much care for losing my temper."

"You lost your temper?"

"I mean, I didn't yell at him or anything," I hedged, "but I could certainly feel a flood of adrenaline, and I'm a little hot and dizzy now."

"You're such a *girl*."

I hadn't locked the truck. I hadn't locked much of anything since I'd been back in the mountains. But Andrews stood at the passenger door waiting for me to unlock it—the product of an urban life.

"It's open," I mumbled, climbing into the driver's seat.

"Oh." He pulled open his door. "Look, Taylor notwithstanding, I've got some news about this painter Cotman that you're not going to believe. I think, if the portrait was actually painted by him, it was probably worth a lot more than you might think."

The engine roared and I pulled out into the street, turned toward home.

"As a matter of fact," I responded, "I found a document at Taylor's that said it sold for two hundred and fifty thousand dollars. Can that be right?"

"It can," he confirmed. "And let me tell you why."

He pulled out his notepad as I stepped on the gas.

Andrews delighted in sharing his research. I felt it gave him the illusion of momentary superiority, and I did not disabuse him of his folly.

"John Sell Cotman," he began, narrating the PBS special that was so obviously in his head, "lived from 1782 until 1842. He was a landscape painter, leader of the so-called Norwich School."

"And that is?"

For some unknown reason, I was suddenly enjoying the drive. The air was glass, the sky was polished, and I'd had a fine moment of blood boiling to invigorate me. The road wound easily around plunging blue vistas, through soaring evergreens.

"Well." Andrews was absolutely reveling in his role as expert. "Cotman's early paintings, before 1804, were very Romantic, with a capital *R.* Read dark and stormy. The style was a bit of an imitation of the Norwich painter John Crome. One of his paintings from this period—didn't write down the title—was notable because he reversed the normal direction of light you would usually have found in paintings of the day. The sun is behind the artist, rather than below the horizon. He used a gray underpainting."

"I think one of the documents I just read may have mentioned that."

"It made the color all thick and brushy. Most people at the time didn't care for it."

"*Brushy* is an accepted art term?"

"It cast a dull pall over the painting, rather than letting the light shine through." Andrews was ignoring me. "This muddy style was deemed absolutely appropriate to Cotman's rather grim interpretation of rural life. And that, in very simple terms, is the Norwich School."

"Ah."

"I saw some of these, actually." He sat back and set his spiral pad in his lap. "I mean I saw them in real life, these paintings, when I was a kid—a fairly large collection, in fact."

"Where?"

"There's a place called the Castle Museum in Norwich that has—I don't know—lots of them. I thought they were kind of boring. All sort of orange and brown, nothing happening—not the sort of thing a boy of my ilk would have cared for."

"You liked . . . ," I encouraged.

"Van Gogh. You've got a choice between a tedious painting of a bridge or a self-portrait of a man who cut off his own ear. Which one do you go for? Not to mention the way van Gogh's paint seems to be moving, actually crawling across the canvas."

"Good, good, you liked Van Gogh," I interrupted. "For me it was the Towers of London by Monet that I saw in the High Museum in Atlanta when I was younger. But we digress."

"You asked."

"About Cotman," I insisted.

"I did find it impressive," Andrews said, picking up his pad, "that Cotman was a drawing instructor in a London school where Rossetti was a pupil."

"Really." I was impressed, as well.

"Then," he went on, a bit more mysteriously, "around 1804, something seems to have happened to our boy Cotman. His style went through a complete transformation. Suddenly, he's all filled with light and, it says here, 'serene planes of transparent color.' The new, improved technique is made up of three parts. First, he started working without the gray underpainting and went more to a sort of wash—all on watercolor paper. Second was his arrangement of light and dark—sometimes putting the lightest and the darkest things in the painting right next to each other, side by side. Very dramatic. And finally, he achieved a greater sophistication in his work with these contrasting combinations against a sort of interlocking approach to his images. Apparently, it's also important to note that he had a keen control of his edges."

"Pardon?"

"His edges are very precise, something about the way he handled the white paint."

"Any idea what happened to him that made such a big change in his work?"

"No one knows."

"*That's* interesting."

"But as it happens," Andrews went on slyly, "around that time he seems to have traveled a good bit, including tours of Normandy and, perhaps, Wales."

"No kidding."

"Small world," Andrews agreed. "Anyway, the guy ended up with a huge output, including architectural drawings, which are supposed to be quite good, too. He had very strong drawing skills."

"And taught Rossetti," I repeated.

Andrews flipped a few pages in his pad.

"He was married in 1809," he droned, less interested in the rest of the man's private history, "came home to Norwich, and assumed a career as drawing master. Ended up a bit broke, somehow, and was dogged by his creditors. He didn't handle the family thing well and began a fairly significant battle with depression. He died in complete obscurity. His work wasn't appreciated, really, until the late Victorian era. Since then, an appreciation of his watercolors and etchings has grown. Hence the museum to which I was forced to go as a child."

He flipped his pad closed, a job well done.

"Wait." I slowed the truck a bit. "No mention of portraits."

"Correct." He slapped the dashboard for emphasis. "Cotman didn't paint any portraits."

"What do you mean?"

"I really looked. Cotman never painted portraits. Not a single mention of anything like that in any one of the dozens of books at my disposal."

"Well."

"Exactly," he agreed. "*Now* we see why the painting sold for so much money. If it was really by Cotman, it was undiscovered, and most likely unique."

I found myself slowing down even more. Trying to concentrate on driving and on what Andrews was telling me began to prove more than I could accomplish.

"Conner was smart," I began, "but I'd be willing to bet a million dollars that he didn't know this much about the painters of England."

"Better just bet two hundred and fifty thousand," Andrews told me. "Apparently, you're good for that amount."

"I mean, what the hell did Conner know about that portrait?"

"I know. That's the question."

Andrews suddenly reached out and honked the horn of the truck.

"You're driving, like, five miles per hour," he complained. "You're a menace on a mountain road. Speed up."

"Oh." I stepped on the accelerator and we lunged forward.

"Any way we could check on the painting a bit more," he suggested, "like find out who bought it or—hang on. How did you know it was worth two hundred and fifty thousand? You saw something in one of the folders at Taylor's office."

"A London gallery sent an appraisal letter, but they said it wasn't worth much. If I could just remember the name of the gallery, we might be able to get in touch with them."

"If they're still in business. It was quite some time—"

"Wait a second!" I almost ran the truck off the road.

"What? Jesus, watch where you're driving! You may have a death wish, but I have things to do later this month."

I was inadvertently giving Andrews a bit more of a "scenic overlook" than he could accept at the moment: The truck veered dangerously close to the edge of the road. There was no shoulder, only a hundred-foot plunge into blue oblivion.

"Sorry." I righted the truck. "I just remembered something. The painting was of someone called Lady Eloise Barnsley, and it was completed *circa 1804.*"

"That's something." Andrews leaned forward. "You think it might have been an encounter with her that changed his style, you mean? *Cherchez la femme?*"

"There might even have been a bill of sale somewhere in the folders, but I was interrupted by a lawyer."

"Still." He began tugging so hard at his earlobe, I was afraid he might pull it off.

"What are you thinking?" I knew his habit quite well.

"I was just— You know, there's a place near Adairsville called Barnsley Gardens, right?"

"There is?"

"Yes. It's a world-class resort. I mean *world*-class. *Condé Nast* called it one of the best places to stay in the *world.*"

"Stop saying *world.*"

"We should go." He seemed very excited by the idea.

"Near *Adairsville?*" It wasn't that I didn't believe him, exactly, but

I was almost certain he was confused about something or other. A *Condé Nast* resort of international proportions in my *neck of the woods* didn't seem remotely likely, especially since I'd never heard of it.

"You really live in your own little world, you know that? It's a historical landmark. I thought you'd have heard of it. They have over a thousand acres. Some famous architect built the place before the Civil War, and the landscape design is supposed to be a big deal. They've made it, now, like a nineteenth-century English village—except that there's an eighteen-hole golf course."

"And, no doubt, a phenomenally overpriced restaurant."

"I believe it has three Michelin stars," he informed me. "Plus, there's a spa, so—"

"How do *you* know about it?"

"I take vacations. Sometimes I travel with a companion. Sometimes I want to impress said companion with, you know—"

"Please," I interrupted. "If you're going to regale me with tales of your lurid trysts—"

"*Trysts?* That's the word you came up with? What century is this?"

"Aside from the coincidence of the name, I don't see what—" I stopped talking instantly and hit the brakes of the truck.

"What are you doing?" Andrews lurched forward. "You actually have to *drive* this truck or I'm walking back to your place."

We came to a complete standstill on the road.

"What if the auction where Conner purchased all three items," I said, "was at Barnsley Gardens?"

Eleven

I was of two conflicting minds by the time we got back to my house. I hadn't been worried about the police while I'd been gone, but once Andrews and I clattered up the porch and through the front door, a certain dark mood took hold of me. When I walked into my living room, the entire matter of dead bodies and murder investigations made it difficult for me to find solace in the comforts of hearth and home. And I had a shiver thinking about lawyer Taylor and the Atlanta police.

"Are you hungry?" I glanced toward the kitchen, trying to remember what I had in the refrigerator.

"I don't know." Obviously, Andrews was battling a mood of his own, or he would never have been ambivalent about food.

"I could wait." My eye was on the kitchen phone. "I really want to know more about the painting. And now, thanks to you, we also have to find out more about this Barnsley Gardens place."

"Not to mention finding out more about the coin." Andrews matched my abstracted tone almost exactly. "Speaking of which, where is it now?"

"Hidden."

In my mother's room, there was a loose windowsill. I knew because I'd seen her hide things there when I was little—when I'd been spying on her. On all those nights when she'd come home late, I would, on occasion, crawl out of bed as silently as I could and watch her. Those moments, sadly, were my favorite memories of my mother, watching her when she didn't know I was there. Sometimes I would see her pick up the board of the windowsill and put something there in the hollow under the window frame.

After any one of those incidents, during a long period when both parents were gone, I would steal into my mother's room to see what she had hidden there. I only looked in the spot a few times. I'd like to think that I matured eventually and didn't need to discover what secrets she was keeping from me, but the truth was probably based more in my discomfort at what I found in her secret place.

The first time, I found an old love letter from my father to her; the second time, I found a small plastic bag with a white powder in it. I didn't know what it was at the time, but it was almost certainly cocaine. The third time, I found a loaded gun. That was sufficiently strange to keep me from ever looking in her hiding place again while she was alive.

It seemed an oddly appropriate place to hide the coin, considering that it was the room where Shultz had slept. His things were still in the room.

"Right now, I feel I would trade everything about that damned coin to know who killed Shultz." I glared at Andrews, as if it were his fault that I was filled with questions.

"Then why are we wasting our time on this painting?" He was responding to my scowl.

"The coin and the painting are a part of the same package." I tried not to sound as if I thought Andrews were the slowest man on the planet. "Someone wanted the coin enough to kill Shultz for it. The coin and the painting are linked. I believe that the murderer is interested in the painting, too. We have a million things to find out about it. Who bought the painting from my father? Why did the London gallery say it wasn't worth much, when, in fact, it sold for two hundred and fifty thousand dollars? Why did Conner acquire it in the first place?"

"Okay." Andrews stopped me before I could rattle on. "So we're abandoning our quest for more information about the coin?"

"No. God. The painting, the coin, and this Indian thing—whatever that was—aren't three separate things. Not for our purposes, I mean."

"Then what are they?" He glared. "Are you coming unhinged?"

"They're all pieces of one puzzle, and the puzzle is clearly—"

"Cursed," Andrews concluded. "That's the watchword, really."

I sighed. "I was going to say that even though the pieces fit together, the final picture of the puzzle is still impossible to see."

"I like my idea better."

I ignored him and started up the stairs.

"Where are you going?" Andrews stood staring up at me.

"I am going into my father's room," I told him, "to rummage through his trunk—an enterprise I dread."

"Upstairs? The trunk is right here." He pointed to the dark corner, farthest away from the front door.

"No," I corrected as patiently as I could manage, "that's Conner's trunk. It's empty. You may recall, I've been robbed recently. Whereas my *father's* trunk, upstairs—"

"Why are you looking in your father's trunk?" He was about as short with me as I'd been with him.

"In the hope of finding some way to contact my relatives in Wales. Obviously, they could answer some of our questions."

"Leave me out of it," he mumbled. "They're *your* questions. Your loony questions."

"I seem to remember a packet of letters from Wales. I never really paid much attention to them, but they could be something."

"Fine, then." He put his hands in his pockets. "And what am I doing?"

"You're finding out more about the Barnsleys and their alleged garden."

I wouldn't admit to Andrews what I could barely face myself: that I had no idea what I was doing.

It did seem remotely plausible that Shultz's murderer was someone who wanted the coin, and that the coin and the other two items Conner had purchased along with it were somehow related. They were certainly related to me. But apart from those patently obvious observations, I was flailing, grabbing at straws.

A significant failing of the human psyche is the inability to admit that so much of existence is random hazard.

I knew it was just as likely that a passing stranger had come into my house. Since I hadn't actually talked with Shultz, and could no longer trust lawyer Taylor, if I ever had, my supposition that there was a connection between the coin and the murder—and, by *that* implication, between the coin and the other two members of our sad trinity—was only the mind's vain attempt to make sense of a senseless tragedy.

Spill a small box of kitchen matches on a table, and the brain will find a pattern—*invent* a pattern where there is none. That's just how desperate human beings are for meaning in a meaningless universe.

Still, any action is better than inaction—a phrase fast becoming a mantra.

Andrews had acquiesced to my assignment silently and gone to his laptop computer, preferring to sit at the kitchen table than in the more comfortable seats in the living room.

I had gone upstairs to rummage through my father's old trunk—

Again.

The theory of *the eternal return* originated in ancient Egypt, later refined by Pythagoras. The basic idea is that time's not infinite in a linear fashion; instead, we repeat a finite series of actions over and over again throughout eternity. All time is cyclical.

This idea is basic to Hinduism and Buddhism, represented by the Wheel of Dharma: an endless repetition of birth, life, and death. But even in the European Middle Ages, this same symbol was found in the image of Ouroboros, a snake eating its own tail, the alchemical representation of eternity. Time is constantly devouring itself, never finishing the meal, always hungry.

The round nature of time, we are told, exists because the universe is always in the process of becoming and will never arrive at a final state of being. Eternity consists of an infinite number of identical circles.

I was fourteen years old when I discovered this idea, and I had nausea for three months afterward. I was depressed for the better part of that year. I wanted to kill myself, but, of course: what would have been the point? I'd just end up killing myself over and over again. What escape was there? *This* was a truer vision of Hell to me than anything Dante or a snake-handling preacher could invent. Just the idea that I'd have to repeat my high school experience even once more in eternity was enough to render me catatonic.

Over the years, a balanced regimen of philosophy and alcohol had eased the panic, but as I opened the lid to my father's trunk, the same stomach-churning ennui I had felt when I was an adolescent swept over me, and I had to sit on the floor.

Because there I was, participating in my own eternal return, going through my father's trunk once more. I took a moment to look around the room, hoping to calm my swirling brain. Andrews had already managed to demolish the thorough cleaning job I had given the place. Clothes were everywhere, and there was a half-eaten sandwich on my nice antique quilt at the foot of the bed.

I couldn't escape the sensation that I was still trying to fathom the meaning of meaningless events, as I had when I was young—still trying to make sense of a random series of events, hoping, ultimately, to find out why something had happened, when, in fact, there would never be an answer.

And the same old things were there in the trunk.

I picked up my father's flash ring and tried it on. The last time I had done so, the ring had engulfed my finger, but it fit just fine at that moment. The silver ring had a small open container compartment, about the size of a raisin, that was to be worn on the palm side of the hand. At the edge of that container was a circular flint that would spark enough to ignite a bit of flash paper that had been stuffed into the container. The result: fire.

My father could make balls of fire fly out of his hand at the audience; he could ignite an entire white screen onstage, which would vanish in an instant, revealing my mother, dressed as a harem girl, wrapped in a huge snake.

I dropped the ring back into the darkness of the trunk. I reminded myself that I was looking for a specific item this time, not vague, impossible clues to the existential dilemma.

I dug down to the bottom, underneath a heavy cloak, gnarled gloves, a copper pot. I found a small packet of letters, perhaps five or six envelopes. They had always been there, of course, but had held little interest for me when I was a boy. They were tied with white kitchen twine; all of them were from Wales.

Light slanted into the room through the window, but I turned on the glass lamp by the bed, as well. I sat back in one corner of the room, where the sunlight and lamplight collided.

The top letter was from a Professor Devin Briarwood. He had apparently written before. The return address was University of Wales, Aberystwyth, King Street, Aberystwyth, Ceredigion, SY23 2AX, Wales. The envelope proudly declared: *Founded in 1872, the first university institution established in Wales.*

The letter began, "Dear Mr. Devilin, Thank you for your charitable response, I did not, myself, believe that the coin would be in America."

It went on at some length about "the coin of Saint Elian" and its value to Welsh history. Some unnamed person had told this Welsh professor that my father had come into possession of the coin, but apparently my father had denied it. Considering how secretive everyone in my family had always been, I thought it quite plausible that Conner had, in fact, never told my father anything about the coin.

Still, it seemed that Professor Briarwood, very possibly a distant relative, though he himself didn't seem to realize that possibility, was the ideal person with whom to start my inquiries. The letter indicated that he knew much more about the coin than I, perhaps more than anyone alive.

The other letters in the bundle were less promising. Three were from lawyers attempting to find out about Conner's will. The last one in the bunch was a bizarre and somehow heartbreaking handwritten genealogical chart of the Briarwood family. As far as I could tell, it started some time in the Middle Ages and one of the bottom lines ended with Conner, but it was mostly an incoherent mess. The note attached to it provided the emotional tug: "If you are Conner B., don't let our family die in America. Have you children? Please, please tell. Many questions." It was unsigned.

Who could say how many years these letters had sat in the bottom of my father's trunk. I assumed they had gone unanswered, or there would have been more.

I tied up all but Professor Briarwood's missive, nestled them in a snug corner of the trunk, and closed the lid. I realized I was wishing, as I left the room, that I could have done the same with everything else having to do with my family—our tree.

Nearly an hour later I had made at least seven long distance calls, mainly encountering anger, ire, and unbelievably rude behavior, not to mention a plethora of curses in Welsh that had surely made a small black cloud easily seen from outer space. My Welsh was so bad that I couldn't make myself understood no matter how I pronounced the words, and I didn't know enough profanity in the language to keep up with the various Briarwoods I encountered.

Their general complaint, as far as I could manage to figure it out, was that there *were* no American Briarwoods, that Conner's family were Satan's spawn and, finally, that I should please rot like a mossy log in hell. One of the men actually used the words "mossy log." The general attitude seemed a combination of economic covetousness—they all assumed that everyone in America, yours truly included, was richer than Midas—and a genetically encoded national pride: no true Welshman would abandon his native land for so paltry a place as America. I tried to explain that Conner had been wanted for murder. They all knew that. It was the only trait of his that they admired. They assumed he'd died in Ireland.

My first call had been to the university, but an answering machine had told me that Professor Briarwood was on sabbatical and would not be back before Christmas. I left a message with no hope of its ever being returned.

So I dialed information and took a stab at speaking with the distant kin, resulting in frustration and the aforementioned cursing.

I had long since chased Andrews out of the kitchen. He'd gone up to his room, my father's bedroom, to continue his research.

In absolute desperation I tried calling the university again. The phone rang for a while before a woman answered in Welsh.

"Oh, hello," I stammered, hoping she'd take pity, "it's Dr. Devilin calling from America—I left a message earlier."

"Oh, I see," she said, in English. "You're lucky you caught me this late, and on a Saturday—I wouldn't ordinarily be about, but we're in pre-semester planning and its chaos. I did pick up your message, though. I'm afraid—"

"Would you mind if I told you why I'm calling? It may make a difference. Do you have a moment?"

Maybe she knew something about the Professor's work and would be willing to help. I decided to eschew further reference to my possible familial relationship to him, in light of the rage it seemed to inspire.

"Of course." She waited.

"I may have come across some information of interest to his work," I began, not certain what to tell her, "concerning a certain silver coin."

"Oh, my God." She dropped the phone. It clattered on her desk a moment. Then: "Hello?"

"Yes." I didn't know how to proceed.

"I dropped the phone."

"So I heard."

"I dropped the phone because—are you talking about the coin of Saint Elian?"

"Well, I think so, yes."

"Oh, my God!"

"So Dr. Briarwood—"

"You have to— Wait just a moment." She was apparently gathering pencil and paper, or so it sounded. "I have got to figure out how to get in touch with him now. He *never* believed it was in America, or at least that's what he always used to say. He just didn't know exactly how to find out more about it. And now, here you are."

"Yes." I switched ears. "Here I am. Look, I'm actually hoping for a bit of information exchange. I can give him some very valuable information about the coin—and I know this sounds like a complete change of subject—but I was hoping he could tell me something about a certain portrait, a woman who lived in Wales in the 1800s whose name—"

"Wait," she interrupted again. "You don't mean the painting of Lady Barnsley."

I tried not to change my vocal demeanor.

"In fact, I do."

"Mary and Joseph."

"I see." I held my breath a moment. "The portrait is important?"

"You don't know the story? You don't know the ancient family tale?"

"Um . . ."

"Jesus, I would have thought you'd at least have heard, if you know anything about the portrait at all." She was obviously amazed.

"What is it?" Ordinarily, with someone who knew a story that I wanted to hear, I would have been terrifically wily. I couldn't believe that I had blurted out the question as I had.

"The story?" She sighed. "Well. Have *you* got a moment? That's the question. It's a pretty good story, but you *are* calling long-distance."

"I'm fine. What's the story?" There it was again: complete lack of guile. What was going on in my brain?

"The long and the short of it is this." Her voice relaxed a bit and I recognized a mode of speech setting in, a style of speaking that said she had told and retold this story hundreds of times. "It began over two hundred years ago—and it hasn't ended yet."

"Andrews!" I bellowed the second I hung up the phone.

I heard stirrings before I heard his voice. He'd fallen asleep.

"What is it?"

"Can you come down, please?" I stood to make some espresso. "I have a story to tell you that you are *not* going to believe."

There was a rumbling sound like distant thunder, then the sort of stagger stumble a drunken man might sound were he coming down my stairs.

"You've got nothing on me, mate." He yawned. "Before my little nap, I found out about the Barnsley brood *but good.* They may be the unhappiest family this side of yours. Around 1828—"

"Stop! I have a tale out of Thomas Hardy."

He appeared in the doorway to the kitchen.

"Mine's more Poe."

"Have a seat. I'll make espresso. Just listen."

He shrugged, not at all awake.

"By all means." He scraped a kitchen chair across the floor and sat at the table. "Bore me."

"Not this time." Pouring bottled water into the reservoir, I snapped on the espresso machine and it grumbled to life. "Are you comfortable?"

He nodded, eyes almost closed.

"It all began at the turn of the nineteenth century." I leaned against the kitchen countertop. "A distant relative of mine fell on hard times in Wales and sought work in England. He was, according to the legend at least, a master gardener, and he was hired to work at none other than the *Barnsley* household around 1803."

That opened his eyes.

"I'm just getting started," I said before he could interrupt me. "This Briarwood was apparently something of a wonder in other ways, as well. When the lady of the Barnsley household became pregnant, the lord suspected that my relative was responsible, as he had not *been* with his wife in several years. From that moment on, her husband never spoke to her, lived in a separate part of the mansion, took her out of his will. The servants began calling her 'the Barnsley Widow.' "

"Widow?"

"Because her husband was dead to her."

"Your relatives in Wales told you this story?" Andrews eyed the espresso machine longingly.

"No. They wouldn't talk to me at all—nor, incidentally, even believe they were my relatives. But this particular story is a part of Professor Devin Briarwood's ardently swashbuckling history of the family, soon to be published in England. Everyone knows the story. I got it from his secretary."

"You're kidding."

"It's a great story, if you'll let me finish it."

"Sorry." He slumped in his chair, a sullen version of paying attention.

"The lord of the house accused Briarwood of dallying with his wife; Briarwood neither confirmed nor denied it, so Barnsley challenged Briarwood to a duel."

"Seriously? Your family gets into more trouble."

"Briarwood refused." I ignored Andrews. "He countered with a wager. He bet his innocence on a horse race."

The espresso machine shot out a breath of steam.

"A bit strange and chancy, wasn't it?" Andrews stretched.

"It seems he knew a jockey," I went on, "and was certain he could rig the race. But Barnsley found out about the jockey, had said jockey beaten, then drugged all the horses but *his own.* Barnsley's horse won the race by a mile."

"Jesus."

"The bet was very public, and Barnsley insisted on payment as well as an admission of Briarwood's guilt. Briarwood said he had nothing of value with which to pay his debts, and Barnsley said, 'What about that silver coin that you wear around your neck?' Briarwood objected violently. He told everyone it was the last thing of value in his entire family and that he would sooner part with his life than with the coin. But Barnsley won out. Not hard to see why: A dallying Welshman owed a debt to an English landowner. So Briarwood yanked the coin from his neck and threw it on the ground at the feet of the jealous husband."

"It was our coin?"

"Yes, but there's more!" I failed to prevent my volume from rising. "As Briarwood was leaving, he put a curse, a Welsh curse, on anyone who held the coin, and, in fact, on the entire Barnsley family and all their descendants."

"Wait." Andrews was fully awake. "He was even cursing his own child, right?"

"Exactly. He was cursing his own child."

"Unbelievable."

"And when it came her time, the wife endured an agonizing seven-day labor and died shortly after the child was born. With her last dying breath, she repeated the servant's curse, only in English, so that everyone was certain to understand every syllable, with her own poison addendum. She included the Briarwood family, as well, and all *their* descendants."

" 'A plague on both your houses.' "

"The lord of the Barnsley house shunned the baby, of course. And when the boy-child grew to very early manhood, the father all but threw him out of the house. That boy was Godfrey Barnsley, who came to America."

"You're not going to believe my story." Andrews sat full up. "It's about Godfrey Barnsley!"

"Wait, I still haven't gotten to the punch line."

"There's *more*?"

"When Godfrey came to America, he brought the only things that mattered to him: the Briarwoods' cursed coin of Saint Elian and a portrait of his mother."

I waited for the last bit of information to sink in.

Andrews only took a moment to realize where I was headed.

"No." He almost stood up.

"He brought a portrait of his mother," I concluded, "painted by a young landscape artist named John Cotman. Cotman had come to paint the English countryside in his typical dark manner, but the image of the woman in his one and only portrait is so romantically portrayed that when it was done, there was speculation that Cotman, not my relative, was the actual father of the troublesome child. And, P.S.: After that, Cotman's style completely changed from dark to light, as you were telling me."

"Godfrey brought the portrait to America with him?" Andrews was still trying to catch up.

"Yes. The painting was presumed to have been lost in the Civil War when Yankee troops destroyed the Barnsley estate here in Georgia."

"Wait," Andrews protested, "now you're getting into my story—it's about the Barnsley estate during the war, and believe me, that family *was* cursed. But aside from roving the countryside, what was Cotman doing on the Barnsley estate long enough to have painted a portrait and dallied with the lady of the house? Any ideas?"

"Yes: more irony. He was known for his architectural drawings, as you discovered. He had actually been hired by Barnsley to produce renderings of that family's estate."

"Damn."

"At least." I put one of the white demitasse cups under the spout of the espresso machine and pressed the button.

The satisfying *whoosh* ensued.

"The woman." Andrews stared out the kitchen window. "Lady Eloise Barnsley—she must have been something."

"*Something?*"

"Made a man lose his last dollar, inspired another to paint his one and only portrait, and finally killed her husband's spirit—not to mention laying down a family curse."

"A widow's curse at that." I turned toward the machine.

"She wasn't really a widow."

"And there's no such thing as a family curse," I countered. "But if there were, it would be worse; much more *effective* coming from a widow than a disgruntled former employee. It's her repetition of the curse that would really made it take hold."

"Why's that? Wait. You have some kind of folk crap to back you up. Is my espresso ready?"

I handed him the cup that was sitting there steaming at the machine.

"In general, widows have often been thought to possess a degree of witchcraft in the folk community."

"Why?" He slurped his espresso.

"My particularly feminist take on the subject is basically that a widow didn't fit into the general sociology of a male-dominated world—she was, necessarily, independent, not herded by a father or husband. Usually, the accusation of witchcraft would come from some argument about stolen corn or a bad wheat crop. If someone told you that you were to blame for a bad harvest, what would be your response?"

"A very English 'Sod off,' I would think."

"Exactly. And then the next bad thing that happened anywhere close by would be blamed on that curse."

"Not fair." He finished his espresso in a final gulp. "More?" He held out his cup.

"But the worst of it was that a widow's curse could be ensured by the power of God."

"What?"

"Book of Exodus. God warns you not to bother a widow. If you do, and said widow calls upon God, He will hear them, and His wrath shall wax hot, and He will kill you with the sword, and *your* wives shall be widows. So don't mess with a widow, seriously."

"Jesus."

"Not really." I took the cup from his hands. "We're still in the Old Testament with Exodus."

"But, I mean, damn." He sat back. "And P.S.: How do you remember all this stuff?"

"Speaking of curses." I set his cup back under the nozzle of the espresso machine and pushed the button. "My brain is littered with thousands—with *piles* of that sort of thing. I'm inhabited by the Ghost of Research Past. I can't get rid of it."

The espresso machine made its own little ghost, a wisp of nearly transparent steam.

"You need so much more help than I can offer you." Andrews shook his head and held out his hand for the cup. "But I do have a terrific companion piece to your story. It starts when Godfrey Barnsley comes to America, and the curse really settles in."

"So you're buying the concept of the widow's curse."

"You will, too, once you hear my story." He blew on his espresso and sipped a bit.

I didn't bother to remind Andrews at that moment that as a descendant of Briarwoods, I was included in the curse.

Twelve

"Godfrey Barnsley," Andrews began, "was penniless—for reasons you've just mentioned—when he came to America from England in 1823. But ten years later, he was one of the richest cotton magnates in the South."

Andrews had run upstairs and retrieved his laptop, to which he was referring for exact information.

"So much for the curse." I turned toward the espresso machine, at last making a cup for myself.

"So you would think. He married well, a young woman named Julia Scarborough, who was the daughter of a wealthy shipping merchant in Savannah. But she didn't like the heat in Savannah, with its attendant threat of yellow fever and malaria on the Georgia coast, and talked our boy Godfrey into buying nearly four thousand acres of land in the solace of a higher elevation."

"Near Adairsville, to be specific," I assumed.

"Right. And he got the land at bargain basement prices *because*?"

"No idea."

"Really. I thought you'd know this, Mr. I Remember Everything."

"Wait. This would have been around—what, late 1830s?"

"Correct." Andrews seemed to delight in my struggle to recall my history lessons.

"The Cherokee." I sank back into the counter. "The Trail of Tears."

"We have a winner." Andrews set down his cup. "Godfrey acquired the land—Cherokee land, and sacred in the bargain—just after the tribe were taken from northwest Georgia."

"I think I'm remembering this correctly." I strained. "The Indian Removal Act barely passed the 1830 Congress. I think—I'm pretty sure Davy Crockett railed against it; might have destroyed his political career. It was clearly insane to relocate the Cherokee. They'd built roads and schools; they were farmers and cattle ranchers. Oh, and there was Sequoyah's *alphabet*—"

"Do you want to show me how much you know," Andrews interrupted, "or do you want to hear the story?"

"Sorry. But the Trail of Tears—it was one of the worst—"

"Right," he broke in again, "but it was good for Godfrey and his family, and that's all he thought of."

"Good, you mean, because he got the land he wanted and didn't have to deal with the real owners."

"Or so it seemed." He glanced at his screen. "By 1841, Barnsley had moved the family up here, added another six thousand acres to the estate, and started work on his mansion. And I do not use the term loosely. Here's a letter from him that says the place had 'six or seven different styles of windows, giving variety, yet harmonizing. All the walls are of brick. The campanile is three stories high. On the first floor is the drawing room, library, vestibule, hall, dining room, breakfast room, pantry, bathrooms, with the cistern above a large closet and a room-size safe.' He used black-and-white Italian marble for the mantels, had everything handcrafted in Europe. Doors came from London cabinetmakers—cost a fortune."

"*But?*" I knew there was a punch line.

"Wait, I'll get to the *but* in a second." He stared at his screen again. "He also acquired every known variety of rose for his garden, and the gardens were designed by somebody famous, or in the style of somebody famous. Anyway, the place ended up with twenty-four rooms, looked like an Italian villa, and it had hot and cold running water."

"How is that possible? In 1841?"

"He had some sort of copper tank close to the chimney that supplied the hot water to bathrooms, and a tank in the bell tower provided cold water to the rest of house and gardens."

"Unbelievable."

"Also his wine cellar was famous for—"

My turn to interrupt impatiently. "Would you *please* get to the *but.*"

"*But,*" he said instantly, reading from the screen, "he had built the whole bit on an acorn-shaped hill, which, and I quote, 'was reputedly *cursed,* and Indian legend warned it should be avoided as an unlucky site.' "

Andrews sat back, once again delighted with his own research.

One of the things I always found most irritating in the academic world was an easy ability to fall in love with one's own research, and then to mistake that research for the point of the story. I certainly had fallen prey to the lure of that siren myself, many times.

"Curses everywhere" was all I said.

"Barnsley didn't care about a local legend." Andrews shook his head. "He should have."

The day was beginning to cloud over again and a cold wind had come up. Quick black shadows darted across the lawn and through thick pines outside of my kitchen window, like great lost souls, I thought, seeking in vain for some bit of sunlight.

"Godfrey's good life was upset somehow, then?" I knew Andrews would go on with his story whether or not I prodded him, but asking him questions now and again assured him I was interested in his tale.

"Exactly." He shifted something on his screen. "After he built his mansion on the Cherokee land, where he should not have, everything went downhill. Very shortly after the family were installed in the manor, one of his infant sons died, and not long after that, wife Julia was lost to tuberculosis. Daughter Adelaide died in the house in 1858 and—this is absolutely the best—his eldest son, Howard, was killed in 1862 by, no kidding, Chinese pirates."

"We've passed over into the land of fiction." I set the espresso machine to its maximum yield and pressed the button.

"Seriously. Godfrey had sent the boy out to scour the world for exotic 'Oriental' shrubberies for the grand gardens around the manse, and Howard was killed by *pirates* on the quest."

"Unbelievable." I took my cup and sipped.

"After that, it appears that our boy Godfrey became obsessed with the mansion and the gardens. He went all over Europe to find things for the family home, even though it was, by then, bereft of family."

"A sad ending to your story," I agreed.

"Not nearly." Andrews leaned forward, scanning his computer screen excitedly. "That's not nearly the end. We're up to the Civil War now, and the Union troops found Godfrey Barnsley, all alone with his Italian marble and his hot and cold running water and his half-finished dreams. Sherman's men were headed for the estate on May 18, 1864. Some Confederate colonel tried to warn Barnsley that the Yankees were on their way, but the colonel was shot down in the garden before he got to the house. And even though orders were given forbidding the sack of the house, the Union troops did just that. All Godfrey's handpicked furniture was burned, and the Italian statues were toppled, dinner plates smashed, wine drunk. The place was an empty husk by the end of the war. So Barnsley went to New Orleans to try to rebuild his fortune and promptly died there."

"But his body was brought back to the mansion," I guessed.

"Right, but the curse did *not* die with the man. In 1906, a tornado tore the roof off the main house. Then Godfrey's granddaughter Adelaide bore two children: one grew up to be a modestly famous boxer called—and here we have a bit of Damon Runyon—K. O. Dugan. And *K. O.* killed his brother and went to prison, hastening their mother Adelaide's death in 1942, when—swell the music, dolly in for a close-up—everything left in the estate was sold at auction, and the entire place was covered over by kudzu, as if it had never been there at all."

He looked up at me as if he had just discovered a new book of the Bible.

"Well." I conceded a bit of a smile. "I can't top that."

"Damn right." He gave one last look at his computer screen. "The epilogue is pretty funny. Who bought the place and turned it into the world-class resort it is today?"

"No idea."

"In 1988—I am not making this up—it was purchased by Prince Hubertus Fugger."

He couldn't hold back a bit of derisive adolescent laughter at the expense of the royal name.

"I'm betting that on your Web site there, you've got a bit of 'even today the ghost of someone or other can be seen lingering'—that sort of thing."

"Oh, absolutely. You can see ghosts everywhere—even the Confederate colonel has been known to make an appearance in the gardens. But I also have to say that from the English point of view, the whole Barnsley family is significantly haunted in a way that might not be immediately obvious to an American. I would think that they represent the worst, really, of the so-called yeoman farmers that date back to the Middle Ages and became, in fact, a certain segment of the English middle class."

"Why would that make them haunted?"

"Families like the Barnsleys, lots of them, developed into the Dickensianly cruel bosses, vicious factory owners, heartless landlords of the past several centuries. The upper classes merely ignored poor people or hired them as servants. But the middle classes felt that they had bettered themselves economically and therefore had earned the right to abuse and take advantage of poor people, deliberately keeping them impoverished so that they, the middle class, could get rich."

"While your bizarre brand of Marxism *is* interesting—"

"Sorry, I only meant to say—"

"That the punch line is," I declared, "the auction of 1942 would be where Conner acquired our three items."

"I do." He closed his notebook. "Yes."

"Of course it's possible." I sipped.

"You're not going to start again with the—"

But before Andrews could continue to berate me, the telephone rang.

"Five dollars says that'll be Skidmore checking up on me." I reached for the phone. "Hello?"

I would have won the bet. His voice was light but firm.

"Good. You *are* there. Now I don't have to get all *manhunt* and release the bloodhounds." Skid seemed in a more jovial mood than he had in some time.

"I've seen those dogs," I agreed. "They *are* pretty tired."

"So. What've you been doing?" His sad attempt at nonchalance failed completely.

I hesitated.

"Fever?" He had lowered his voice.

"How much do you want to know?" I matched his tone. "I mean, just enough to convict me or enough to make you an accessory after the fact?"

"Quit that kind of talk," he said instantly. "I'm not fooling with you."

"I went to Pine City." Best not to make matters worse by provoking him—or lying to him. "So did Andrews. We've uncovered what we feel is relatively amazing information."

"You have." It wasn't a question—more an accusation.

"First," I hurried on, "I have discovered that my family is cursed."

"I could have saved you the trip to Pine City on that score."

"In the matter of Mr. Shultz," I went on, "I can tell you that it's possible the coin he brought me was minted by my Welsh ancestors, and it was a prized possession of my family until it was lost in a bet to the Barnsley family—"

"As in Barnsley Gardens?" he interrupted.

"Am I the only one who doesn't know about that place?"

"Yes. What about the Barnsley family? Man, *there's* a family with a troubled history."

"You know about this?

"Everybody knows about the Barnsley curse, Fever," he told me wearily. "It's a great story and most likely good for business over there."

"Well, that saves me telling you about the research that Andrews has done. Except that my great-grandfather—"

"Conner," he injected.

"—might have gotten the coin in question back from the Barnsley family, along with a very valuable painting and, for some reason, an Indian artifact at auction in 1942. So if the coin or the disposition of the coin is the motive for Shultz's murder, things don't really look that good for yours truly."

"Right." Skid shuffled some papers on his desk. "I'm sure there's more to your story."

"Including," I interrupted, "the weird fact that some lawyer named Taylor over in Pine City will lie or has already lied to the police about a phone call I received from Shultz just before the murder."

"Preston Taylor?" Skid sighed. "The one you were talking about with Huyne?"

"Don't know his first name. But it's Taylor and Taylor in that big house on—"

"Preston Taylor is about to run for governor, Fever."

"Of Georgia?"

"He'll most likely win, too. He's got enough money to buy the one or two connections he doesn't already have. He's a part of the old-style machine that you always hope is gone from Georgia politics but isn't, really."

"Yes. I thought that, in slightly more coherent fashion, when I first met him."

"Well, congratulations: You're dead. If he's got his sights set on you, he'll kick your butt *good.*"

"Your language really has degenerated since you became sheriff."

"Uh-huh. All this so-called research you and Andrews have done—has it gotten you anywhere?"

Had it? Before I could think, I heard myself coming to conclusions as I told them to Skidmore.

"I believe that the three items Conner bought at auction are related, and I must also now assume that they are related to a family curse in which I am involved. That the curse has actually attached itself to the coin, at least insofar as it is deemed valuable both economically and emotionally. Ergo, I conclude that someone in the Barnsley brood is trying to get the coin back in an effort to a) change their economic fortunes or b) improve their lot in general. J'accuse some Barnsley. There should be plenty of the descendants around here somewhere. I mean, I found out from my own Welsh relatives that the memory for this kind of thing is genetic and really long-lived. *That's* where my research had gotten me."

Andrews was staring at me as if I had lost my mind. Doubtless, Skidmore was on the other end of the phone with more or less the same facial concern.

"One of the Barnsleys killed Shultz?" Skidmore was the first to react.

"Are you insane?" Andrews followed suit.

"Family legends take root." I was looking at Andrews but speaking into the phone. "Someone in the Barnsley clan blames their family's ill fortunes on the cursed coin. In a time of need, someone in Blue Mountain allowed the coin to be sold. Now the Barnsleys have to get it back."

"Why?" in stereo from both men.

"In order to rid themselves of the curse." I tried to make it seem the most obvious thing in the world.

"Fever," Skidmore began, irritated as he could possibly be, "you know I usually indulge your ideas because I believe they have a real meaning for you, and maybe for me, too. But if you think—"

"What I think is irrelevant," I interrupted. "I'm not remotely saying I believe in this sort of thing. I'm only saying that some people do, and one of those people might be a Barnsley, and if he or she is, that would be reason enough to go to almost any lengths to get the coin back."

"Why do they need to have the coin in their possession to get rid of the curse?" Andrews leaned forward onto the table.

"I heard that," Skid said on the phone. "I'd like to know the answer myself."

"Because the coin *contains* the curse." That much was obvious, surely. "So when an object carries this much bad luck, the ancient ways are, I think, the best. Let's say we revert to Celtic lore. Get a black feather from a rooster, go to a crossroads, and, holding the feather and the coin, call out the name of the goddess Áine three times."

"Stop," Skidmore insisted. "Which goddess am I calling out?"

"Áine. She's one of the original Tuatha de Danaan, offspring of the goddess Dana—first tribe of Celts." I watched Andrews shake his head. "She'll help you with the curse."

"Right." Skid was, I believed, on the verge of hanging up on me.

"And we revert to Celtic lore because?" Andrews spoke loudly enough for Skidmore to hear him.

"Appalachian folklore has its roots in a more ancient belief system brought to America by the Scots-Irish settlers in these mountains. That system belonged originally to the Celts. The people with whom we're dealing in this instance span the ocean, are genetically associated with both European and American variants of these beliefs, ergo—"

"Haven't I told you never to say the word *ergo*?" Skid broke in.

"Sorry."

"Look, Fever," Skid allowed, "I don't really care that you left the house when you weren't supposed to, or that your explanation for the murder belongs in an old-timey song more than in a crime investigation. But I am interested in the fact that you believe the Barnsley family has something to do with our situation, in light of what I've just found out."

"You don't wonder if the Briarwood curse has anything to do with the Barnsley bad luck? You said yourself that everyone—with the apparent exception of myself—knows the stories about the Barnsley family foibles. So why wouldn't that same curse have something to do with the murder of Mr. Shultz? I'm talking about the *psychology* of a curse—nothing metaphysical whatsoever."

"Do you want to hear why I called you?" Skidmore sighed, somewhat indulgently. "Or do you want to go on and on like a college professor?"

"'Like a'—that's hitting below the belt a bit, isn't it?" I complained.

"I'm calling," he insisted, losing patience with me, "because I've busied myself with a little actual police work. Melissa and I have been checking phone records, just like they do on television. And you might be interested to know that we discovered Mr. Shultz was called from England not long before he called you the first time. I recognized your number, of course. Right before that, someone in England called Shultz over a dozen times in two days."

"From England?"

The surprise in my voice prompted Andrews to come to attention.

"What is it?" Andrews sat up straight.

"Someone called Shultz from England," I told him, "shortly before he came up here."

"Who called? Does he know?" Andrews asked.

"Melissa's still checking," Skidmore answered, "but as far as we can tell, every call came from a household by the name of Barnsley."

I moved to sit down at the table with Andrews.

"Who called?" Andrews insisted.

"He was called by the Barnsleys. In England." My voice sounded hollow even to me.

"Hang on," Andrews said slowly, suddenly tugging at his earlobe. "Hang on."

"That's right," I said, reading his mind.

"What's right?" Skid mumbled into the phone. "What's Andrews saying?"

"He's not saying anything," I answered, "but I'll bet he's thinking the same thing I am. If you're right about those calls, then Mr. Shultz may have known a whole lot more about all of this business than we thought. Than he ever told us, I mean."

"I'm not sure I understand that." Skid's voice had gone quiet.

"Andrews and I have spent our considerable—as you so offensively referred to it—college professor prowess on research to come up with the Barnsley/Briarwood connection. Barnsleys called Shultz. What reason would they have for that except to ask him about the coin because they had somehow found out that his father had purchased it? They would have at least told him something about their family's claim to it just so Shultz would talk to them."

"Got it." Skid paused. "That's most likely how the Shultzes know that the coin used to belong to your family. Where does Shultz's father fit into this, by the way?"

"I'd like to know that myself." I could feel myself grinding my teeth. "I'm assuming our Shultz didn't live with his father. I mean, you were checking our Shultz's phone, right?"

"The victim lived alone. Not with his father."

"Hang on." Andrews seemed stuck in a particular loop.

"What is it?" I asked.

"What if Shultz knew the murderer? Invited him to this house? Isn't that what Taylor said before he started to lie about us?" Andrews sat back, sheet-white, looking right at me. "Maybe the killer was here for you."

"He's right, you know," Skid said softly into the phone. "I heard that."

What was more: that person could still be about somewhere, perhaps even nearby in the pine shadows just outside the sunlight in my yard.

Thirteen

Skid wanted to send someone over to the house, maybe Crawdad. As delightful as the prospect was, I declined. Andrews was with me, I would lock my doors for a change, and Skid was only a short drive away, no matter where in Blue Mountain he was.

The sun was going down by the time Andrews and I had finished talking over all our research, strange ideas, theories, guesses, and accusations: Shultz was evil or Shultz was innocent; lawyer Taylor was evil or he was in league with someone else to wrest my inheritance from me; Taylor was a small-town politico with pretensions too large for his capabilities; Taylor's secretary, Becky, was very attractive.

The final theory was almost exclusive to Andrews.

For my part, the more we talked, the less convinced I was that any rhyme or reason remotely applied to the facts as we knew them.

"Nothing makes any sense; nothing *means* anything," I concluded. "Do you know what I was doing when Shultz called the other day, in fact?"

"What?" Andrews barely indulged me.

"I was moving big heavy rocks from one place to another. Rocks that will surely tumble back down in a very short time to the spot where they were in the first place."

"Fine," Andrews moaned. "You go ahead and be Sisyphus; be Camus or Genet or whichever depressed French existentialist it was who came up with the concept that life is meaningless, backbreaking work and then you die. Me? If it has to be French at all, I prefer the more bacchanalian Greek derivative: eat, love, drink more wine. And *cherchez la femme* all over the place."

"I see."

We had sat all afternoon at the kitchen table. I'd scrambled some eggs late in the afternoon. They went well, somehow, with the bottle of Veuve Clicquot that Andrews had given me last Christmas. I had been saving it for some New Year's Eve. Empty plates had been shoved to the middle of the table; empty glasses stood mute before us.

"But despite yourself, you were right about the connections among all of these things, you know," Andrews went on. "I see the patterns now."

"I was just thinking recently that if you spill a box of kitchen matches on a table, your brain will invent a pattern where there actually is none. That's how desperate we are for meaning in a universe that doesn't really offer an objective order at all."

"God." Andrews craned his neck around as if he had a crick.

"What?"

"You love this melancholy like a bleeding Frenchman. Is that your heritage, too?"

"In fact—"

"Look, I don't want to hear it!"

Even Andrews, I could tell, had been surprised by the sudden vehemence in his voice.

"All right." I let out a slow breath.

"Sorry." He looked around as if someone else might have yelled, not he. "I guess I'm a bit on edge. What the hell is the matter with me?"

We both glanced toward the living room for an answer.

"We're like two of the dwarves that didn't make the Snow White cut," he said, obviously attempting to lighten the mood. "You're Gloomy and I'm Grumpy."

"I think Grumpy actually *was* one of the seven."

"No," he corrected me breezily, "Dopey, Sneezy, Doc, Goofy, Happy, Gallant, and Dumbo."

"Half of those aren't right."

"I don't care."

"And you know the actual story of Snow White—I mean, I could tell it to you if you're in a mood—"

"Not if you paid me one thousand dollars." He sat back. "I've changed your name. You're not Gloomy; you're Snoozy."

"Sleepy was one of the real dwarves, wasn't he? I think that's who I am right now."

Night birds and dark wind filled the air outside my house. A pale moon struggled up the sky. Andrews and I did our best to ward off the night with deliberate laughter.

As human beings have always done, even before the discovery of fire.

Deeming it best to turn in early, we left the kitchen light on—our version of leaving the fire burning—checked all the windows, locked all the doors, and retired upstairs.

"I'm thinking of sleeping with my cell phone in my hand." Andrews yawned at the top of the stairs. "I put Skidmore's number on speed dial."

"I'm thinking of not sleeping." I followed him up.

"Fever." He didn't turn around, but his voice flooded the house with warm concern. "You have to get some sleep."

I stopped on the stairs for a second, because it was the first genuinely kind utterance from Andrews in recent memory. I had the impulse to cry—a testament to how right he was about my need for slumber.

He went to his room; I went to mine. We both closed our doors.

Instantly, every sound outside, every creak of the floorboards, every thump on the roof took a beat out of my heart. I was more awake than I had been all day, and I could actually feel adrenaline diluting my blood as it pounded through me.

I kicked off my shoes and lay down on the bed fully clothed and on top of the covers. The little glass lamp on the bedside table didn't give much light to the room, but I left it on.

I tried to breathe slowly, counting my breaths as I exhaled, but every sound broke my concentration and caught my breath in my throat.

I felt hot.

I spent ten minutes trying to decide what to read, but nothing seemed interesting. I thought of getting out of bed and doing a few sit-ups and push-ups, but inertia kept me in bed.

Every time a random thought would leap out of the shadows and into my skull, I'd have to fight it off as if it were a bat trying to eat my brain.

I couldn't say when I finally drifted off to sleep.

But the violent explosion of breaking glass is what woke me back up.

I threw myself out of bed. Still in my clothes and my stocking feet, I moved as silently as I could to the door. I glanced at my watch. It wasn't even nine o'clock yet.

As I turned the handle of my bedroom door, I could hear noises downstairs. Every sound I made was like thunder: floorboards complaining, hinges screaming, my own breathing like a hurricane.

I was hoping I'd find Andrews in his own doorway, but his door was closed. By the time I stood at the top of the stairs, I could clearly hear someone walking around in my living room.

I stood for a moment, trying to plan how I might attack the intruder.

I heard him in the far corner of the room; I heard him lift the lid of Conner's trunk.

What was he looking for there? He'd already cleaned it out. Maybe he thought there was a secret compartment. He would never know that the secret compartment was in my mother's windowsill. That thought made me consider going back into my room, barring the door, and waiting until the intruder went away, frustrated at not finding the coin.

But of course I had to stop him. He'd murdered a man; he would stop at nothing.

I drew in an enormous breath and called on all the demon anger I had stored at the back of my brain.

"Stop!" I bellowed.

I heard the man downstairs stumble and take a short gasp.

I also heard Andrews fall out of bed.

"Don't move!" I shouted, almost as loudly as before. "Sit down on the floor."

I started down the staircase, blood pounding in my ears, skin tingling with rage. Before I was halfway down, I saw the man bolt past the bottom of the stairs, heading toward the front door in the clear kitchen light.

"Stop!" I screamed again, so violently that it clawed my throat.

The man was desperately trying to figure out the lock. The front door was still secured. I took a few more steps down and could see that he'd gained access to the house by smashing in the living room window that looked out onto the front porch.

Suddenly, I heard Andrews behind me.

"We've got a gun," he said, clearly still half-asleep.

"We don't have a gun," I said instantly.

The man turned. He was carrying a cricket bat. He snarled but did not speak. He was something trapped in a corner, less than human.

Shadows obscured his face. He was dressed in thrift-store rags—torn jeans, a flannel shirt three sizes too big, a wool cap. The look made his weapon surreal. But it was just the kind of thing to use if you wanted to break a thick window and didn't care about the noise—or if you wanted to make a dent the size of a brick in the back of someone's head.

"We do, in fact, have a gun." Andrews came up beside me on the stairs, aiming a small silver barrel at the intruder. "Hey! He's got a cricket bat!"

"I know," I said, trying to get my bearings.

"Put it down and have a seat on the floor," Andrews said calmly, pointing his weapon directly at the man's chest.

The intruder erupted, a howl escaping him that shook what was left of my windows. He spun around to face the door again and with one crashing blow of his bat knocked the handle and the lock off my front door.

It was a wild, desperate gesture. The locking mechanism remained intact, and of course the door opened inward, so it would have been nearly impossible for him to force it out. When it wouldn't open, he screeched again and came toward us with the bat, pounding the stairs.

Andrews fell backward; I wondered that his gun didn't fire. Whether I was too frightened or too stupid to move didn't matter ultimately. Standing my ground seemed to confuse the man at the bottom of the stairs.

He grunted, not quite knowing what to do next.

"I'll shoot!" Andrews managed from his reclined position.

The man snorted, shook his head, and walked toward the window he had broken.

Andrews got to his feet and sighed.

"You're not going to stop him?" he asked me.

"You're not going to shoot at him?" I countered.

He held out his hand. He showed me his cell phone. It had a thick antenna, which almost looked like the barrel of a small pistol. I remembered his telling me he had to use it when he was making calls from the mountain, a special attachment of some sort—good for communication, completely useless as a firearm.

The man was scrambling out the window. A bit of his shirt caught on a shard of glass. I thought he cut himself a bit on the back of his hand. He thumped onto the front porch before Andrews and I were able to mobilize.

We clattered down the stairs, only to see the man lumber across the lawn in the early moonlight.

"Well, if you can't use that thing to shoot at that man," I stammered, glaring at Andrews, "could you at least call Skidmore? Didn't you just say that Skidmore ought to be on your—"

But he had already hit the speed-dial button.

Skidmore was in the process of asking us to describe the events of the break-in for a third time when Melissa came into the kitchen.

"Got a blood sample and a tissue sample," she said, holding up what looked like small sandwich bags. "Also threads from the shirt, or whatever he was wearing."

"So he didn't speak," Skid said, making doodles on his notepad around the few words he'd jotted down. "He was dressed like a homeless man, and he had a cricket bat in his hand?"

"Torn jeans," I said as I had twice before, "flannel shirt—mostly red and gold—and a wool cap."

"And a cricket bat."

"It doesn't matter how many times you say it." I glared at Skidmore. "It won't make any sense."

"Sorry, Dr. Devilin," Melissa said gingerly. "But I don't believe I've yet heard you mention his shoes."

"Shoes?" I looked at Andrews.

"Hang on." Andrews raked his hand through a blond wreckage of hair. "He wasn't wearing sneakers or work boots or anything that went with the rest of his outfit."

"He wasn't?" I was at a loss.

"He was wearing Marks and Spencer oxfords." Andrews could not believe what he was saying, and he was more pleased with himself than I had ever heard him. "He was wearing dress shoes from England."

"What?" I thought I'd heard him wrong. "Are you sure?"

"They were my first adult footwear; wore them for my confirmation. They don't look like any other shoes in the world, and I'll never forget them."

"Confirmation?" I blinked. "As what?"

"In the Church of England, when a boy turns twelve," Andrews began.

"Could we stick to the shoes for a minute," Skid intervened. "You're saying he was wearing fancy dress shoes from England?"

"The jeans and work shirt were a disguise." I was certain of it; I found I'd suspected it all along once I said it out loud. That would explain his not speaking and deliberately odd behavior, I thought.

Skidmore stared at me, waiting.

"I've been developing a theory that doesn't hold much water," I admitted, "but here it is: Some Barnsley is after the coin, as I've said. He followed Shultz up here—your discovery of the phone calls to him might confirm that. Once here, he demanded the coin from Shultz. When Shultz didn't have it, they argued and Shultz got the thick end of that cricket bat. Have a look at his skull, the way it's caved in. I think you'll see I'm right. That Barnsley came back tonight, dressed in such a manner as to hide his true identity. He's the murderer."

"Because of this old silver coin from England." Skid hadn't moved.

"Wales," Andrews corrected.

"Because of a curse that one of your kin put on it." Skid shook his head and folded up his notepad.

"All right, then," I countered, "because it's worth however much money Detective Huyne said it was."

"Shoot," Skid said, "you're just guessing. You're trying to make sense of something that's most likely a random event."

I turned a jaundiced eye on Andrews.

"Please," he begged Skidmore. "Now you're just feeding his angst."

"I don't know what that is," Skidmore said, standing, "but Melissa's got some real evidence, and my plan is to use it to get Dr. Devilin out from under suspicion of murder and, in the process, get the aforementioned Atlanta policemen off my ass."

"Your language really has gotten worse since you've become sheriff," Andrews said absently.

Skid stared.

"Do you two make these things up before you see me just to vex my mind?" He squinted.

"What?" Andrews didn't know what he'd said to vex the sheriff.

"You got some plywood you can nail up over that window for tonight?" Skid was on his way to the door.

"I'll find something."

He stopped with his hand on the open, broken front door.

"I'm going to leave Melissa's squad car in your yard tonight," he said without turning my way. "That's why we brought two cars."

"It's locked, though, so you can't get anything out of it," Melissa volunteered.

"You know you can't go anywhere now, right, Fever?" Skid still wasn't looking at me. "I mean it this time."

"I understand what you're saying," I responded.

He offered me a low, exasperated mumble—completely unintelligible—then pulled the door open and headed toward his car.

Not five minutes later, I was on the road to Hek and June's house. I knew I would wake them, but I was angry enough to break down the door if I had to.

Andrews had all but stood in the doorway to prevent my leaving, but when I told him to come with me, he declined.

I insisted. I wasn't going to leave him in the house alone.

"Aren't you afraid the guy will come back?" Andrews said, arms folded tightly against the chilled air.

"With every light in the house on and a police car on the lawn?" I said. "Not likely."

"What about the open window?"

"Close the curtains and shove a chair up against them to hold them shut until we get back. I'm not planning to be gone long."

Without much more argument, Andrews gave in, pulled on a jacket, and ran after me out the front door to my truck.

I spun the tires and scattered mud, some of it onto Melissa's squad car.

"What do you think you're going to get out of Hek and June that you haven't already?" Andrews sank down into the passenger seat.

"You don't understand." I ground my teeth around the words. "They know everything. They know about the coin, the painting, the murderer, God knows what else."

"What? You're losing your mind." He swallowed. "They don't know all that."

"They know *so* much more than you think they do."

"No." He was firm. "They know so much more than you *wish* they did."

"Maybe."

The road was all black water, a snaking river. Clouds cut and bisected the air, sliced at the moon. The wind was cold as a silver nail and twice as biting. Stars had no hope in the wilderness of that night and seemed to have blinked out, waiting for a more opportune sky.

Andrews and I traveled the rest of the way to Hek and June's house in silence. By the time we pulled up close to their door, I was tense as a bowstring, ready to snap.

I shot out of the car. Andrews barely caught up with me as I bounded up the porch steps and began pounding on the door with the back of my fist. Yellow light from an upstairs window spilled onto the lawn and my truck behind me, but I kept pounding on the door.

"Stop." Andrews was whispering for some reason. "They're up."

I stood poised right at the threshold, shaking a little. The rage I had built to help me deal with the intruder and the leftover adrenaline still spoiling my blood were causing minor tremors. I must have looked like a demon when Hek opened the door.

He stared at me for less than two seconds, then nodded as if he'd been expecting me. He stood aside and opened the door wide enough for me to shove past him.

Andrews followed, nodding politely.

June was already in the kitchen at the percolator, wrapped in the same navy blue robe she'd had for decades, hair somehow perfect even under the circumstances. She didn't look up.

"What happened?" She didn't stop scooping coffee into the metal basket inside the pot.

It wasn't at all a strange first thing to say to me. In Blue Mountain if the phone rang after midnight or, worse, someone came to your door, it only meant something wrong had happened.

Nothing good ever came to the door after midnight.

"Someone just broke into my house." I sat at the kitchen table, more from habit than from a genuine desire to sit down. "He broke out my living room window, went through my house, and threatened my life."

"Mine, too." Andrews sat beside me, not certain of the proper behavior for such an odd convocation.

"You remember Dr. Andrews." I inclined my head in his direction.

"We heard about your Mr. Shultz," Hek said, taking a seat opposite me at the table.

Hek had thrown a flannel shirt on over his T-shirt, but nothing covered his long johns. He was wearing indoor/outdoor slippers that, obviously, someone had given him for Christmas.

"Bad business." Hek stared at the tabletop as if he were trying to read it. "So what is it you want to know?"

"What is it I want to know?" I repeated, hoping to drive my astonishment into his brain. "I want to know all the things you wouldn't tell me about this mess when I came over here just the other day."

"About Conner." June plugged in the percolator.

"Yes." I could barely keep myself from exploding. "About Conner."

"He's upset," June explained to Hek, taking a seat beside him. "Coffee be ready in a minute."

"Ordinarily, I stay calm about this sort of thing," I began, voice strained, "and I believe I'm very patient."

Hek coughed. It turned into a laugh immediately.

"You can believe the funniest things about yourself," he finally managed to tell me. "You don't have the patience God gave a moth."

"I don't know what that means and I don't care," I began.

"He's unhappy because somebody broke his window." June was doing her best to inform Hek.

"No," I insisted. "I'm unhappy because someone killed a man in my house and then came back to try and kill me. This has nothing to do with a window."

"I've got some glass out in the shed," Hek told me calmly. "We'll see what we can do about that window tomorrow or the next day. You got some plywood you can put up over it in the meantime?"

"I'm not here about the window!"

The percolator responded with a gurgle. The rest of the room remained silent.

"He wants to know about Conner," June said at last. "About those things."

"I expect he does." Hek took in a deep breath. "That coffee ready?"

June got up and stood by the pot, hoping to make it work faster.

"I believe it was 19 and 42," Hek began. "Now, you understand Junie wasn't hardly born yet and I was no more than a mite."

"So how do you know this story?" I leaned forward. "How do you have this information."

"From your dad," June said quietly. "Mostly."

The "mostly" implied someone else. I assumed it was my mother. June rarely talked about her.

"Okay." I was willing to let that part go if Hek was going to tell me what he knew. "In 1942—"

"Conner, it's been said, was strangely compelled to travel over to Adairsville, to the Barnsley estate. They were having an auction."

"The family had almost nothing by then." June stared at the coffeepot. "Funny how having lots of money and then losing it seems sadder than never having money at all."

"Conner went to the Barnsleys'." I tried not to sound as irritated as I was.

"Yes, he did." Hek nodded once. "He was said to have gone there to bid on several items at that auction."

"Said he wanted to buy some thing that were of 'immense personal value' to him." June put her hand on the handle of the pot. "That's the phrase he used: 'immense personal value.' "

"Of course that didn't make a lick of sense." Hek sniffed. "We didn't hardly know anything about the Barnsley estate, nor the family. Nobody had the least idea what Conner was talking about. Still. He traveled to the Barnsley auction, which was a trek in those days."

"He went by mule." June seemed satisfied with the progress of the coffee and began taking down snow-white cups and saucers from the cupboard in front of her.

"He bid on three items, outbid everybody—no telling how much money he gave. Then, without a single word to explain himself, he came home, locked the items in a trunk, and was never heard to speak of them again."

Hek's telling of the story had the sound of a well-worn bit of gossip.

"Never spoke of it again." June piped up in confirmation. She began to pour the coffee.

That was all I was going to get.

"You were right," Andrews whispered. "They do know everything."

"What?" Hek's hearing wasn't what it used to be. "What'd that boy say?"

"He asked me why you won't tell me these things unless there's a life-or-death crisis." I sat back.

"No," June said gently, handing Hek his coffee. "He said Fever was right."

"About what?" Hek's voice had become angular.

"Obviously, these three items are the things we saw evidence of in Taylor's office—the coin, the painting, and the thing."

"Taylor?" Hek's coffee cup had stopped halfway to his mouth.

June had also frozen on her way to fetch more cups.

"Over in Pine City." I shot Andrews a quick glance. "Do you know him?"

"He's no good." Hek had spoken. "Anything you found in his office is tainted. He's a liar and a thief. Don't go near him again."

Rarely had I heard Hek string together so many negative sentiments about another human being.

"Too late," Andrews chimed in before I could stop him. "We went there, found out about Conner's trust for young Fever Devilin, and in the meantime learned that Taylor is, in *fact,* a liar. We got a phone call from Shultz—"

"But if we could stick to the subject," I interrupted. "What do you make of Conner's strange behavior?"

I wanted to know what Hek had to say about lawyer Taylor, but I simply wanted to know about Conner *more.*

Collecting folk information is sometimes like sifting through sand to find one tiny diamond. I may be looking for a specific diamond, but the informant doesn't know what I'm looking for, may not even know that it's there in the first place. So I often have to guide the sifting process.

This same technique, I had found, could work almost as well in any situation when a group of people were sitting around a kitchen table just chatting, but I wanted to know something more particular. Always direct the conversation back to the point. I generally did it with more finesse when I was speaking with strangers, but with Hek and June, I could use a degree of shorthand that they understood.

"Conner was a strange man, by any accounting." Hek sipped. "Your dad never understood him."

"Conner's wife never understood him." June poured more coffee, her back to us. "Poor Adele."

Adele, Conner's wife, had been driven mad because when Conner died, his last request was to be buried with several reminiscences of Molly, the woman he'd loved in Ireland—long dead—instead of anything remotely having to do with Adele.

"But I can tell you this," Hek began softly.

Here it comes, I thought to myself. Everything in Hek's demeanor revealed that he was about to tell a secret.

"Conner loved his family more than anyone knew." Hek looked up at me. "He set you up pretty good, when you were barely more than a sprite—didn't hardly even know you. He helped your mom and dad, and I'm not supposed to ever tell you that. And he gave a good deal of his time to the church."

"Your church?" I couldn't believe it.

"He never came to service." Hek smiled. "But he helped me put up the new building."

Hek's new building, nearing fifty years old, was a white wooden square with a roof in the middle of the woods. Tall pines and giant rhododendrons surrounded it, and various members of Hek's strange congregation had added bits and pieces to it. It was a kind of church that filled a certain kind of person's spirit without ever discussing theology, rarely mentioning the tenets of any religion despite long, perfectly remembered Bible quotations.

When the time would come for Hek to die, the work of his church would be done. The congregation would drift to other churches and the building would return, in time, back to the earth. At Easter, a near-perfect circle of red rhododendrons would bloom enough to please the spirits of everyone who had ever known Hezekiah Cotage.

That would be his legacy.

"Everything Conner did in his last years," Hek said, rousing me from reverie, "was done for the family. Best to keep that in mind."

"It was almost an obsession." June set a cup of steaming coffee in front of Andrews.

"Look," Andrews said, nodding a thanks to June, "far be it from me to suggest something useful, but I wonder if we shouldn't try to find out who bought the painting from your father. Maybe they have some sort of useful information, and maybe they don't. But wouldn't you at least like to see the portrait of the face that launched your little ship?"

He stared directly into my pupils.

I understood.

Andrews had come up with an idea that he didn't want to talk about in front of Hek and June, for some reason.

"In fact, I would like to see that portrait," I answered, "now that I realize how seminal it has been to my path. Unfortunately, I wasn't able to find a bill of sale in the shambles that Taylor called 'my files,' and I'm not really going back to his office, so I don't know how we'll find out who bought the thing."

Andrews and I both turned to Hek and June at the same moment.

"Unless the two of you know," I said softly.

Hek returned his gaze to the tabletop. June concentrated on her coffeepot.

"We don't like to say," Hek said softly.

"It was a private matter," June agreed, not looking at me.

Andrews almost rose out of his seat, but I shook my head quickly. The fact that they had said anything at all only meant they wanted coaxing.

"Of course the details would remain my father's business," I said calmly. "But you can understand my curiosity—to see the picture that sent me to college, changed my life so profoundly. Surely you see that. I would be concerned only with the name of the person who bought it. Nothing else."

This was a ploy occasionally used to good effect: let them know that they could still keep secrets, even imagined ones, while helping out the troubled boy.

June looked over at Hek.

"That would be all right." She held onto the coffeepot but did nothing with it.

Hek nodded once.

"It was a rich man your dad knew from the show." Hek sighed. "They say he was sweet on your mother."

June fumbled with her coffee cup.

"Name of Spivey." Hek scratched his left cheek.

"Duncan L. Spivey." June whispered the name as if it were a hex.

They would say no more.

And I knew it was best not to dwell on what stories might exist behind that name in combination with the misbegotten details of my mother's escapades. I'd dug up enough of those particular dead bodies to last me a lifetime.

Fourteen

The ride back to my house was more silent than the trip to Hek and June's had been. I knew Andrews was working something out in his mind, something about Hek and June, I thought. I left him alone to do the work. I did my best to concentrate on the road, the starless night, watching for possums or raccoons that might cross the road—anything to keep myself from thinking about my mother.

The arrival in my front yard was dismal. Nothing more had happened, but it was tremendously depressing to me to see my broken window, the squad car, and—for some reason—all the lights on.

I gunned the truck engine before I turned it off, vaguely thinking that the noise would ward off further evil action or scare away any lingering menace.

Andrews sighed heavily getting out of the truck.

"How many Duncan L. Spiveys could there be in Atlanta?" He trudged up the stairs behind me.

"I'm hoping there's only one." I didn't see how I could face the conversation I'd have to produce in order to get information I wanted out of Mr. Spivey. I certainly dreaded doing it more than once.

I pushed on my front door and it clattered open.

"I hadn't realized how exhausted I was until I sat in June's hot kitchen. Really made me sleepy. And that coffee. It's caramel-colored water. Is there *any* caffeine in it?" Andrews rubbed his eyes.

"No." I stood just inside the doorway, trying to decide what to do.

"Aren't you sleepy?" Andrews yawned.

"I didn't even notice how hot it was at Hek and June's, I'm so used to it, but I know they keep their house twenty degrees warmer than I keep mine."

"At least." He sniffed. "Look. I've been thinking."

"I thought I heard machine noises coming from your head."

"When I suggested going to have a look at Lady Barnsley's portrait," he went on, ignoring me, "I realized we'd have to go into Atlanta. That involves the Atlanta police, potentially. What's the guy's name?"

"Detective Huyne."

"Right. I'm not prepared to mess about with him. I was thinking I could call some people in Atlanta and *they* could have a look at the portrait, snap a digital pic, send it to me by e-mail, and Bob's your uncle."

"*Bob's your uncle*?" I glared at him. "What century are we in? Do people actually ever say that anymore?"

"I just did." He folded his arms. "But it was said ironically."

"Oh. Was it ironic." I hadn't so much asked a question as made an accusation. "And P.S.: I'm not remotely afraid of Detective Huyne. I don't want to see a digital picture of the painting that changed my life; I want to see the real thing. And lastly, I'm not sleepy. I'm thinking about driving to Atlanta now."

His shoulders sank.

"Christ." He shook his head. "You really are in your existential period."

"Why do you say that, exactly?"

He numbered off his thoughts on his fingers.

"Don't care about the law, have to experience it for yourself, and apparently something of a death wish—all foibles of the late, great Jean-Paul Sartre."

"I'm not certain you understand the existential ethos."

"I'm not certain I wouldn't rather kick your ass right now than argue about the existential ethos."

"Well." I arched my brow very deliberately. "You could certainly *try.*"

"I play rugby. You do research. I'd kill you." He yawned. "Though I'm too tired to kill you tonight. Besides, you don't even know if this Spivey still has the painting. He bought it some thirty years ago, right?"

"He could tell us where it is if he doesn't have it."

"How will you get in touch with him.?"

"I'll call him on the telephone. Damn, why are you vexing me? You don't think he has a phone?"

"You're going off—as I believe the expression is—half-cocked. There may well be more than one Duncan Spivey, for example."

"I'll call them all."

"Why don't you call them now? From here?"

"Because if I call from your place in Atlanta, it won't be a long-distance charge, *and* when I find him, I can go right over instead of having to say 'Great, be there in three hours.' Immediacy is important."

"*My* place?"

"Where else in Atlanta would we go?"

"*My* place?" he repeated, jaw jutted.

"You could sleep in the truck." I pulled my keys back out of my pocket and jangled them in front of him, mock-hypnotically. "Sleep. Truck."

"You really are an immensely troubled soul." He jammed his hands in his pockets. "You're just going to leave your house open to the elements? What are you going to do when Melissa comes tomorrow morning to collect her squad car and sees that you're gone? What are you going to say to Skid? To say nothing, no kidding, of this Detective Huyne, who already thinks you're the killer."

"In reverse order: Huyne won't think I'm the killer once he hears about the bat-wielding psychopath with the expensive shoes; Skid will be mad, but he'll understand because he knows who I am; Melissa will shake her head and smile, which is a trademark gesture of her great spirit; and at the moment, I don't care what else happens to this house. How much worse could it get than having a dead body where I sit to read, where I eat, sometimes, in front of the television, where my friends—"

"All right." He nodded once. "You drive. I'll sleep."

Without another word, he headed for the door.

The trip from Blue Mountain to Atlanta usually takes two and a half hours during the day, even though it's all downhill. But I discovered that when you're traveling after midnight, it's a much quicker trip.

Everything happens faster after midnight.

Careening down a mountain road with only your own headlights to guide you, the moon hiding behind black clouds, can be a liberating experience. For a span of time, all I thought about was keeping the truck on the road, trying not to kill Andrews or myself—twisting the wheel, squealing the tires, defying inertia.

But eventually, the winding asphalt leveled off, straightened out, and I was on an expressway, surrounded by other late-night drivers. Then the hollow energies of insomnia flourished, kicking at my nervous system, prompting my brain to think about things I really didn't want to.

What lay ahead of me was a tête-à-tête with a man who'd had an affair with my mother. That in itself was, alas, not unique. I'd spoken with many men over the years in Blue Mountain with whom my mother had dallied. What made this Spivey unusual was that he had paid an enormous amount of money to my father for a painting that might not have been worth it. At two o'clock in the morning, I fancied he'd done it out of guilt. But what would make a man like that have a quarter of a million dollars' worth of guilt?

Andrews lived in a very nice faux English cottage close to the university. Built in 1937 out of cratered old brick and salvaged wood, it was solid, lovely, and, under the current owner, ill-cared for.

The paint on the upper half-timbered gables was peeling; the cement walkway and steps leading to the front door were cracked and mossy. The yard was a disaster: all chickweed and wild violets.

Still, inside it was cozy. The living room presented a fine fireplace with built-in bookshelves on either side of the mantel, and the dining room was large and filled with light in the morning.

It actually had three bedrooms, but for Andrews there was one bedroom, one office, and one room where everything that confused him lived. The junk room held an assortment of Christmas gifts, unwanted furniture, boxes yet unpacked from his move many years before.

It was still the middle of the night when I pulled into the driveway.

"What?" Andrews jumped forward with a start.

"You're home, that's what." I turned off the ignition.

We sat in the truck a moment, too tired to move.

"That was quick," he said finally.

"You slept the entire way."

"Hope you didn't." He opened his door. "Come on. You can get a couple hours' sleep before you begin your campaign of harassment."

He yawned, fished in his pocket for his keys, and stumbled toward the front door.

I got out of the truck and started to follow.

"Lock your truck," he said wearily, not bothering to look back. "This is a good neighborhood, but you should still lock your truck."

I did. He opened the front door.

"Well, it was a short, piss-poor vacation for me." He flipped on the porch light. "And now I'm home."

"I'll just stretch out on the sofa for an hour or two." I lumbered past him into the living room. "Until morning."

"Right." He yawned again. "I think I'll have a bit of a crash myself."

He disappeared almost immediately into his bedroom.

I found myself on the sofa before I completely realized that I was in a mental twilight. I saw two hooded figures standing guard at the front door, but they turned out, on startled further examination, to be a coat rack and an umbrella stand. Certain proof of my deep need for sleep.

I laid back, hoping I would sleep without dreaming.

Before my second breath, I was wrapped in silent ink black oblivion. Possible proof of the existence of God.

I awoke with a start, stabbed by a golden spear of sunlight. For the merest instant, I had no idea where I was. Two blinks reminded me I was in Atlanta; the third brought down the crushing realization that I would not have espresso to drink.

I sat up on Andrews's sofa. His living room was relatively free of clutter. A vase of dried flowers—the only kind, surely, he could tend—helped to sophisticate the mantel between two well-burned candlesticks. The flowers were miniature ruby roses; the candles were white as snow. I studied their composition, trying to gather my thoughts enough to stand.

To my great surprise, Andrews appeared in the hallway

"I'm up!" he announced to no one in particular. "Inferior coffee and strange toast are on the way."

Not daring to imagine what "strange toast" might entail, I somehow managed to achieve a standing posture and stagger toward the kitchen, where I knew the telephone and phone books would be.

I could hear Andrews running water in his bathroom, splashing it on his face, groaning. It seemed the perfect music for the morning's moment.

His kitchen was a tiny affair riddled with Sears appliances and cold Formica countertops. There was a small breakfast bar that made the room seem even smaller, at which he had placed two bar stools—stools actually stolen from a bar. I sat precariously on the one next to the phone and rummaged through the wreckage of papers, take-out menus, and jotted notes before I found the Atlanta residential phone book.

The print was so small, and my eyes so unawake, that it was nearly impossible to read the pages in the dim light of the kitchen. I leaned out to flip on the overhead globe and nearly fell off the stool.

"I hate your kitchen," I called out to Andrews.

"I know."

The light helped enough for me to find the Spivey pages. Certain Spiveys in Atlanta were moneyed. One had given what was perhaps the most acoustically perfect concert hall in the south to Clayton State University just south of the city. There was also a Lake Spivey. I assumed that our Duncan Spivey was one of these.

Before I could make it to the exact page, Andrews lumbered into the kitchen, hair wild, eyes to match.

"Must have coffee." It was almost a prayer.

"Ah!" I'd found it. "Duncan L. Spivey. The only one."

I reached for the phone.

"Stop," Andrews commanded. "It's not yet eight o'clock. And I'm not certain, frankly, what day of the week it is."

I thought, but I couldn't recall the day, either.

"Well, what time is it?" I glared in the direction of the little clock set into the stove but couldn't make it out.

"It is seven-forty-seven." He pulled his Mr. Coffee machine toward him on the counter by the sink.

I was very glad to see that he also had a bean grinder and fresh black beans. While he busied himself with the coffee, I tried to imagine what I would say to Mr. Spivey. Everything I could come up with at that moment only made me a lunatic—even more so than usual.

By the time the coffee was placed before me only a few moments later, I was regretting the entire trip to Atlanta.

"How am I going to explain anything to Spivey?" I stared down at the red coffee mug.

"Don't try." Andrews leaned on the counter. "He doesn't need your life story. Keep it simple: 'My father sold you a painting and I've never seen it. I wonder if it would be possible to pop by—' "

"All right." I reached for the phone. "But I'm at least going to tell him that the proceeds put me through college."

"Why?"

"So he'll know it's not just idle curiosity. He'll understand *why* I want to see it."

"No he won't." Andrews sipped the brew he'd concocted.

I was already dialing.

"You know he'll have a machine," Andrews mentioned casually. "He won't answer the phone. Not at this hour."

"Hello."

Someone had answered, and after only one ring—an older man, by his voice.

"Hello," I stammered, "I'm calling Duncan Spivey."

"I'm sorry," he said immediately, "I'm expecting a very important call from my doctor."

"My name is Devilin."

There was a dark pause at the other end of the line, and then the man let go a breath as heavy as the silence had been.

"Fletcher?" he asked.

My father's name.

It was a ghost question, and the man's voice was mostly air.

"No." I struggled with what to say next. "Fletcher was my father—he's dead."

"Dead?"

I instantly wished I had said it better.

"I'm Fever." I cleared my throat. "Dr. Fever Devilin. I believe my father—"

"You're Dolores's son?" he interrupted, barely comprehending.

My mother's name.

"I'm afraid so." I tried to regroup.

His voice sounded so . . . shaken.

"Your mother—," he began.

"My mother's dead, as well," I said quickly.

Andrews looked up from his coffee, but I avoided eye contact.

"I was only going to say," Spivey began, "that I knew them both, a number of years ago."

"Yes." I was absolutely at sea as to how to proceed.

"You're probably calling about the portrait that put you through college," he said, every syllable hollow.

I looked up at Andrews then, eyes wide.

"As a matter of fact, that's exactly why I'm calling."

Andrews set down his cup. "No," he whispered.

I nodded.

"How could you possibly guess—"

"I have been waiting for this phone call for a great many years," Spivey said, tone unchanged. "I thought you might call me when you were in college, or even when you were teaching at the university. But now here you are."

"I meant—"

"When Fletcher sold me the painting, he told me what the money was for."

"Oh." I stared at the phone.

"So." He sighed. "I suppose you'd be wanting to know why he sold it to me. Or why I bought it. It's not, as you may know, a particularly interesting painting. As a portraitist, in my opinion, Cotman made an excellent landscape artist."

"You didn't care for the painting?"

"No, I liked it. And I supposed that it might be worth something one day. I had heard Cotman's name. But upon further investigation—after I purchased the piece—it wasn't as valuable as I'd imagined."

"What investigation?" I didn't want my voice to sound as dull as it did, but I couldn't force it to be anything other than colorless and plain.

"I contacted a gallery in London that specialized in Cotman." He, too, seemed almost completely uninterested in this particular part of the conversation.

"Wait," I said suddenly. "Was it the Ashton Gallery?"

I couldn't say what had made me remember the name of the gallery from the file I'd seen in Taylor's office.

"As a matter of fact," he said slowly, a bit energized.

"They said it was nothing of value."

"They did indeed." He blew out his breath; it was like thunder in the phone. "Look. You may be wondering why I paid so much money for a painting that was of little genuine worth."

"I'm calling—," I began, hoping just to get to the part where he'd let me come to his house to see the thing.

"I gave Fletcher a lot of money," Spivey said, voice torn, "because I knew it was for you—and I thought I might be your father."

There it was: the exact sentence I had been hoping to avoid, not because I thought this man might actually be my father, but because I wanted to avoid the part of the conversation where I had to explain to him that any one of two or three dozen men might have had the same suspicion about me. Around the time I was born, my mother had been in a prodigiously promiscuous period. The fact that I looked almost exactly like Fletcher Devilin—and, from evidence of old photographs, a good bit like Conner—belied all such suppositions. But Spivey had never seen me, at least as an adult, and so would not know that.

"Mr. Spivey." I struggled to sound reasonable and, somehow, professional. "I really only want to see the portrait, strictly idle curiosity. I happened to be in Atlanta visiting a friend—"

"Oh." Such a hopeless syllable.

"So I was wondering—," I tried again.

"I sold the painting." He said it as if I should have known. "I didn't even hang it in the house when I brought it home. I sold it several years ago when I was cleaning out a part of the house so that—I was doing some renovation, and making a master suite in the upstairs part of the house. Doesn't matter. I came across the painting, advertised in the proper places, then sold it to a private collector."

"I see." I bit my upper lip. "You wouldn't mind telling me how to contact that person, then, would you? So I could see the picture."

"What?" His mind was obviously elsewhere. "Wait, yes. I think perhaps—" And he set the phone down without further words.

"He sold it," I told Andrews, still staring at the phone.

"Sold it? When?"

"Couple of years ago." I swallowed. "He's gone to find the name of the—"

"Hello?" Spivey's voice was harsh in my ear.

"Yes." I sounded calm.

"Diana Dandridge and Kristin Shaunnesy," he said quickly, "at Seventeen Amsterdam Place. It's in midtown, I think."

"No phone number?" I barely recognized my own voice.

"No." He hesitated. "Look. Fever. Dr. Devilin. I'd like to see you."

"If only I had the time this trip," I told him as breezily as I could manage, "but my schedule's really tight at the moment. I just have time to pop by and see the painting before I'm called hence. But the very next trip to Atlanta—"

"We could have dinner," he finished the sentence.

"Absolutely." I leaned my head nearer the phone, ready to hang up. "The very next time I'm in Atlanta."

"This isn't the conversation I was hoping to have," he began.

"All right," I sang into the phone as if I were brushing off a telemarketer. "I have to run."

His silence made the phone heavy in my hand.

"You're not going to call me." His voice was a vapor.

"Bye now." I hung up.

Andrews stared.

"You're white as a sheet." He seemed a little alarmed.

"I'm certain," I told him in some misguided attempt to maintain a carefree facade, "you'd come up with something less of a cliché if it weren't so early."

"What was all that with Spivey?"

How could I tell Andrews that I'd spoken with a particular kind of ghost—not someone who was dead and had come back to haunt me, but someone who was alive and had been haunted by my existence, a man turned into a ghost by guilt and longing, by half a lifetime of unanswered questions: a distant past, barely remembered but vividly painful? There was no explanation for that kind of suffering. And I only that moment realized he'd been waiting for a call from his doctor, a fact I had not remotely addressed or even acknowledged.

"I told you," I managed. "He sold the painting."

I reached for the phone book.

"It had something to do with your father. Your mother."

One of the problems with having a good friend is that it's difficult to hide something from him even when you want to.

"He told me where the painting is." I looked through the *D* listings.

"You'll tell me eventually."

"Because you'll needle it out of me," I agreed. "But could we let it go for the moment? I don't think I can—"

"Where's the painting now?" he said instantly.

"In midtown." I was very grateful, in that moment, for a friend's willingness not to pry.

Even if it was somewhat predicated on a very short attention span.

Diana Dandridge and Kristin Shaunnesy lived in a particularly nice midtown neighborhood, on a hill, with a view of the Atlanta skyline through tall pines. My phone call had roused them, but Diana was astonishingly kind about it, and once I explained my situation, she practically insisted that I come right over. At least that's what I told Andrews.

"This is outrageous, you realize," he said as I pulled my truck up in front of their house.

The front yard was surrounded by a black iron fence and the walkway to the door was lined with huge rosemary plants, flowering blue.

"She said it was all right." I climbed out of my seat.

"She was being polite. Christ. I wasn't even born here and I can recognize southern hospitality."

"We'll only be a moment."

I was already headed for the iron gate.

I realized as I trudged headlong toward a stranger's house at 8:30 in the morning that I was almost overcome with a desire to have a look at the portrait. The feeling had come on gradually, a slow dawning, but the light was hard and clear now. I was about to see the painting that had changed my life.

Andrews followed behind reluctantly as I stumbled through the gate and up the path.

Before I was halfway to the door, I heard the dogs.

Dogs.

I turned.

"They have dogs." I glared at Andrews.

"Serves you right," he said as he nudged past me on the path.

He knew my fear of the animals. He'd seen it in action. All canines belonged to Satan; nothing could have been clearer to me.

Andrews had achieved the front steps and tapped the doorbell before I could tell him I'd changed my mind about the entire matter.

The door flew open and a hundred dogs appeared, teeth gleaming in the early-morning light.

"Dr. Devilin!" The woman offered one hand and held the hounds at bay with the other. "I'm Diana."

"I'm Dr. Andrews," he corrected, taking her hand. "The wee timorous cowering beastie behind me would be Dr. Devilin."

"That's Robert Burns," Diana announced proudly. " 'To a Mouse'—what you said."

"Absolutely correct!" Andrews beamed. "Very impressive for this time of morning."

"We play a lot of Cranium," Diana explained. "Come on in."

"Come on in, Dr. Devilin," Andrews called, mocking me.

"Yes." I didn't move. "Absolutely."

"He's afraid of dogs," Andrews confided to Diana.

"Oh. God. Right. Kristin!"

There was a commotion from within, and short moments later, the dogs had vanished.

"It's safe now." Andrews indicated the way.

Diana appeared in the doorway again.

"Well, then." She held out her hand.

I moved as quickly as I could to take it.

"You can't possibly imagine," I began, squeezing her hand a bit too hard, "how much your kindness means to me in this regard."

"Please." She dismissed the entire notion of our boorishness. "This is kind of exciting, knowing something more about the painting. Kristin bought it, really. Kristin!"

"They're put up," a voice called from another room. "The dogs are all in the basement."

"No. Come here and meet Dr. Devilin." Diana pulled me into her house.

Andrews followed, all smiles—mostly at my expense.

Kristin came into the living room as I was getting my bearings.

Diana's chestnut hair fell over one eye, a dark Veronica Lake. Kristen's short blond crop was a perfect contrast. They were both dressed for work.

The living room was a *House & Garden* display: perfectly filled spaces, fresh-cut flowers, original art, and a display case to the left of the door filled with, quite possibly, the most extensive collection of antique corkscrews on the planet.

Kristin saw that I was staring at them.

"I collect." She smiled.

"I see that." I looked around the room. "This is all quite remarkable."

"The portrait is out here in the garden room." Diana moved immediately to the room beyond the one we were in.

"I'm going to be late for work," Kristin said, delighted.

"I'm Fever Devilin." I offered her my hand. "I really can't tell you—"

"Hey." She took my hand, still smiling. "I really want to hear the story. I'm *happy* to be late to work."

"Winton," Andrews said, waving at Kristin.

We were all moving toward the garden room.

It had been a porch at one time, but it was closed in on three sides with windows and sat under the heavy shade of a flowering almond tree. The windows on the side of the room that faced the house next door were simple stained glass. The others, facing the street, were antique X-patterned affairs, giving the effect of a place from another time. There was a delightful array of plants in the room, including a huge Victorian-era palm in one corner.

But the focus of the room was the painting on the only solid wall. Under its own light, the face, pale and fragile, glowed with supernatural aura. The skin was poreless and perfect, the eyes brimming with the overwhelming melancholy of unattainable desire. But the desire was written onto the expression as clearly as if the face had been outlined with the word *passion* written a thousand times in the dark background of the painting.

She was no Mona Lisa, no mystery on her lips. Her secret—a bursting cry she had hoped to hide in the chambers of her heart—was made clear with every brushstroke. Fully clothed in a neck-high aubergine dress, she was naked—and ashamed to be discovered in such a state. Misery had swallowed her, and she was lost.

"How could anyone think this picture wasn't worth a million dollars?" Andrews whispered, obviously seeing what I saw.

"I know," Diana whispered back. "I got it for a steal.

"And this belonged to your father?" she asked me.

"Not exactly." I wanted to sit down.

Lady Barnsley would not stop staring at me. I could feel the sting of her sorrow, the wretchedness of her regret. I understood her curse. It had nothing to do with evil events or catastrophic fates. It was much worse than that. She had bequeathed us all her pain: always wanting—seeing joy and contentment just barely out of reach—and never attaining.

I knew that emptiness all too well.

"Belonged to his great-grandfather, actually." Andrews, too, was still staring at the painting, though obviously less affected than I.

"Conner Devilin," I began, only a little in a daze, "was born in Wales."

I gave Diana and Kristin the shorter, more poetic version of the story as best I could, occasionally helped by Andrews: murder in Ireland, mayhem in Wales, a family curse, the education of Fever Devilin. We omitted any reference to Shultz. A murder in the past is a fascinating story; an ongoing homicide investigation was an entirely different matter.

"Unbelievable." Kristin stared at the painting. "All because of her."

That conclusion had not gelled in my mind exactly, but I considered that Kristin's observation was at least partly correct. Eloise Barnsley was indeed in some way responsible for even the events of the preceding days.

If that's not a curse, what is? I thought.

Diana shuddered. "I need more espresso."

Andrews and I both turned to her instantly.

She read our faces. "Can I offer you some?"

"We couldn't." Andrews had pitched his voice perfectly. It said, Ask me again and I'll take five, please.

Alas, at that exact moment, the hellhounds, having burst their confinement, marauded the room.

I was surrounded by, perhaps, seventy animals, by my now-conservative estimation.

"Why do you have so many dogs?" I failed to keep the terror from shining through every word.

"Five's not that many." Andrews had knelt and was clutching one, a Dalmatian-looking puppy, the most energetic of the lot.

"There are only five?" I was trying not to look.

"I know they're all over the place—sorry," Kristin told me sweetly, grabbing two dogs and holding them away from me. "But it's a good thing we have them. We think they might have kept someone from stealing this painting."

"What?" Andrews stood.

"About a month ago." Diana was holding a blond older dog and a more peaceful shepherd of some sort.

"We only had four then." Kristin patted one of hers on the head. "Dogs."

"Someone broke a stained-glass window in here while we were gone to Publix. Tried to get in."

"The house alarm went off, but I don't think that would have stopped them." Kristin stared at one of the windows. "They could have been in and out before the police got here."

"When we got home, the alarm was ringing like all get-out." Diana was looking at the paining. "We came rushing in, and all the dogs were in this room barking at the broken window."

"They saved your painting." Andrews glowed.

I glared at the animals.

"I see." I managed a smile in Diana's direction. "Well. I think we should be going. We've inconvenienced you two enough. Can't tell you how much I appreciate—"

I began backing out of the room toward the front door.

"No espresso?" Andrews cast a forlorn glance my way.

His look had little effect on my retreat. I could see the dogs' eyes. They could see mine. The rending of flesh and the snapping of bones could scarcely be far behind.

Andrews properly read my face.

"We really should go," Andrews admitted, shaking hands with Kristin.

"Sorry about the dogs," Diana whispered to him.

"Please don't apologize. Dr. Devilin here is a biological experiment," Andrews explained calmly. "We don't usually let him meet the public. He'll be much better once we get him back in his cage and sedate him."

"Thank you again," I called to them, hand on the front door, clearing my throat, "for letting me see the painting. Sorry about leaving like this. They really are lovely dogs. It's not them; it's me."

I threw open the door and ran from the house, gasping, toward the truck.

Fifteen

The ride back to Blue Mountain was a blur. Andrews slept the entire way. I tried desperately not to think too much about Mr. Spivey and ended up obsessing about Eloise Barnsley's portrait instead.

We arrived back home, only to discover the presence of not one but three police cars in my yard *and* a dark sedan that could only belong to Detective Huyne.

Andrews woke with a start when the truck came to a halt. He rubbed his eyes before he noticed the plethora of constabulary vehicles.

"Christ on a crutch!" He slumped down in the seat. "We're going to jail."

In something of a wild moment, I thought I might just turn the truck on again, throw it into reverse, and careen down the mountain. Maybe I could lose myself in the woods, but I didn't think Andrews would survive. I could have shoved him out of the truck, but before I had a chance to act on any impulse, Skidmore appeared on the porch, shaking his head and motioning me into my house.

"We're not going to jail." I didn't even sound confident to myself; I'm certain Andrews didn't buy the sentiment.

I climbed out of the cab and moved with great deliberation right toward Skidmore, brimming with aggressive energy.

"I'm glad you're here." I leapt up the steps. "You're not going to believe what we found out."

Skidmore sighed.

"I know you think that your option here is to try for 'The best defense is a good offense.' " He bit his lip. "But I told you not to go anywhere."

Detective Huyne appeared in my doorway.

"I'm thinking of shooting you." His eyes were glued to mine. "Just in the leg. Nothing serious—but you won't be able to get around anymore."

I turned to Skidmore.

"I saw the painting." I hoped he could read my mind—or at least part of it. "And P.S.: Someone tried to steal it recently."

"Look." Huyne came onto the porch. "The fiber evidence we found on your broken window seems to match the evidence we already have, and the blood we found in there isn't a match for your type or Dr. Andrews's."

How he knew what blood type I was—or Andrews—was a riddle I chose to ignore.

"Detective Huyne is changing his mind about who might be Shultz's killer." There was a hint of light in Skidmore's eyes, almost disguised by the blur of his official demeanor.

"It's not changed yet, and I could still have you arrested for leaving your house when I told you not to," Huyne grumbled.

I moved so quickly, I surprised myself. I was almost nose-to-nose with Huyne.

"In fact," I growled, "you could not. I believe you I told you that Deputy Mathews would have to hit me with a tranquilizer dart to keep me from going where I wanted to. The same concept applies to arresting me. I've found a dead body in my house, I've been attacked by a lunatic, and now I'm being threatened by an out-of-town policeman. That's about all the distress I can eat at the moment. So unless you're going to get out your little gun, step aside. I'd like to go into my house and wash my hands."

"Davis!" Huyne bellowed, staring at me.

The other detective appeared in the doorway.

"Those notes we got in Pine City." His voice was granite. "What was it the lawyer said? About the phone call?"

Davis fished in his threadbare suit coat pocket, found a small spiral pad, flipped through it, and began to read the third page.

"Mr. Taylor stated that he received *no* phone call such as the one described by suspect Devilin—"

"Stop," Huyne ordered. "Now why, Sheriff, would your friend lie about a thing like that?"

"My assumption would be that Mr. Taylor is lying." Skid sniffed. "I'd spend a bit of time trying to find out the *why* of that."

"Just because Devilin here is your pal—"

"Got nothing to do with that," Skid said calmly. "I've a great mind to lock Dr. Devilin up myself for leaving his house last night. But the fact is, I know Dr. Devilin's patterns and I know Mr. Taylor's patterns. Fever doesn't lie, because it doesn't occur to him. While this character trait seriously impairs his ability to interact socially, it does make him a fairly reliable commodity. On the other hand, Taylor is a lawyer whose business—and, as far as I can tell, his life—is predicated on the well-placed lie, the political expediency, and the sociological misdirection."

"*Political expediency? Sociological misdirection*?" I gaped at Skidmore. "Where the hell—"

"All a part of the seminar in Alabama," he explained to me, then turned again to Huyne. "So, based on prior knowledge and years of local experience, I would have to call Taylor the liar, whereas Dr. Devilin is merely the idiot."

"Thank you." I nodded ever so slightly to Huyne. "There you have it."

"I *hate* this place!" Huyne spun around, talking to no one.

"The feeling is mutual!" Andrews called, still sitting in the truck.

Skid stared at me.

"You're a big troublemaker, you know that?" He almost succeeded in sounding serious.

"I don't know what it is about that person that rubs me the wrong way." I watched Huyne grab the notebook out of his subordinate's hand.

"Oh, I expect he affects everyone that way." Skid stepped off the porch and into the yard.

I knew he wanted me to follow him.

"You know you *really* ought not to have left home." He wasn't looking back. "It was dangerous in a great many ways. Why don't you just meddle in things around here the way you usually do?"

"Well, as it happens, the environs you call 'around here' don't contain all the information I need."

"So are you thinking of flying to England next?"

"It had occurred to me."

It had not, in fact, but I was assuming a certain belligerence toward the concept of policemen telling me what to do. A trip to Europe was obviously a part of that demeanor.

"Even though you have work to do around here?" Skid was still staring off into the woods.

"My work—"

"I mean about all this mess. About Shultz." He sighed and turned to face me at last. "I believe you're forgetting an important element of your . . . I don't know what you'd call this. Your business?"

"What are you talking about?"

"Weren't there three things your great-grandpa bought at the Barnsley auction?"

Three or four sentences jumbled in my mind; all of them jammed up when they got to my tongue. A single syllable escaped, alone and without content.

"Ah."

"What?" He blinked. "I've got you speechless? Is this really happening? God, I'd pay ten dollars for a witness to this moment."

"How did you know about the—I don't remember telling you that there were three things." I stood my ground, trying to gather my thoughts.

"When you were ranting and accusing some nameless member of the Barnsley family of killing Shultz, you mentioned something about it." He smiled. "But I actually do a little investigation of my own every once in a while. You do remember that I actually am the sheriff, right? Swear to God, you don't give me a lick of credit for that."

"I do," I began hesitantly. "I just forget how good you are at it sometimes."

"Whereas I take in nearly everything you tell me." He sighed. "How many times have you drummed into me the idea, for example, that the number three is important? Whenever I tell you it's just superstition, you tell me that it's more than that. You say—let me see can I remember the exact words— 'Mythology reflects the world.' Do I have that right?"

"Sounds like one of my more pompous pronouncements," I agreed, properly chastised, "and I'm impressed that you remember the phrase. I think maybe—"

"Because every time the number three appears," he said, having a good time teaching me a lesson, "it makes a triangle, and a triangle is a universal symbol—"

"Will you please stop." I put my hands over my ears.

"That's how you go on." He drew in a heavy breath.

"How do you put up with me?" My own voice sounded a bit thin to me.

"Sometimes it isn't easy."

"I can't believe you remember my ravings."

"I remember them," he said quietly, catching my eye, "because I know it means something to you. So I pay attention."

I broke eye contact, gave a quick nod—too much emotional content for me in his words, too much to think about.

"The third object in question," I began, erudite to a fault, "is a Cherokee artifact. Its disposition is unknown to me at the moment."

"Maybe it would help to find out about it. You've gone to great lengths to investigate the other two." He shrugged. "Or maybe I'm just trying to get you to stick around your house long enough for me to get you completely shed of a murder charge."

"Either way." I smiled.

"How are we going to find out anything about that Indian thing?" Andrews yelled from the truck.

I turned his way. "Have you been listening to our conversation?"

"As much as I could hear." He finally opened his door. "You both mumble too much."

"I'm going back inside." Skid headed for the house.

"I suppose," I said to no one in particular, "I could start with my father's trunk. Again."

The most fascinating thing to me about my father's trunk when I was younger was its seemingly endless hidden places—pockets in black velvet, envelopes inside of hat linings, false heels on well-worn two-tone shoes. If he'd wanted to, I always believed, my father could have hidden our mountain in his trunk. He had done something more powerful to me already: He had hidden himself in it.

When I'd returned to Blue Mountain as an adult, years later, I did as little exploration or rearrangement of anything in either parent's room as I could without turning into Dickens's Miss Havisham. Still, I had been going through my own house, my little town, my troubled mind since I returned to Blue Mountain, looking for clues about my life—and every other mystery had been a metaphor. But I'd probably looked in that trunk more since Shultz's visit than anytime in the previous several years.

As I opened the lid that day in the darkness of my father's room, the familiar revulsion danced in my stomach. It occurred to me that it was, in fact, the third time I had looked inside the trunk since Shultz had first called me—was it only days ago?

Now, I thought, where would my father hide something about a Cherokee artifact?

I'd played the game since I was seven or so, trying to find rhyme or reason to his method, even long after it had become obvious that there was none.

Still.

I had a hopeless, sinking feeling, realizing I had been over and over everything in this chaos a thousand times or more. I would have noticed anything remotely resembling an Indian piece of art long before that day.

Still.

The lining of the trunk had long since been explored. The envelopes had recently been ransacked. Pockets and chambers and secret drawers had all been discovered. Every secret, surely, had been revealed—and the greatest of these was that there were no secrets at all, only tricks.

I sat on the floor, just staring at the thing before me. A sudden and completely inexplicable impulse to weep washed through me; then I thought I might actually throw up.

One last try, I thought, if only to defeat the intense and baffling emotional circus barreling through my rib cage.

Summoning preternatural powers of concentration, it occurred to me, only slightly, what a great reader of Poe my father had been. Could it really be that the now-exhausted cliché of hiding a thing in plain sight had been in his consciousness?

I tried to stare into the trunk and take in the whole of it, not its parts. I tried to see the contents as a single image rather than a disordered assemblage of dozens of individual puzzles.

Rolled up in a corner of the trunk, there was a sheaf of perhaps ten maps. I'd looked at them several times as a child, dismissing them as an adult. The most interesting was a map of Blue Mountain made by a government surveyor at the beginning of the twentieth century and amusing as much for its inaccuracies as its misspelling of our part of the mountain, which was recorded as belonging to the "Deverling" family. The rest were copies of older maps, some made as early as the 1700s. The whole affair had held little interest for me as a boy, and I had not looked at them since I'd returned home. What could be more boring than an old map?

A good trick that the mind plays is that it can disregard what it does not like. Furthermore, what it disregards can then become invisible.

Hence my dismissal of the coil of maps tied with yellowed string.

I plucked them from the corner and worked the string off them. The knot was too old to disturb.

I did my best to lay them out in the bad light of the room and began to search each one for anything resembling a clue, not for a second expecting to find anything.

One of the maps—entitled "Georgia, 1835," a date that seemed significant in the back of my brain—had strange markings on it. Some of the letters looked like ornate medieval script; others weren't letters at all, just calligraphic designs. The note had been written on the map. It hadn't been part of the printing. I was about to move on to other maps, when I realized I was looking at a note written in "Talking Leaves," Sequoyah's Cherokee alphabet.

Andrews, Skidmore, and I had been gathered around the map on the kitchen table for nearly an hour before Andrews stated the obvious.

"We'll never be able to read this." He sat back.

"Why does 1835 seem a significant year?" I was talking to myself.

Skidmore sighed.

"Didn't you *ever* pay attention in elementary school?" He rolled his eyes. "The Treaty of New Echota was signed in December of 1835, and it ceded the last remaining Cherokee territory in Georgia."

It came to me. "You're right!"

"I know I'm right," he groused.

"A little rusty on my Georgia history," Andrews said, raising his hand.

"President Andrew Jackson wanted to remove all the Indians from Georgia to Oklahoma or somewhere, take away their land," I said.

"It went through the courts, but eventually it all came down to the Trail of Tears." Skid stared at the map.

I had a great moment of melancholy realizing that nearly everyone in the world to whom that alphabet had meant so much was now gone—passed into history and longing.

"This sounds familiar." Andrews sat back. "We talked about this before, in connection with the Barnsley estate."

"We did," I said to Skid.

"But this alphabet—," Andrews began.

"It is amazing." I stared down at the impossible letters. "Sequoyah took twelve years to complete it. He was a silversmith, you know. All he wanted when he started the project was a way to sign his own name to the work. He tried pictographs first, but he realized that his alphabet would have to be thousands of letters, so he created a symbol for every syllable in the spoken language."

"Like the Japanese," Andrews interjected.

"Actually Phoenician in origin," I corrected, "but the point is, he developed something like eighty symbols, and it became the written language of the Cherokee nation."

"It's a very poetic name, Talking Leaves." Andrews couldn't take his eyes off the mysterious words written on the map.

"In fact," I pointed out, "it was primarily derisive. The Cherokee felt that most English words would dry up and blow away like leaves when the words were no longer suited to a political purpose."

"Really an amazing thing to have done," Skid said, "if you consider that this man put together an alphabet in a few years, when it took most other civilizations on the planet a couple of thousand."

"And it was apparently easy for the Cherokees to use. If you could speak the language, you could learn to read or write it in a few weeks."

Andrews touched one of the letters.

"But who can read it now?" He looked up. "They're all gone, aren't they?"

"A forlorn question," I admitted, "but I've been thinking about just that. As luck would have it, there's a happy answer. When I was in graduate school, I was fascinated by a bit of oral folk collection done in the late 1800s by a man named James Mooney. I must have read his 'Fifth Annual Report of the Bureau of American Ethnology' a hundred times. It prompted me to seek out a man named Dan Battle, a Blue Mountain resident, who clamed to be a descendent of several Cherokee families who hid in these woods around here and managed to avoid relocation."

"How did they do that?" Andrews was surprisingly fascinated.

"It wasn't hard," Skid said before I could. "The Treaty of New Echota was signed in 1835, but the so-called legal relocation didn't happen until 1838. That gave a lot of the Cherokee time to figure things out."

"Where did you say they were supposed to be relocated to?" Andrews scowled.

"Oklahoma." Skid shook his head. "They were marched from Georgia to Oklahoma."

"And that's the Trail of Tears."

"Right." Skid swallowed.

"Jesus," Andrews said a little too harshly, "it's a wonder they *all* didn't die. The United States government—I mean, sorry, but where do you people get the nerve?"

"I would imagine it comes from the same source," I countered slowly, "that allowed the English government to annex India."

"Point taken." Andrews sat back.

"The first guy they got to take the Cherokee away," Skid went on, "was a general named John Wool."

"Can you tell history was Skidmore's favorite subject in school?" I asked Andrews.

"He resigned his command in protest," Skidmore went on. "The general they got to replace him, Winfield Scott, had seven thousand men with him. In the summer of 1838, the United States Army began what could only be called 'the invasion of a sovereign nation.' "

I stared at the map, going over all the parts of it that said, plainly, "Cherokee Nation."

"But some of them evaded Scott, you're telling me." Andrews nodded, also looking down at the map. "I can see how that could happen. There must be a thousand places just around your house where a whole group of people could hide."

Skid nodded.

"And your friend—what was his name? He was one," Andrews said after a moment.

"Well, his family was. Dan Battle is his name."

"And he can read this." Andrews tapped the map.

"He once told me he could." I sighed. "He's a sort of self-styled Cherokee shaman."

"Then why are you still sitting here with us? Call the man."

"Right." I stood.

"You're not going without a police escort," Skid said casually.

"What?" I was about to argue.

"If you go anywhere else without telling me for the next six months," he said plainly, also rising, "I will hunt you down with my pistol in my hand. So I believe I'll get someone to carry you over there to Mr. Battle's. Just to avoid the appearance of impropriety."

Andrews and I both glared.

"You really have taken to this sheriffing business," I accused. "That's the sentiment of a politician."

"You make your call," he responded wearily, "I'll make mine."

Sixteen

Less than a half hour later, I was in a squad car with Crawdad Pritchett, map in hand.

"I'm really glad the sheriff called me," Crawdad said for the third time.

"You told me that." I was still a bit perturbed about having an escort.

"I mean, Dan Battle is kind of a hero of mine."

Crawdad's eyes were locked onto the treacherous mountain road. We were climbing through thick pines on a dirt road. A darker gravity was jealous of our assent toward light and did its best to prevent it.

"He is?" I couldn't imagine why.

"I mean, what he does and all."

"Dan Battle is a real estate broker." I tried not to sound too condescending.

"Naw." Crawdad laughed like a teenager. "That's just what he does for a living."

"I'm not sure what you mean, then."

"Sure you do." His smile seemed a permanent fixture. "You more than most. What he *really* does is, you know, magic tricks."

He'd whispered the last two words so softly that I wasn't certain I'd heard him correctly.

"I mean, his stories are great and all," Crawdad went on, "and I could listen to them all day. I expect you've heard every one. But when he does those tricks—they say he's as good as your dad was back in the older days. Your dad was the best, everybody says. Of course, I never saw him."

The road had gotten even steeper. It was little more than a rut, and I feared that gravity might win our war. Great granite boulders were beginning to replace the pine trees, a certain sign that we were achieving the top of the mountain. The day was opening up, but it was too soon to tell if the sky would clear; low-flying rain clouds were moving in.

A few words from a boy named Crawdad, and my entire nervous system had sizzled. In the first place, I was chastising myself for thinking of Dan Battle as a real estate salesman instead of a folk genius, the living repository of invaluable information. In the second place, I was confused by Crawdad's reference to my father's magic act. And finally, I was embarrassed that I didn't know anything about Dan's life other than the stories I'd gotten out of him years before, preserved for my files on a trusty Wollens tape recorder. At that moment, I could not even have told anyone alive where those tapes were in the jumble of my office.

Crawdad seemed to sense my discomfort, if not its source.

"Sorry, Dr. Devilin," he said, easing up on the accelerator. "I ride up around here all the time and I forget the road can be a little— You got you some carsick?"

"No." I rubbed my face. "I'm fine. I didn't know Dan Battle was a magician."

Confession is good for the soul.

"You're kidding! Everybody knows that."

Also good for derision, apparently.

"Our discussions were more along the lines of his Cherokee heritage." I was hedging.

"That's what I'm talking about."

Crawdad slowed the car almost to a stop, and I realized that the landscape around us was suddenly golden. We'd made it over a ridge, and the car had leveled off. Accustomed as I was to the so-called scenic overlook, what I saw out the window absolutely stopped my heart for a beat or two.

We were above the clouds. All around us, the sun was glazing everything, blazing rocks and blasting shadows. White birds of light filled the sky, and I could barely tell the difference between land and air.

Clear light shocked the tops of the clouds, turned them to roses and wheat. They looked solid enough to walk on, and I had the light-headed sensation that we were in another world.

"God." It was the only syllable that seemed appropriate.

"Yeah." Crawdad, too, was mesmerized.

After a moment, I deliberately turned my concentration to the matters at hand.

"Dan Battle used to be in town when I knew him." I looked around for a cabin. "He's up here now?"

"That place in town, it's just for the tourists in the summer." Crawdad opened his car door. "This is where he lives."

Crawdad started off toward a large granite outcropping, and I spent a foolish moment wondering if Dan Battle lived in a cave.

"It's over here," Crawdad called.

I got out of the car and followed. It was still a bit difficult to see anything in all that light. I rounded the edge of one of the biggest boulders, and there was his home.

Designed very much like a Tudor bungalow, wood beams and raw stone, the house was perfectly set in nature. It faced due east; a small mountain stream ran close by on the southern side; tall shade trees at the west kept hot afternoon sun from troubling the place. There was a stone walkway leading to the front door, lined with white impatiens. The garden bed in front of the house was more adventurous: Strange celosia rose over black sedum, burgundy-leafed cuphea shot white spires into the air, and some sort of flowering moss acted as perfect groundcover. I barely had time to remind myself that I would never have known any of those plants but for Lucinda, when Dan Battle appeared in the doorway, beaming.

"Fever!"

Dan was dressed in purple Hawaiian shirt and old blue jeans, but clothes did not belie his true bear nature. Before I knew what was happening, he had moved down the walkway and crushed me into a near-fatal hug. I was trying to think of what to say, when he moved away from me.

"Crawdad!"

Crawdad received the same greeting.

"Skidmore called and said you'uns would be up this way." Dan turned without looking and strode back into his house.

Crawdad followed; I stood dazed for a moment.

The Dan Battle I remembered was a mysterious, nearly wordless sage, given to darker moods. The man who had just crushed me was an American Santa Claus on summer vacation.

"Come on in," he called from the recesses of his home. "I've got martinis!"

It didn't take long to suss out the reasons for Dan Battle's personality shift. In town, he was sober, even grouchy, answering tourist questions about Indian history and great conflicts. Even when he had talked to me in my official capacity, he'd been rightly guarded. I was twenty, and my questions had carried with them all the arrogance of youth. As I sat in his perfect living room, filled with antiques, sipping something called a lemon martini, I understood why Crawdad held him in such high regard. His greatest magic trick had been his native persona. The real Dan Battle was, without question, the most delightful man I had ever met.

"Mr. Battle," Crawdad was explaining to me quietly, "takes him a feather, any feather, and he can turn it into a bird. I'm serious with you. I seen him do it."

Crawdad had eschewed a martini in favor of cherry Coke, complaining that he was on duty.

"Wasn't hard." Dan winked at me—actually winked. "God's the one who got it started. He made the essence of the bird and put it in the wing. I just finished the job for Him. He's kind of busy at the moment."

"Bird flies off," Crawdad told me, nodding. "Right up into the sky. Best trick I ever saw."

"Dr. Devilin didn't come here to talk about magic tricks," Dan said, smiling. "He's got something interesting to show me."

Dan's living room was larger than I'd expected when I'd been looking at the outside of the house. Hardwood floors were covered by ancient Persian rugs. The fireplace seemed to have been carved from a single huge stone and the design was ornate, almost medieval. The ceilings were high, and light poured in, but the room was cool. It could have been a finer home in any city in the world.

"I do have something of a conundrum." I unfurled the map and turned it so that Dan could see.

"Say." He moved closer, setting down his martini. "That's Talking Leaves."

"That's what I thought." I handed him the map.

"And this is the last map—I mean, it's a copy, but it's the last official map of Georgia that includes Cherokee land."

Except for the coast and a few lowland holdings, most of Georgia had been marked "Cherokee Nation" on the map.

"Let me see." Dan held the map closer to his face, leaned back, adjusted the angle to get more light.

A few moments of silence passed. The air in the home was clean and clear, filled with oxygen. I noticed what looked like a large sunroom filled with plants toward the back of the house.

"This is really something." He wasn't smiling. "I think this is a note from your dad."

"My father?"

Crawdad sat up.

"Something about a Cherokee artifact."

"I didn't know he could write in that language." I hadn't meant to whisper, but I couldn't seem to make my throat work properly.

"Yeah," Dan said, staring at the map, demeanor darkening. "Says so right here: Your mom was frightened by the thing, the artifact, for some reason. She said it was bad luck and made your dad bury it out in the yard. Your backyard, I guess."

"It's buried in my backyard?" Repetition is the earmark of the dumbfounded.

He stared at the letters of the Talking Leaves.

"Says right here: 'between two cedars next to the mossy boulder.' " He looked up. "That make sense to you?"

I think I nodded.

"Well then, you have to go dig it up. You have to take it back where it belongs."

"What? Why?"

"This particular object," Dan said, "if I'm reading it right, was used in a very nasty way."

"What way?" Crawdad managed to ask, nearly as hushed as I was.

Dan looked back down at the map, smile completely gone.

"It was very potent." Dan set the map down on the table between us. "A water curse. Of course, we wouldn't have used the word *curse* exactly, but it comes out to the same thing. It could kill."

"Come on." But my protestation was halfhearted at best.

Dan started to say something, clearly thought better of it, and changed tack.

"It's up to you, since the item is in your possession. You have to find out where it was originally placed, what water it was cursing, and take it back there, if you can. This is very important, Fever. I'm not fooling around. You can't have that thing in your yard. It's doing you a lot of harm—maybe has done for a lot of years."

All I could think of at that moment was how strange my family life had been, how silent my father was, how wild my mother became.

"How the hell did you dad get ahold of it?" Dan's face was ashen.

"My great-grandfather, Conner, bought it at an auction a long time ago."

Dan's eyes narrowed, and I could tell he was about to ask me more.

"How in the hell—excuse my language—could you ever find out

where that thing had originally been put down? I mean, how would you ever know what body of water it was meant to curse?" Crawdad shook his head.

"You could ask any Cherokee you know." Dan's face was carved in granite; there was not a hint of levity. "But it's up to the owner, the one who possesses the thing. Personally, I'd like to find out a little bit more about how your kin got ahold of this in the first place—and why. Can you help me with that, Dr. Devilin?"

"Are you saying you know where this belongs," I asked him slowly, "but you can't tell me?"

He nodded.

So Dan Battle was a genuine resident of Blue Mountain, a trove of hidden treasure, as stubborn and mysterious as Hek and June Cotage.

I did my best to keep my face from revealing what my mind knew, as well. At that moment, I felt I absolutely had to keep it all a secret.

Seventeen

There may be a moment in everyone's life when the idea occurs to them that they come from a cursed family. Every family is cursed. I'd held that belief since I was seven, and thought about it often as an adult. But it was quite another venture to be confronted with clear evidence of the concept.

I should have stayed at Dan Battle's house longer than I did. I should have asked him the kinds of questions, the sort of dialogue I might have had with any true folk informant, but once he'd told me where the artifact was buried—and that it looked like a cross bound with cloth or vines—I couldn't get Crawdad to move fast enough.

My father had described, in the Talking Leaves language, where he'd buried the Cherokee artifact. I knew the exact spot. I saved any question of how he knew that language for another day.

I knew what I had to do.

Dan had really wanted me to stay, but I think I retreated into my mind a little, and I can't quite remember what he said at the end of our visit, what excuse I made to leave his house—or how I got into Crawdad's car.

"Well, that was weird," Crawdad said after a moment of bumpy downhill jostling.

I had no idea how to respond.

"I have to get home," I said after too long a pause.

"Right."

Crawdad didn't speak for the rest of the way down the mountain.

By the time we'd rolled onto the blacktop and were headed back to my place, I thought I knew what to ask Crawdad.

"Did you ever have the feeling that there was a curse on your family?"

"Me?" He grinned instantly. "Naw. I guess you're talking about my uncle Harbey being kicked in the head when he was at that wedding party. He ain't been right since. But that's because he's stupid. Don't have a thing in this world to do with a curse."

I let a pulse beat go by.

"How did your uncle get kicked in the head at a wedding party?"

"He was bothering the mule."

Some things, I decided instantly, are best left alone.

"So you don't think your family has a curse?"

"Definitely not. Just the opposite way around, I reckon. I believe we've had a great share of blessings." He inclined his head ever so slightly my way. "I can see how you'd think that, though, you know, about your own family."

"Yes."

"Is that inappropriate?" He winced. "Sorry. Sheriff is all the time telling me that my comments are what they call 'inappropriate.' "

"Sadly," I assured him, "your thoughts on the subject are not in the least—You really think your family is—"

"What did you want to leave so quick for?" He was doing his best to ease the conversation. "You all but run out of Mr. Battle's place."

I swallowed.

"I want to go dig up the thing, the cross."

He nodded. I don't think he realized that he stepped a little harder on the accelerator.

"You know where to take it." His voice had gone quiet. "I mean, you know where that thing belongs."

I did my best not to give an indication of anything, but that in itself was a giveaway.

Andrews was sitting on the front porch when Crawdad's car pulled up in my yard, and he got up and came into the yard before the engine was off.

"So?" He was tight-lipped.

"We found out where the thing is buried," Crawdad gushed, "and *what* it is." He lowered his voice. "And Dr. Devilin knows what to do with it, too, I believe."

"You're not going to believe this." I was headed for the garden shed in the back of my house. "Is Skidmore still here?"

"He went into town. Detective Huyne is still here, and there was something about the blood they found on your window from the lunatic with the cricket bat. Where are we going?"

"There." I pointed to a moss-covered boulder between two ancient cedar trees in the backyard.

Crawdad nodded and I was off.

My yard slopes down behind the house and is eventually lost in tall pines, thick undergrowth, and steep angles. It's shady, and a little difficult to navigate when the incline gets too intense. There was a barbecue pit, a stone oven and chimney, about twenty feet from the back door. I have no idea who built it and I had never seen it used. Fire would probably never touch the stones again. Lucinda had planted some creeping ficus around it the summer I'd first come home, and it was climbing the rocks quite nicely.

The garden shed was a rustic affair, built by my father out of scavenged barn wood. It had a padlock on it, but I never clicked it shut. I went straight for the shovel; Crawdad and Andrews watched.

Andrews complained.

"What are we doing?"

"That's where the thing is buried," Crawdad explained, hushed. "We're going to dig it up."

"The Cherokee artifact is buried in your backyard?" Andrews was very amused. "Why?"

"Apparently, my mother was frightened by it," I told him, striding toward the boulder. "She made my father bury it back here. She thought *that* would ward off the evil."

"But Dan says it won't work," Crawdad went on. "We've got to get it back to where it belongs."

"And where is that?" Andrews caught up with me.

"He's not saying," Crawdad allowed, "but he knows all right."

"Exactly what is this thing?" Andrews tried to catch my eye.

"It's a water curse," I said, not looking at him. "Can you believe that? It's a cross-shaped object that the Cherokee put near a stream to curse the water."

"You're *kidding.*" Andrews stopped. "What does Dr. There Is No Pattern 'Cause It's All Random think of *that*?"

I turned to face him.

"Would you mind?"

He read my face.

"Fever? Are you all right?"

"Not remotely." I hoisted the shovel.

Forty-five minutes and three sizable holes later, I had nothing to show for my efforts but the derision of Dr. Andrews and pain from my sciatic nerve.

Crawdad had gone reluctantly when a call over his police radio demanded his attention. He didn't say what it was about—or maybe he did and I just didn't pay attention. Either way, he'd made Andrews promise to call him the moment I found the cross.

Andrews had gone into the house for a Guinness—he'd brought a twelve-pack with him, apparently, and squirreled it in his room—and come back out, only to lean on the boulder and make pirate noises.

"The note from your father wasn't very specific, then." He sipped.

"Well," I answered, leaning on the shovel and breathing hard, "who knows what's happened to this piece of land in twenty years or more? Things grow; others shift. I'm in the right area."

"Unless someone's already dug it up."

"We'd see that." I stared down at the ground. "We'd notice the disturbed earth."

"Not if someone dug it up in the years you were going to university, or teaching there. A couple of seasons of growing and shifting can cover a lot of 'disturbed earth.' "

I hadn't thought of that.

"What if it's not even here anymore?" My voice sounded shaky to me.

"That's what I'm saying." He took another healthy sip. "Why don't you come on in and let's think about food. I'm hungry."

"You go on in," I told him, "I'm just going to try a bit longer."

"God." He finished his Guinness and headed for the house.

I have no idea how much longer I stayed in the backyard digging useless holes, losing hope that I would find the impossible object. Shadows were long, the sun was nearly down, and rain clouds threatened the horizon.

I leaned the shovel on the boulder, wiped my forehead with my sleeve, and started thinking about what would be good for dinner. I had some fresh trout in the refrigerator—just caught. My mind was occupied with lemons—trying to remember if I had any.

I barely heard the rush of running feet or the heavy breathing coming my way.

By the time I realized someone was there, he was on me, grunting and snarling, tackling me, knocking me back against the boulder.

With the breath knocked out of me, all I could do was drop lower when I saw the cricket bat headed toward my skull. The bat landed hard on the rock, and the impact must have stung his hands. I grabbed my shovel and poked it into his stomach as hard as I could, and he doubled over.

The shadows were too deep for me to see his face, but he was clearly the man who had broken into my house. And he was mad as a loon.

I scrambled away from the boulder, holding tightly to the shovel. When I got far enough away from him, I stood, planted my feet, and hefted the shovel to swing at him.

But he had recovered from the blow in the stomach and jumped back. He began swinging the bat in front of him like a scythe, back and forth, very quickly. He lumbered my way, head down, eyes up—

a terrifying, mindless expression on his face. There was no reasoning human being in that body, only anger and the power of lunacy.

I cocked the shovel and let it swing, tip outward, with all my weight, knocking it against his bat. The impact stung us both. He howled; I hissed. But we both held on to our weapons.

If I could have gotten my breath, I would have hollered for Andrews, but I was afraid to use any effort that would distract me from defending myself.

The madman raised his bat over his head and shrieked, instantly running toward me, a Viking berserker.

I managed to get the shovel raised just high enough to bash the side of his head with the back of it on my upswing. It caught him under his jaw. It wasn't as hard as I'd wanted it to be, but it stopped his progress.

Hadn't Andrews heard his howling?

He stood a moment, dazed by the bash in his head. I used that pause to get a better grip on the shovel and plant my feet.

"The next one will take your head off," I told him, trying to keep my voice low and threatening.

He squatted, started pounding his bat on the ground, apelike.

I relaxed—my mistake.

He leapt up suddenly, whirled the bat over his head, and sent it flying toward my face. I didn't have time to duck. If I hadn't turned away, the bat might have taken my eye out. As it was, it rocketed into my temple and I went down like a shot buffalo.

I fought to remain conscious, knowing the man would kill me if I passed out. I flailed the shovel blindly, hopelessly trying to fend him off. I could hear him moving around me, but I couldn't concentrate—moments or hours might have passed.

Without warning, the back door of my house slammed open and I heard Andrews on the steps.

"What the *hell* is going on out there?"

I scrambled up.

I could hear someone slithering toward me in the grass, but my vision was cloudy.

I held the shovel in front of me.

"I'm going to cut your head off with this shovel," I growled.

It didn't remotely sound like my voice.

The movement stopped.

"Fever?" Andrews kept his distance.

I blinked several times. My vision cleared a little. There was only one figure.

"Andrews?"

"What are you doing?"

"Heads up," I whispered, "there's someone else here. He just clubbed me. Look around."

"What?" Andrews took a step in my direction.

"Look *around.*" I backed up to the rock, scanning the yard in the failing light.

"There's no one else here." Andrews moved closer. "Put down the shovel."

"Oh." I dropped it. "Sorry."

"Jesus, look at your head!" He came to me instantly. "What happened?"

"The man with the cricket bat was here again!" I searched the ground around us for the weapon. "He threw it at me. It should be right here."

"There's nothing." Andrews shook his head. "But you already have a nasty bump there."

"It's affecting my eyesight." I closed my eyes.

"Oh my God," Andrews whispered.

My eyes snapped open.

"What is it?"

He pointed. I turned.

Just under the boulder, about where I'd leaned on it, I could barely make out the top of a burlap sack.

In my kitchen, under the bright light, the Cherokee cross was beautiful, not threatening at all. Two carved branches of a river birch had been fixed in a cross with what appeared to be braided reed green cloth, very sturdy. There were several feathers woven into the pattern, making a circle around the nexus of the sticks. I couldn't figure out how it had survived for so long intact.

There had been nothing else in the burlap bag—no note, no clue, no hint.

"Why was it buried out there, did you say?" Andrews couldn't take his eyes off the thing.

"My mother was reportedly frightened by it." I sat back, vision still a little on the jagged side. "But they say anything shaped like a cross makes a vampire nervous."

"Stop it." Andrews roused himself. "So—dinner?"

I glared in disbelief.

"You're still hungry?"

"You're not?" He tapped the cross. "You think you have to do something with this right *now*?"

"Yes."

"No." He reached for his cell phone. "I'm calling Crawdad."

"Hang on." I rubbed my face. "I was thinking of trout."

"That'll take forever! Cleaning and boning—"

"How about some of the leftover duck?" I shot back.

"It's days old!"

"We'll put it in a cassoulet, add some sausage, double-cook it, slather bacon on top."

"I guess."

"Rugby players don't care about food poisoning."

"Right," he agreed, "but English professors do. I stride two worlds."

"Do you want the cassoulet or not?"

He sighed heavily.

"Good, you get out the duck," I instructed, "and I'll get this cross out of the way, put it someplace safe."

He went to the refrigerator.

"The bacon's in here somewhere?"

"In the meat-keeper drawer on the bottom," I assured him.

He mumbled something.

I picked up the Cherokee cross and headed for the living room. Before I knew what I was doing, exactly, I'd grabbed a light jacket out of the coat closet beside the door and stumbled out onto the porch.

I was in the truck with the engine running, cross beside me on the passenger seat, before Andrews appeared in the front doorway. He was yelling something, but I couldn't hear it. I turned the truck sharply and ground a rut into my yard getting to the dirt road that led down the mountain.

Adairsville was at least an hour away, but that's where Barnsley Gardens was, and that's where I was going.

Eighteen

So that's how I came to be standing in the moonlight in the middle of Barnsley Gardens on an odd September night.

What was left of the estate rose into view as I walked up the hilltop. A full moon made the mansion a skeleton, something from a grotesque animal more than remains of an antebellum home: a vision to match the story of its curse. A razor of wind cut across my fingers and kicked up leaves; I thought they might have been footsteps following behind me.

I'd parked my truck near the business office but hadn't found anyone in it. The only other vehicle parked in the lot was a rented Mercedes, and I wondered how the place could make any money with only one guest.

I half-expected to be stopped by some sort of security guard as I wandered past the guest cottages onto the road that inclined toward the mansion, but I saw no one.

There were big open fields on either side of the road, and in the darkness and moonlight, all that open space seemed alive. Several deer were grazing so casually that they didn't even lift their heads as I passed by. Fireflies, crickets, tree frogs, bats, and night birds all made their presence known. The wind gusted suddenly, hard enough to scramble the smaller pebbles in the road behind me, and it did sound like someone was following me.

But the silence in between all the noise was where the true menace lay, I figured.

Up the road and into a more wooded part of the land, I ran into a maze of dwarf boxwoods. In each open part of the design, different mass plantings had been established: roses, white gardenias, tall cleome and shorter cockscomb. The path twisted through the plantings enough to slow my progress, even if I hadn't been fascinated by the flowers.

Once through the maze I was faced with stone steps, a pathway, and the front of the ruins. Only brick walls were left, no roof, no doors—an American Parthenon. But the places where windows had once been made it clear that the mansion had been comprised of several stories, and some of the windows at the front of the house had obviously been placed to overlook the maze and the steps, allowing residents to assess all visitors as they approached.

The air bit harder, and I completely gave over to the presence of Barnsley ghosts, my distant cousins. I carried the Cherokee cross in my right hand, but I had no hope that it would ward off any evil. It was an instrument of evil; it might even attract foul spirits. Leaves swirled on the ground around me, and for the third time I had a sensation that I was not alone, that someone was close to me in the shadows.

I stood staring up at the house, one more visitor the ghosts could evaluate, suddenly wondering how I'd gotten myself to that black moment, and, yes, I found myself in the middle of a very basic ontological dilemma: Who was the man standing in the dark garden holding on to a Cherokee curse?

I began to imagine myself standing in the upstairs window of the derelict mansion, looking down on myself. How did the man down there, I wondered, get to that desperate garden, wanted by the police and pursued by a murderer?

I moved slowly toward the house, replaying in my mind the whole history of the doomed Barnsley family, lamenting their great sadness as if it were my own.

Just as I stepped onto the stone stairs, I thought I saw something moving inside the mansion. I froze.

Wind batted tree limbs; here and there, it drove more leaves to the ground. Tree frogs and crickets had gone silent. The moon was suddenly bound by black clouds and the night was plunged into a deep well.

Just as I was considering walking very quickly back to my truck, I saw it again: a shadow moving in the shadows, a rustle of footsteps in the ruins.

I took a few steps as soundlessly as I could in order to get a better view just as the moon was released from its bondage. Light broke forth, poured into the mansion, and I saw, quite clearly, a woman in a neck-high aubergine dress, folds flowing in the wind. She was walking past one of the huge fireplaces.

I thought she must be an employee of Barnsley Gardens, a historically dressed figure who would lead tours and ooze charm. What she was doing wandering around in the dark at that hour, I had no idea—though I didn't know what time it was. But I thought she might at least direct me to the springs that had once provided the mansion with its water.

"Hello?" I called.

She did not pause, heading toward the rear of the ruins.

"Sorry to bother you," I stammered, taking a few more steps in her direction. "I was wondering—"

My plea was interrupted by a strange sound. I stopped, listened. The woman was crying.

"Are you all right?"

She paused, and I thought she'd heard me.

I made it to the front of the house before she moved again. I stood where the door would have been, holding the Cherokee cross; the moon was bright in the house, and she turned my way.

It was Eloise Barnsley.

She looked away quickly, tears in her eyes, and moved toward the back of the ruins.

I stood, baffled, for a moment before I followed, telling myself that the good people who ran the Barnsley Gardens Resort had outdone themselves in research and commitment to accuracy. The woman looked almost exactly like the portrait of Eloise Barnsley I had just seen.

"I'm trying to find the springs," I called out.

She disappeared down some steps at the back of the house.

I followed her as best I could through the house, but the moon didn't reveal everything. I tripped over stray bricks in the shadows, darker corners hid huge wisteria vines blocking doorways, and odd hidden steps jolted me downward twice. It all combined to make it more difficult to navigate through the ruins. By the time I reached the back of the house, she was nowhere to be seen.

The hill sloped down again behind the house. To my left, there was a gazebo and a rose garden. The wind filled the ruins with their scent, so rich that I closed my eyes for a second, taking it in.

Below me, down the hill, there were several outbuildings and what might have been a stream. To the left, there might have been a marsh. I let my eye wander in that direction and spotted what looked like might be a well house.

I was certain that the woman had gone the other way, but if the water for which I was searching was to the left, what was the point of following her? I told myself that she was going back to the office to change and go home.

I walked along the path that led to the gazebo behind the house. Huge blue hostas lined it on one side, and a perfectly manicured lawn bounded it on the other. I had a momentary vision of the grandeur of the place in its prime: stunning gardens, hilltop view, hot and cold running water in a time when most people didn't bathe. Nothing but a very strong curse indeed could cause such beauty to come to such desolation.

The gazebo may have been a more modern touch; it looked to be in very good shape, but it was hard to tell in the moonlight. Beyond it, there were steps that descended to a large reservoir and an old stone building—clearly, the well from which the house had once gotten its water.

As I made my way down the stone steps toward the well house, I was certain I heard someone else in the surrounding woods. In a sudden shift of cloud and wind, the moon revealed a moving shadow in the trees. I moved more cautiously, hyperalert to every sound around me and every motion in the corner of my eye.

By the time I was standing on the rim of the water, every muscle in my body was tense.

I paused for a moment, feeling the crush of my heartbeat, hearing how loud my breathing sounded, wincing at the thump of blood in my temples. I had no idea what to do with the cross.

The sudden snap of a twig not ten feet away from me made me whirl around, and I saw the man in the darkness between two trees. I couldn't see a cricket bat, but I was certain I knew who was there.

My lungs exploded with an involuntary noise, and my first reaction was to get to a more tenable position for a confrontation—one where I wasn't backed into a black pool of water.

I leapt across a small channel and down onto a docklike walkway that led to the stone house. I thought if I could find a big loose stone, I might have something to threaten the man with.

I was holding so tightly to the cross that my hand started cramping. The pounding of my feet on the wooden walkway thundered. I thought I heard the man mumbling something, but I couldn't understand what it was.

I made it to the well house just in time to turn and see him coming down the slope toward the water. The moon backed him, so he was only a silhouette, but he was moving fast.

Light on his feet for such a big frame, I thought giddily.

I looked around for a rock or a branch, anything to use against him, but the place was tourist-clean. There was a cast-iron plaque on the well house that likely told its story. I stepped inside.

It was black as pitch. I could smell the water, not an unpleasant scent, almost verdant. I thought perhaps I could hide from the man, but as my eyes adjusted to the lack of light, I realized it was a dangerous place to be: little foot room and lots of water in which to drown. There was an exit on the other wall, and I made for it.

I could hear the man on the wooden walkway outside just as I cleared the exit and began to run into the woods.

The way sloped up again, and there was a path, both sides of which were incredibly lush, and I realized it was a woodlands garden. I couldn't make out anything but the ferns and hostas, but it was so thickly planted on both sides with specimens I didn't recognize that I couldn't help but think how much attention had been paid to it. I remembered Andrews's strange revelation that one of the Barnsley sons had been murdered while he was on an expedition to find exotic plants for these gardens.

I was sweating, despite the chill in the air, and I was beginning to tire from running uphill. The path went through a darker part of the wood, through tall trees, and I destroyed three spiderwebs, feeling their sticky irritation on my face, fearing their poisonous residents.

But I kept running.

At last, I came to the top of the slope. It opened onto a small family graveyard.

Ten or twelve grave markers stabbed through the mossy earth, reaching for, but failing to gain, the sky. There was a bench at the end of the path, and another plaque that clearly said BARNSLEY. I thought that perhaps a spot of more open ground might provide more light, and that I could see my attacker.

I set the cross down on the bench and looked around for a weapon. If I could have pried loose one of the sections of rusty iron fencing that surrounded the cemetery, I would have done that, but I was afraid it would take too long.

I frantically cast my eye about for a sturdy branch. I suddenly caught sight of a shovel leaning against a tree close by. It didn't even occur to me that this would be the second time in a single night I would use the grave digger's tool to fight for my life. I merely raced for it.

Surely, I thought, no one has been buried here in over fifty years. This must be an gardening implement.

Dizzy from the running, a parallel occurred to me, a warning about my state of mind: Plant a seed, grow a flower; plant a body, grow a ghost.

Just as that thought was boiling in my brain, I saw the man lumbering up the path toward me. He didn't seem to see me.

I positioned myself in the darkest shadow I could find near the top of the path, hoisted the shovel over my shoulder, and waited. I was afraid that my gasping would give my position away, so I concentrated on slow breathing.

The man was grumbling in such an incoherent manner that it removed any doubt from my mind. This was not a security guard. This was the man who had murdered someone in my house and had just tried to kill me. He'd waited in the shadows behind my house and followed me to this spot.

I bent my knees, tensed my forearms. A strange rage, born of terror, clamped my chest, and I realized I was capable of killing the human being who was coming my way. That realization only added to my madness.

The man drew nearer, and I could barely hear his babbling for the pulse pounding in my ears. Thorns of sweat burned my hairline, and my fingers began to shake.

At last, he gained the top of the path, and with an explosion of breath I swung the shovel directly at his head.

Effortlessly, he ducked, my shovel flew from my hands, and the man rushed me, palm to my chest, foot behind my right ankle. I went down on my back with a bellowing thud.

Before I could scramble up, eyes squinting to see his next move, I realized he was calling me by name.

"Fever!" It was his third attempt to engage me. "God damn it, what the hell are you doing?"

I blinked. The buzzing cloud of berserk adrenaline that had rampaged my brain began to dissipate. I strained to confirm that the face matched the voice I fancied I'd heard, but it was the Hawaiian shirt that gave him away.

"Dan?"

He reached out his hand to help me up. I took it.

"You could have killed me." He was breathing hard. "That shovel. It could have took my head right off."

"I thought—"

"I know what you thought." He grasped my hand and got me to my feet. "You thought I was the man who murdered that Mr. Shultz in your house the other night. I don't blame you. But didn't you hear me calling your name?"

"All I heard was some kind of incoherent mumbling." I made it to my feet. "What was that?"

"Yeah, that would be *prayer,*" he chided. " You don't recognize the sound of praying, you heathen?"

"You're calling me a heathen?" I couldn't stop shaking. "What were you praying about?"

"I was scared!"

"So what are you doing here, exactly?"

"Me? I came straight here after you left my house. I've been waiting for you. You looked so weird when you left, I could tell you'd figured out where the water cross needed to go. I was pretty sure you'd come here tonight."

"How did you—wait, how did you know about Shultz's murder?"

"You can't be serious." He headed for the bench where I'd set the cross. "Everybody in Blue Mountain knows about that. That kind of gossip? Travels faster than the speed of light in our little town. Damn. I have to sit down. You really gave me a start."

I followed along behind him. "But how did you know where the cross was supposed to—"

"Once again I say," he told me, sitting down on the bench that faced the graveyard, "you have to be kidding me. First, lots of people, especially the Cherokee that still live in these parts, know about the curse. And most of us know about your great-grandfather's buying the cross. It's common knowledge."

"Not common to me." I joined him on the bench.

"Well, you've heard the thing about how you can't tell the forest for the trees? It's even harder if you're one of the trees."

"You mean other people can see my family history better than I can."

"Something like that." He coughed for a moment. "Damn it. I

need to exercise more. One little chase through the woods and I'm hacking up a lung."

I commiserated, panting. "I know."

"You don't know," he countered. "You're not sixty-seven years old."

"Neither are you," I insisted.

"June ninth." He sighed. "I'm a Gemini."

"You are *not* sixty-seven."

"You want to argue about my age?"

"No," I said, getting my wind back. "I want to know what you're doing here."

"Same as you." He was just on the edge of being irritated. "Only I came to make sure you put this thing back the way it belongs, the Cherokee way."

He tapped the cross.

"Yes," I shot back, "exactly *why* do we have to do that? I've just figured out that all the Barnsleys who were cursed by this thing have been dead for over fifty years. The curse has done its work—it killed them all."

I indicated the nearby graveyard as proof positive.

"Typical." Dan patted his thighs with his palms. "Absolutely typical."

"What are you talking about?"

"The curse, ignoramus, is on the water, not on any person in particular."

"It wasn't intended to kill the Barnsleys?"

"Well, yeah." He shrugged.

"And by the way, why was that, exactly?"

I may have asked him that just so I could catch my breath.

"You want to do folk research *now*? Let's take the thing down to the well house and I'll tell you the whole rigmarole while we do the ceremony. I think I got my breath back now."

He grabbed up the cross and stood.

"Ceremony?"

"I got to take the curse off the water now, and we need the cross to do that. I have to explain everything? Like you said, the curse did its work, so let's get it off the water and go back to my place for a nightcap. What do you say?"

"I'd say I'm speechless, but the fact that I'm talking—"

"Are you coming with me or not?"

"I don't know. My first thought was that you were a security guard. I've seen other employees around here. I'm not sure I want to get arrested for trespassing and vandalism at my age. Especially not with a sixty-seven-year-old man."

"Shut up and bite me," he explained calmly. "And by the way, there aren't any employees around at this time of night; there's only the kid in the business office, and he's asleep in the back room there."

"No," I told him, "I saw a woman dressed in—"

"Shh!" he commanded with superhuman force.

He'd also stopped dead in his tracks. I thought he saw someone in the woods, and I strained my eyes to see if I could discover where the person was.

"Don't talk about that," he whispered.

"Don't talk about what?" I glared at him, confused.

"Don't talk about the thing you saw. I saw her, too, but you can't pay her any attention. *None.* I'm serious. She wants attention; that's her food. The more you give it to her, the more she bothers you."

"I—" There were no words that could express my bafflement.

"It must be a Barnsley." He said it staring at the graveyard, and so softly that I almost didn't hear him.

"*What's* a Barnsley? That woman?"

"The thing you saw! Damn, you surely can be slow for a bright boy. It wasn't a woman; it was a spirit. And it wants attention, and that's just what we're doing by talking about her, so shut up, come down to the well with me, and have this thing over with so we can get the hell out of here before one of us gets dead."

Without another syllable, he set off down the path, through the moonlit wood, toward the cursed black water.

Nineteen

I didn't quite know how, but the well house seemed even darker than before. By the time I got down the slope and into the cold stone room, Dan was already out the other side and sitting on the dock walkway.

I approached him as quietly as I could. He was obviously concentrating—or praying again.

"Look at this water." He stared across the surface of it.

"Yeah." I sat beside him.

"No, I mean, look and see can you tell where it's bubbling up. I'll be damned if I can."

"What, you mean the ground source of the spring comes up right *here*?"

"Right. And that's where we have to— Wait a second." He leaned forward.

"You see it?" I tried to look where I thought he was looking.

"Over on the bank. Should have thought of it myself. Does that group of stones look familiar?"

"Group of stones?"

I scanned the bank, but I couldn't find any stones, let alone tell if they seemed familiar in any way.

"There." He pointed impatiently. "Right next to that horsetail reed."

I could barely make out, just above the black water, five or six small rocks. They were only a jumble in the mud to me.

"You have to kind of squint," he whispered, "and cock your head, but don't that look a little like a syllable from the Talking Leaves?"

I would never have thought of it myself, but when he said it, so hushed, it seemed obvious.

"It does." I didn't even try to cover my astonishment. "Can you make out what it is?"

He straightened up, turned his face my way, grinning.

"Hard to explain." He was beaming. "But it's a little like the old '*X* marks the spot.' My tribe—they surely could be arrogant in those days, huh?"

"What do you mean?" I could find absolutely no reason for amusement.

"Well," he groaned, getting to his feet, "think how many years those rocks stood there telling everyone who passed by them, Here it is, stupid. It's a double curse, really. If Barnsley or any of his brood had taken the trouble to learn the Cherokee language, they would have known this thing was a curse. They could have taken it out in a second. They probably just thought it was a nice Indian decoration. But it was like saying to them that their own ignorance was as much of a curse as anything we did to the water. That's a pretty good joke."

A joke that, if you believed that sort of thing, had taken the lives of every Barnsley who had ever lived there. I didn't think it was quite right to mention that the Barnsleys would not have believed in a Cherokee curse and would never have been looking for it in their water.

"Let's get to it."

He headed across the walkway and onto the far bank.

I got up, trying to understand what the Barnsleys had done that was so much worse than other families to provoke all the deadly curses they'd acquired.

"So," I began, coming across the walkway, "I gather that the Cherokee at the time didn't like the Barnsleys' being here. But why was there so *much* ire?"

He stopped.

"Are you kidding me?" He turned. "Know much about the Trail Where They Cried?"

The way he said it made me shiver. Suddenly, every plant and every insect, all the night birds; even moonbeams seemed filled with a wailing silence, a welling of soundless tears.

"Treaty of New Echota," he said with some difficulty. "One of the few documents the United States government signed with my tribe that they honored. It gave all our land to the whites, and it took us away."

A sudden massive rain cloud took away all moonlight, everything went silent around us, and the gardens and the ruins weren't real. They were a stage set that had been hastily constructed long ago on a much more permanent, ancient, and ultimately more beautiful stage.

"In 1830, the Congress of the United States passed what they called the Indian Removal Act." Dan's voice was filled with rocks and wind, lightning and roaring waterfalls. "Almost everyone in America—I mean whites, now—was against it, but President Jackson signed it anyway. We fought it. Took it the Supreme Court and tried to establish an independent Cherokee Nation. In 1832, the Court ruled in our favor. In our *favor.* Chief Justice John Marshall ruled that the Cherokee Nation was sovereign, and that made the Indian Removal Act illegal. They only way they could make it work then was if the Cherokee would *agree* to be removed, which, of course, we would never do. So we won."

He stared out across the water, up the hill, to the ruins of the Barnsley mansion.

"So what happened?" I sounded like a small child.

"The Cherokee—I mean, like any other nation, we didn't all believe just one thing. We were a diverse bunch. Your people, your history is filled with disagreements. You have two basic sides, as far as I can see: the more conservative people and the more liberal people. We were divided, too. Most of us liked Chief John Ross. He fought the whites. A smaller group, fewer than five hundred out of maybe twenty thousand Cherokee in north Georgia, went with Major Ridge, who—for reasons of economic greed and demon possession—advocated the removal. He actually wanted his own people to be taken from this world and rubbed out. The Treaty of New Echota was signed by Ridge in 1835. It was completely illegal, but it gave Jackson the paper he needed to remove us."

"Jackson just put it into law? On the basis of such a flimsy document? Without Congress?"

"No." Dan's voice had grown soft, a volume without hope. "It had to be ratified. People spoke out against it."

"Davy Crockett." I remembered talking with Andrews about it, and I felt a sudden pang of guilt for leaving him behind at my house without an explanation of where I was going. Clearly, I wasn't in my right mind.

"And Daniel Webster." Dan sighed. "But it passed anyway. It passed by a single vote."

"What?"

"The irony there, of course," Dan said, managing a wry smile, "is that if your friend Davy Crockett hadn't left Congress all mad and hurt before that, he could have cast the tying vote and Jackson might not have gotten his way. But he did. In 1838, the United States invaded my country and began to take us to Oklahoma. Without a thought for our houses or our things, we were supposed to leave the land we'd lived on since the beginning of time and walk from Georgia to Oklahoma. You're not in terrible shape—how do you think you'd fare if you had to walk that far?

"Not well."

"Now imagine if you had Hek and June with you, trying to help them along."

The very thought of June Cotage being forced to abandon her house, walk though the mountains, across the desert, and into Oklahoma—it churned my stomach.

"We weren't allowed to forage for food, so a lot of us starved on army half rations. Those of us that made it got to Oklahoma just in time for the killing winter of 1839—still the worst on record in that state. Over four thousand of us died on the way, and an unrecorded number died right when we got to Oklahoma. It's a tough mixture: winter and despair. It ensured the death of my country. Only a very few of us stayed put in Georgia, hiding out, blending in. Kind of like these rocks."

He stared down at the Talking Leaves arrangement of stones near his feet.

"We went unnoticed for decades by the whites, who walked right by us," he concluded. "And now I'm a tourist attraction. Just another way for whites to make money. But I can't look in these woods, or walk though them, without seeing a ghost by every tree, a spirit standing in this very water, silent—cold."

I fought the urge to look into the water.

"So here's the punch line to our story," he said, rallying. "Julia Barnsley didn't like Savannah because it was too hot and there were too many bugs to suit her, so her husband, Godfrey, found this piece of land—high on a hill, cool even in summer, way above the gnat line—and he wanted it. The trouble was, it belonged to us, to the Cherokee. So Mr. Barnsley, a wealthy cotton magnate, and his father-in-law, a rich Savannah gentleman, went to Washington and had dinner with Andrew Jackson. They made a sizable contribution to his reelection campaign—which went into Jackson's private account, of course—and the next thing you know, we have the Indian Removal Act."

"Godfrey Barnsley," I began, dumbfounded, "was responsible for the Indian Removal Act?"

"The irony gets deeper. He wanted this particular plot of land because of this very spring. It was exactly what he needed to make his modern house with hot and cold running water and flush toilets. But this was a sacred spring, like a Cherokee church. What would you do if someone wanted to use your church for a bathroom?"

"I don't have a church," I stammered, "but if I did—"

"So everyone told Godfrey not to build here, not to screw with this water. He didn't listen. So we put this in his water supply."

Dan held up the cross.

"Hard to believe it's held up all these years," I said, staring at it.

"Not really." He looked at it as if it were made of jewels. "It's treated. We had a way of—it was kind of like creosote: sap and a tar-like gunk that you use to seal a thing like this. It'll most likely survive the nuclear holocaust. We knew it would outlast the Barnsleys. And it poisoned their water—every time they drank it, washed in it, cleaned their clothes and their dishes and their faces and hands, they were smearing the curse onto themselves. It got into their genes. It passed from generation to generation, and lived on in their blood even if they moved away from this land."

"Jesus," I whispered.

"I thought you didn't know what praying was."

"That wasn't a prayer."

He shrugged.

"Let's do this."

Dan suddenly squatted on the bank and looked down at the stones.

"The—well, the trouble is," I stammered, "that curse? It kind of got onto my family, too."

Dan froze.

"What?" He didn't look up.

"My great-grandfather, Conner, I believe, had figured out that the Barnsleys and the Briarwoods—how should I say this?—cross-pollinated."

"Briarwoods?"

"That's my real family name. Conner changed his last name when he came to America because he was wanted for murder in Ireland."

"That story's *true*?" He finally looked up at me. "I been hearing that one since I was a kid. I thought it was just something the old man made up to keep people from messing with him. You know, get a reputation as a bad ass, but you don't actually have to *be* a bad ass."

"It's true."

"So how did your kin and the Barnsleys—"

"It's a long story," I interrupted, "but the crux of it is that Godfrey's mother, in England, dallied with a servant named Briarwood—

a gardener, actually—and produced Godfrey. And here's a bit of gothic coincidence: *she* put a curse on both families as she was dying in childbirth with Godfrey."

Dan sat on the bank.

"Man." He shook his head. "What the hell did the Barnsleys do to make God that mad at them?"

"I was just asking myself that same question."

"Double curse." He looked up. "Was the mother's husband alive or dead?"

"Alive." I didn't know why he'd asked that.

"Well, at least it wasn't a widow's curse, then."

I didn't bother to tell him my thoughts on that subject.

"So I believe Conner came here in 1942," I said hesitantly, trying to get us back on some sort of track, "because he was trying—in his own weird and probably misguided way—to remove the curse from his family. I don't think he much cared about the Barnsleys one way or another."

"How's that for the Web of Life?" He smiled.

"I've heard the term, of course, but I'm not exactly certain, in this context—"

"Look," he told me impatiently, "I don't want to get all hoodoo on you, but the universe is like a spider's web, and at every junction there's a bright bead of water, and in every bead of water there's a life—yours, mine, everybody's. You can't touch one part of the web without making something happen in every one of those beads of water, because they're all connected by the web."

"That doesn't sound— Is that Cherokee philosophy?"

"Well, I saw it on one of those Bill Moyers interviews with Joseph Campbell. You know Joseph Campbell."

"He's my spiritual father, and a hell of a folklorist, but you can't—"

"God Almighty, Doctor," he shot back, "could we *please* take the curse off this water so we can go back to my place for a nightcap? We can talk world philosophy all night if you want—but I'd very much like to get away from here. This place give me the willies."

Again, I thought of Andrews.

"What do you want me to do?" I tried to sound a bit more contrite than I actually was.

"See, to take the curse off the water," he began, his tone almost scholarly, "you have to remove this cross thing in the right way. You can't just pull it up out of the ground and sell it at an auction to raise money. The curse is still on the water that way."

"So you figured out that Conner came here for the auction."

"I'd heard stories about this water curse since I was a little boy." Dan was distracted, staring down at the arrangement of rocks, looking for something. "Everybody knew that the sacred— Hey, look."

He fit the cross down into the middle of the rocks, a hidden cavity, and it stayed perfectly upright, like Excalibur in the stone.

"Now what?" I whispered.

Dan took out a pocketknife, opened it, and held up the blade for me to see.

"Look at how the nexus of these two pieces of wood," he said softly, "is kind of like that web thing I was just saying. The place where these two sticks cross is the place where the living thing is. If I take away the junction, the circuit is broken and the energy is dispelled—the magic is gone."

He slowly began to cut the reed-colored cloth that held the sticks together. He was mumbling something—so low, I could barely make out the sounds, but they weren't English.

As he cut, the cross lost its structural integrity and began to fall apart. I realized as I watched, transfixed, that the process somehow mimicked the gradual ruination of the mansion on the hill above us.

A final cord was cut and the crosspiece fell, rolling into the water.

Dan pulled the other piece back out of its rocky cradle and tossed it into the water as well, along with the cloth.

"Let the water have what's left," he said, a benediction like a burial at sea. "The water will eventually absorb the wood and the cloth, and everything will be washed clean. It'll take a little time, but the water will run clear someday."

He nodded, a button on his pronouncement.

"Now," he said, leaning over, "help me pull out these stones. I think we'll take them up there to that graveyard and put them onto some of the graves. Seems right."

I didn't quite know how it seemed right, but I knelt on the bank beside Dan and began to help him pry out the stones.

The moon was out again, and a kind of Latesummer Night's Dream seemed to wash over the landscape. Night doves called out, calming the air around us; a black lace sound of crickets patterned the wind.

I have no idea how both of us failed to hear footsteps in the dead leaves behind us.

Twenty

I saw the cricket bat, blond lightning, out of the corner of my eye just as it connected with Dan's skull. The cracking sound made every cell in my body sick. Dan went down face-first into the water, oozing thick burgundy blood from his head.

I turned just in time to see the bat coming my way. I twisted right, my muscles flexed automatically, and the bat hit my forearm. I was certain I felt the bone crack.

One of the rocks we'd been working to pull loose was in my hand, and I threw it toward the drooling, vacant-eyed face above me. It struck a glancing blow, enough for me to push myself backward into the water, clutching a fistful of Dan Battle's shirt collar.

The pool was deeper than I had imagined, nearly up to my shoulders. I struggled to turn Dan over onto his back and drag him across the water to the opposite bank.

The maniac with the bat recovered quickly but did not pursue me into the black liquid. He moved instead with great staring deliberation onto the wooden walkway, not six feet away from me, and watched to see what I was going to do. He would simply wait for me to come to land, move to that spot more quickly than I could through water, and finish me.

Dan's eyes were closed. I couldn't tell if he was breathing. My feet struggled with the slimy bottom of the well pond; the water was cold.

Without thinking, I began to yell. Surely the woman I had seen in the ruins or a security guard would hear me. I bellowed.

"Help!"

The man with the bat gargled several inarticulate words but did not move.

I knew I couldn't stay in the water with Dan long. I had to get him to a place where he would, at the very least, not drown.

I began dragging him away from the man, toward the reedy shallows that were the likely source of the spring.

The man with the bat moved slowly, apparently wary that I might be deceiving him and feigning one direction, moving another. I used his doubt to my advantage, remembering something Hek had told me when I was a boy: "Dealing with a liar, trick him with the truth."

A man who uses subterfuge will sometimes mistake the truth for a trap.

I headed directly for the spot I wanted, doing my best to keep the murderer in my sight but not look at him directly.

The water got shallower fast, but I stayed low, shoulders below the surface, so as not to give that fact away. I could feel reeds snapping my back.

The murderer determined, at last, that I was going through them to the far shallows, and he headed around the walkway. He was perhaps twelve feet away at that moment.

I got my feet under me and my hands in the middle of Dan's back.

As the murderer stepped off the walkway and onto the bank, coming toward me, I took in a monstrous breath. Without warning, I roared, stood straight up, and shoved Dan's body as hard as I could toward the mossy bank opposite the one where the killer stood. I was in water only to my thighs, and Dan's head and shoulders were securely on something like dry land. It happened in a single move, in a single second.

The murderer was startled, and the sound that had come from my lungs had even frightened me—not human, filled with rage.

He stood frozen for an instant longer, enough for me to slush through the water to the bank where I'd thrown Dan. I had it in mind to drag Dan up onto the land more securely, but the murderer had recovered and was loping my way, back across the walkway, bat cocked over his shoulder.

I scrambled across the moss, slipping and desperate, toward the pine straw–thick edge of the wood. I jumped, and got a more solid footing, grabbing hold of a smaller pine tree, the bark scraping the palms of my hands.

I could hear the murderer behind me, his animal breathing. His footfalls on the dock were heavy and staggering.

I pushed myself off from the tree and dug the soles of my shoes into the upward incline. My own breath sounded panicked and rasping. I thought if I could make it to the top of the hill, I would have an advantage. It occurred to me, deliriously, that I was only replaying a moment from half an hour before, running up the same hill, with the same thoughts in mind, away from Dan.

Giddy, burning flashes of the Eternal Return burst like sweat from my forehead. Despite the fact that I was dripping wet in cool air, I felt my temperature rise, and my forearm was beginning to swell where it had been bashed.

In the spirit of repeating everything, I realized that the shovel at the top of the hill was my goal—the third time that night I would use such an implement as a weapon instead of a tool.

The pine straw skidded under my feet, and the trees were small but thick, a younger growth of pines. I was moving fast and breathing hard and my vision wasn't clear. I knew only if I kept moving upward, I would eventually hit the plateau close to the path that opened on the cemetery.

A thick wall of rhododendrons lay just ahead, threatening to block my progress. I leaned forward, got my body as low to the ground as I could, covered my face with my forearms, and plowed through the branches.

I tried to protect my sore arm, but everything seemed intent on slamming against it. The pain was oddly focusing. I had nothing in my mind at that moment except making it through the tall shrubs and into the opening at the top of the hill.

I had no idea where my attacker was.

After an endless sequence of moments in the verdant crowd of leaves—it could have been ten seconds or it could have been a quarter of an hour—I fell through the hedge and onto a grassy spot. I landed on my bad arm.

Wincing and rolling, I managed to get to my feet and turn around to see if the man had followed me through the shrubs.

There was no one.

I turned a wild eye toward the graveyard, trying to locate the shovel. I couldn't remember where I'd been when I dropped it. I thought it must be near the gate, but the light was too dim to see it, even in the clearing.

I rushed toward the tombstones, heart exploding in my chest, constantly checking the woods for the man with the bat.

As I stepped onto the smoother path, I thought I heard him bashing through the pines. I squinted, trying not to give my position away by breathing too hard, and saw the shovel lying where I'd dropped it.

Thrashing sounds were coming up the path, getting closer.

I sprinted giant leaping steps to the shovel and had it in my hand when I heard his low growling close by.

There, at the mouth of the path, he stood hunched, bat dragging the ground, a shudder of dark sounds in a blacker night.

"Ah," I said loudly, shaking the shovel in his direction, trying to steady my breath. "Glad you're here. I hadn't quite finished taking your head off back at my place. . . ." Then my breath gave out, and my bravado seemed lost on him. I considered that he might be deaf, and that the noises he made were an attempt at speech.

He did notice the shovel. I had the idea that it kept him from lurching right for me.

I had a sudden notion, the kind of idea that can only be born of terror. I backed away from him slowly, eyes steady in his direction, and worked my way past the low open gate and into the graveyard.

He watched but made no move.

I found myself in the cemetery between two larger headstones, towers really, with half-size statues and ornate designs.

I took one more step back and suddenly began to slam the shovel back and forth between the low part of the grave markers, like the clapper of a bell, cast iron on granite. It made an ungodly noise, flat, scraping—a sound of the dead.

The man was at a loss.

Another lesson from childhood: When dealing with a lunatic, see how much crazier you can be. Unfortunately I'd applied that theory so frequently in my life—under the suspicion that everyone was a lunatic—it had become more a general character trait than an individual ploy. Crazy came naturally—especially out of fear—and it seemed to be working at that moment. The man stayed where he was.

My hands and arms began to ache from the impact of the shovel on the stone, and I knew I couldn't keep up the clamor indefinitely. So I stopped abruptly and started digging. I plunged the tip of the shovel hard into the ground between the two graves. I tossed the dirt in the man's direction.

"To save us a little time," I managed to call out, "I'm digging your grave here. It won't be quite deep enough, but then, you won't be quite dead when I put you in it, so it all evens out."

I didn't know whose voice I was using—it was one I'd never heard before. I realized I hadn't slept much in days and was probably on the verge of genuine mental trauma.

The killer seemed to rally, almost reading my mind, realizing I was near the breaking point. Or was that my own paranoia? Perhaps his face hadn't changed at all. Maybe he wasn't inching toward me through the scars of moonlight that separated us.

"I'm ready," I whispered.

He hunched lower, took a clear step my way.

I steadied myself, bent my knees, held the shovel in front of me like a broadsword, eyes locked.

He lumbered forward, bat low to the ground, shoulders slumped—a troll. He was a smaller man than I, and older. Other than that, it was impossible to determine anything about him in the relative darkness.

Without any warning, he suddenly flew toward me, as if on springs, thumping directly into my chest. I rocketed backward too suddenly to comprehend completely what had happened.

The next thing I knew, he was sitting on top of me, with the cricket bat raised high over his head. Miraculously, I still felt the shovel in one hand, though he'd somehow managed to pin my arms with his knees. If I bent my elbows just a little, I figured, I might be able to hit him in the back of the head. It wouldn't have much force, but it would prove a distraction, and maybe I could get him off me.

I flailed, hitting nothing, but his head snapped around in the direction of the shovel. Maybe he thought there was someone behind him. I kicked and rolled, and he was tossed off balance, falling to one side. He landed on his shoulder with a good thud, and I scrambled away from him as best I could.

I tried to put one of the tombstones between us and get to my feet, but he moved too quickly. He was up, snarling and swinging his bat.

I jabbed the shovel at his shins. He danced backward, and it looked to me as if he were smiling wildly.

I tried to quell a growing fear that nothing would stop him. Nothing physical, at any rate—but I hit on another, more psychological ploy out of abject desperation.

I jumped up, shovel in front of me, though much less confidently than I had moments before.

"If you kill me," I rasped, "you'll never find the coin."

He stopped dead still. He could have been one more of the graveyard statues: no movement, no sound, no life.

"The coin is hidden in my house, where you'll never find it. Even in a century, when my home looks like that one up there on the hill, no one will ever find it—unless I show them where it is. If you kill me, if you threaten me, if you so much as hurt my feelings, you'll never see the coin again."

I wasn't certain why I'd ended exactly that way, as if he *had* seen the coin at some time in the past.

Alas, I could not leave well enough alone. "Besides, it belongs to my family."

I don't know what that sentence triggered, but the man exploded in every direction, howling, waving both arms, one holding his bat aloft. It was the cry of an animal caught in a trap.

I was so startled, I staggered backward once more. Red fear pulsed in my burning forearm and I lashed out with the shovel savagely, smashing it into his kneecap with one swing, cracking a rib with another.

I might have kept swinging—I felt at that moment I would be capable of bashing his bones even long after he was dead—but he knocked the shovel from my hands with one casual swipe of his bat.

I tried to keep running backward, but I slammed my thigh into a tombstone and took a tumble, my head thumping hard on the ground.

My mind was swimming, my eyes unfocused. A sudden inexplicable sleepiness swept over me, the kind a drowning man feels, a surrender to black water. My limbs were thick, weighed a thousand pounds. My tongue filled my mouth, blocking the airway. I went deaf—there was no sound anywhere on the planet.

In that moment, I was convinced that a door between worlds lay open, a bright door made of new stars and piercing memories, bits of melody and an intuition of being not quite human. A sensation of serenity washed over me.

And in that same moment I saw quite clearly the golden bat moving infinitely slowly toward my skull.

A popping sound, a champagne cork, roused me from my graveyard sleep. It was followed by cheers and some sort of dancing. An odd moment for a celebration, I thought.

"Fever?"

Jolted out of my rapture by a name I barely recognized, I struggled three times to open my eyes before I saw Skidmore's face.

"Hello." I couldn't think what else to say.

"Thank God." Skid's eyes closed. "He's okay!"

Andrews appeared.

"Andrews," I said dreamily, trying to sit up. "What are you doing here?"

I had no idea where *here* was.

"He hit his head," Andrews said to Skid, as if I weren't there. "Look."

He pointed to a place behind my ear.

I realized that the spot was wet and cold.

I lost a weight of euphoria suddenly, and struggled up on my elbows in the strange cemetery.

"I hit my head," I repeated. My voice sounded like thorns. "Where's the man—"

Andrews stepped aside.

The maniac with the golden bat was sitting on the ground, clutching his right shoulder and rocking back and forth. He was also wearing a set of silver handcuffs.

"Skidmore shot him," Andrews explained.

What was left of my delirium cleared instantly.

"Help me up." I held out my hand to Andrews.

"Should he be lying down?" Andrews spoke, again, as if I were not present.

"I think you're not supposed to let them sleep when they hit their head," Skidmore answered, voice shaky. "Better let him get up."

I finally noticed that Skidmore had his pistol in his hand.

The cemetery was flooded with flashlights' pale fire; the moon had retreated behind a bank of black clouds. Aside from my two friends, I counted three more men in different uniforms, milling about us.

The killer was bent over not five feet from where I sat, his bat nowhere in sight.

Andrews offered his hand and I got myself to a standing posture, dizzy and more than a little confused.

"What happened?" I said it to no one in particular.

"Well," Andrews began immediately, anger rushing into his words, "the second you left me standing on the porch, I went into your kitchen and called our sheriffing buddy. He was almost as mad as I was when I told him you'd taken off after babbling about someone attacking you."

"And after what Crawdad told me about your conversation with Dan Battle," Skidmore went on, "I was pretty sure I knew what you were up to. And I told you that if you went anywhere without telling me that I would hunt you down with my pistol in my hand."

"You two figured out that the Cherokee artifact—"

"Listen." Skidmore's voice was a cold wall. "You spent most of your childhood avoiding the gossip in our little town, and I can understand that. But don't be so surprised when I tell you that I paid attention to it, and it's been one of the three or four most valuable tools I have in my current chosen profession. Stories about the Barnsley curse are famous all over this part of Georgia, and the role of the Cherokee in the curse is hardly a secret. Dan tells you that the thing your great-granddad bought here was a cursing tool, and it has to be put back where it belongs and I put two and two . . . damn it, Fever, you'd have to be a moron not to figure out where you were going tonight. You don't think I'm a moron, do you?"

His words were tight as a violin's E string, and just as ready to snap if they were played too hard.

"I don't think you're a moron," I answered softly, filling the syllables with a genuine astonishment at the question.

"Okay." His hands were shaking a little.

"Skidmore was at your house five minutes after I called him." Andrews was somehow talking to me as if I were a child. "And we were on the road a second later. His car can go really fast, and, you know, he's a policeman, so we weren't really worried about speeding. I'm surprised we didn't get here before you did."

Andrews was talking funny, clearly adrenaline-buzzed himself.

"So *everyone* knew where I was going tonight at the same time I was—wait." I started suddenly toward the path. "Dan Battle's down there in the water!"

One of the uniformed strangers responded.

"The man down in the well house? We've got someone with him, and we called the ambulance man."

"How is he?" I stared at the stranger.

The stranger shook his head; his face betrayed my worst fears.

"I have to go down there." I turned toward the path down the hill.

"You have to stay put and let these men take care of it!" Skidmore barked.

I was shocked by his vehemence.

"This man," Andrews said, pointing to the killer, "was standing over you with his cricket bat, about to make meat loaf out of your brains. Skidmore and I came up the path just in time, and Skidmore *shot* him."

Skidmore shot a man.

That's why Skidmore was so strange, of course. He wouldn't have hesitated in the heat of the moment, but he was a kind-enough soul to indulge in the shock of remorse afterward.

"Skidmore." I tried my best to get him to look into my eyes. "Jesus. Thank you."

"He saved your life." Andrews sounded only a little belligerent.

"I know." I nodded at Skidmore. "He's been saving my life in one way or another since I was nine years old."

Skid looked down at the graveyard dirt. I hoped he knew how I felt.

"So, Mr. It's All Chaos," Andrews chided, "what do you make of the timing of *this* little thing? I mean, you can't think it's only another instance of hazard. There's more to it than that and you know it. You'd be dead if it weren't for Skidmore and me—and something more than a meaningless series of random events."

Instead of pointing out the logical fallacies in his theory, as I would have at any other moment in my life, I was suddenly taken by the image of Dan Battle's spiderweb with a drop of water at every nexus, a human spirit at the junction of every strand.

But before I could elucidate my thoughts, the killer groaned, raised his head, and spoke—impossibly—with the perfectly British voice of Henry Higgins.

"He wouldn't actually be dead, you know." He smiled, an authentically meek expression. "I was only trying to frighten him."

Twenty-one

"I told you the killer was a Barnsley!" I exploded.

The killer reacted with equal force.

"A Barnsley!" He tried to stand, but the handcuffs made it difficult.

Skidmore raised his pistol.

"I don't want to shoot you again," Skid said calmly, "but I will do it if you can't calm down."

"He calls me a *Barnsley*!" the man howled.

"You're not?" I stammered.

"Barnsley" was all he would say.

"You are the one who killed Carl Shultz." I leveled a look at him that I hoped would eat his liver.

"It was a mistake," he moaned, collapsing even closer to the ground, closing his eyes. "That was just—he wanted to call off our deal."

Andrews and I exchanged looks; Skidmore still had his pistol trained on the man.

" 'Deal'?" Andrews mumbled.

I could hear sirens wailing faintly in the distance: the mourning of the dead.

"And you killed Dan Battle." I looked down the hill.

"Who?" The man looked startled.

"The person down in the water whose head you bashed."

"Oh." It was a hopeless sound.

He put his head in his hands, staring at the ground, and began to sob.

"That was an accident. I only wanted—"

But it seemed he could not articulate exactly what he had wanted to do.

"You only wanted to frighten him," I told him as viciously as I could, "the way you were trying to frighten me just now."

"But—"

"I have to get down there," I interrupted, standing as best I could. "Dan wouldn't be hurt—or dead—if it weren't for me."

"You're not going anywhere else tonight." Skidmore's voice was iron. "Sit down and let the medical people and the Barnsley Gardens crew do their jobs. If Dan Battle is dead, there's nothing you can do; if he's not, you'll only be in the way."

I didn't sit down, but I didn't argue, either. He was right.

"Is my fatalism rubbing off on you?" I asked him vaguely.

"Please sit down and shut up." But his voice was softer than before.

"Well, if no one else is going to ask," Andrews began, staring at the killer, "I suppose it's up to me. Who the hell are you and what are you doing in those shoes?"

The man sniffed and glanced at his shoes.

"These? I suppose I should have gotten substitutes where I found the rest of my disguise—at the Goodwill thrift store—but I'm a little fussy about footwear. I got these at Marks and Sparks."

"I told you!" Andrews gazed at me triumphantly.

"I thought it was Marks and Spencers," Skidmore said, at last holstering his gun.

"Marks and *Spencer,*" Andrews informed him, "no *s.* And some people used to call it Marks & Sparks in the old days. Don't know if they still do. Have I been away from England too long?"

"So, you're not bleeding that much," Skidmore said to the killer.

He went to the man and examined the wound on his shoulder. Blood had darkened the material of his coat where the bullet had torn away the seam at the shoulder. It appeared as if the bullet had not actually gone through the flesh, only glanced off it.

"And you don't appear to be in pain," Skid said almost to himself.

"I've had quite a lot to drink," the man admitted almost jovially. "I'm sure it'll feel much worse in the morning, if that makes you all feel any better."

"So I repeat," Andrews insisted, "*who the hell are you*?"

"Sorry," the man said immediately. "You did ask, didn't you. I'm Devin Briarwood."

My knees buckled and Andrews had to catch me to keep me from tumbling onto the ground.

"Dr. Briarwood, actually," the man went on casually. "University of Wales at Aberystwyth."

"Jesus Christ Mahoney," Andrews exploded, actually laughing right in my face. "He's one of yours!"

"I've spoken with your secretary," I said to Dr. Briarwood.

"I know." He responded distractedly, tilting his head at Andrews. "What does that man mean, 'He's one of yours'?"

Sirens were louder, and the tree frogs fell silent. Night doves had gone. Red man-made screaming filled the night instead.

"I think we'll only have time for the short version of the story," I said. "I have things to tell you; you have things to tell me. Fair enough?"

He nodded.

"Are you seated comfortably?"

He blinked.

"Then I'll begin." The sound of my voice was, once again, a stranger to me. "At the beginning of the last century, my great-grandfather fell in love with a woman in Ireland. He killed a man because of her and escaped to America. His name was Conner Briarwood."

If I'd hit the killer in the head with his own bat, I could not have stunned him more. His head twitched and his eyes were as large as the moon.

"You're one of Conner's brood?" he barely managed to say, not quite believing me. "How could I not have known that?"

"Because you're a loony?" Andrews offered disingenuously.

"I gather that when Conner came here," I went on, cold as the tombstone against which I was leaning, "he remained significantly incognito. He changed his name to Devilin and never contacted his family in Wales except through lawyers, who always used the name Conner *Briarwood*—not *Devilin.* But he had children and grandchildren, and, well, here I am. By the way, the trouble with your venom for the Barnsleys is that they are, in fact, our cousins or something. One of our kin sired the man who built that House of Usher up there." I glanced toward the Barnsley ruins.

"I know that." He could no longer look at me. "I know that."

"Then I think it's time for you to tell us a little something about yourself," I hissed, barely able to contain a burgeoning anger.

"Yes." He drew in a huge breath.

"Could you start with the difference between the way you were in Fever's house and the way you are now?" Andrews cocked his head. "I mean, then you were Quasimodo; now you're—"

"Dr. Jekyll." He smiled. "That's my secret power, actually. I could never have done the . . . the things I've done. Not if I hadn't adopted an alter ego. A Mr. Hyde—a Cro-Magnon persona. I am not, by nature, a violent man."

I could only picture the slavering madman who had stood over me with a club not five minutes before.

"In fact," he continued, voice tiny in the huge night, "I've always been accused of being a bit too mousy. Other professors at University were more aggressive, got promotions and tenure long before I did. Grants went to others, too. I languished. But there was one project no one could take from me, because it was mine in my bones—my life's work."

"The coin of Saint Elian." It wasn't a guess; I knew his obsession.

"My secretary told you, I assume. You must know that we were cheated, that the Barnsley scum rigged the race that lost us our coin."

"In fact, as I understand it, our ancestor tried that first. He knew a jockey, I believe. Your secretary told me quite a lot. But Barnsley found out about it and turned the tables."

"Yes!" the professor shouted. "That's how he won—by *cheating*! And then he took our coin!"

"Once again, I feel I must set the record straight." I plowed the air with my words. "Our fabled ancestor, who had cuckolded Barnsley in the first place, threw our coin at Barnsley and stalked away, cursing."

"And Barnsley kept it!" the professor blathered. "He kept what was mine!"

"Fever, stop." Andrews had realized what I already knew: that Professor Devin Briarwood was insane.

But I couldn't stop.

"And when Lady Eloise Barnsley lay dying in her seven-day labor, she repeated our family curse—and included us all: your family, my family, the sad residents of that foul heap there on the hill."

Moonlight seemed complicit with my poisoned thoughts, and it filled the ruins with shadows and ghosts of light, dancing together in the desiccated mansion.

"And what did Godfrey Barnsley bring with him to America? The way my great-grandfather brought his own shame with him when he ran from Ireland? A portrait of the woman who had cursed him, and a coin from the father he would never even meet—the only vestiges of parental evidence he would ever know."

"You have no idea how deliciously appropriate it all is," Professor Briarwood oozed. "The coin of Saint Elian—and it may well be the only one left in existence—was minted by us Briarwoods in silver in the sixteenth century to pay a monk to curse someone or other with the waters from Saint Elian's Well. That also belonged to us, the well. Oh, we made a pretty penny in those days. You see the beauty of that, in a story like this. My book—it'll be nothing short of sensational."

"But what your myopia won't allow you to see, apparently, is the value of the portrait Godfrey had."

"The portrait?" he sneered. "I know all about that. Rubbish. Had it appraised years ago. Gallery in London. Worthless."

"The Ashton Gallery," I confirmed slowly.

"Exactly," he insisted. "Worthless!"

I flashed a look at Andrews. "Want to see a magic trick?" I asked him.

"What?" Andrews may have been concerned about my mental stability. He was still trying to remember why the Ashton Gallery sounded familiar to him.

I turned back to Professor Briarwood. The air was filled with sirens; stabbing white headlights confused the darkness around the mansion.

"You're in quite a bit of trouble," I told the professor dryly. "Should I call your lawyer? Sheriff, do you happen to have Mr. Taylor's number with you?"

"Yes!" the professor replied at once, "call my lawyer, my American lawyer, Mr. Taylor! He'll tell you. I'm *not* a violent man. I'm a university professor—a research analyst. I'm working on a *book*!"

"See." I turned to Andrews slyly. "I pulled a lawyer out of a hat. And I believe said lawyer may also be an accomplice to fraud, embezzlement—even murder. Worst of all, of course, I can't stand the way he dresses."

"Preston Taylor is your lawyer?" Andrews stared at Briarwood.

"*Brinsley* Taylor," Briarwood corrected, "was the family lawyer in America. Had been for years."

"Because of Conner," I whispered to myself, but loudly enough for Andrews to hear. "I can't quite figure how, though."

"Wait." Andrews looked around as if someone else in the woods might have a clearer story. "Taylor?"

"Before we get too far away from something you said a second ago," Skidmore chimed in, "what was that you meant when you said that Mr. Shultz wanted to go back on your 'deal'?"

"Shultz, that fat bastard." Briarwood's energy had shifted again. "His father called me—I can't remember now, must have been fifteen years ago—with a wild story about a coin. He'd collected it in the Georgia mountains—in America—and when he'd done his research, he'd come across several of my articles about Saint Elian's coin, put two and two together. I disregarded it entirely then, because I was convinced that the coin was still in Derbyshire, the ancestral home of the Barnsleys. It couldn't possibly have gotten to America. Spent several years in England chasing rainbows there. Long years, you understand, that brought me to nothing, to a dead end."

"Hence the shoes, however," Andrews whispered.

"Dead end." Briarwood's voice was beginning to sound a bit singsong. "Went back to university without a thing to show. Oh, no one said much, but I knew what they were thinking."

"The deal with Shultz," Skidmore prodded.

"Carl Shultz," Briarwood snarled immediately, "knew all there was to know about the coin long before he visited you a few days ago. He was only supposed to find out from you how, exactly, it got to America, and who sold it to his father. I was paying him a good bit of money. I bought the coin from him, of course—gave him extra to help me. A great part of my book, you see, would be the amazing voyage of the coin across the ocean. That's what I was paying him for, and that's all he was supposed to do. But he couldn't even manage it. He wanted to call off our deal. He wanted me to leave off. He *liked* you, he said. Told me to take the coin and shove off. We argued. I didn't mean to kill him. It was— Call my lawyer; he'll tell you I'm not a violent man. And anyway, there was no real reason to—he needn't have made me kill at all. I had other contingencies, other ways of getting you to tell me the story." Briarwood looked up at us with the grinning mask of lunacy, eyes nearly rolled back in his head, crooked teeth poking through the curve of his chalky lips. "I still do." He had lost most of his humanity in that instant.

"Hey," Skidmore spoke up, startling everyone. "It nearly got out of my head with all that's going on. I believe he's talking about that Detective Huyne."

Andrews and I both turned slowly to look at Skidmore. His eyebrows were arched and his eyes were bright.

"Huyne and his buddy?" Skid went on. "They aren't Atlanta detectives after all. I mean, there actually is a Detective Huyne in Atlanta, but he's retired. The guy that was in your house? He was a private investigator hired by this man, Briarwood. Apparently, the plan was to scare you with the idea of arresting you for murder and getting the story of the coin out of you, far as I can put it all together. I went to arrest the Huyne imposter. He's vanished."

"How on earth did you—" I couldn't finish the question.

"Simple, really. This Huyne didn't have any paperwork, didn't really seem right to me in the first place, so I called Atlanta." Skid sniffed.

"Unbelievable." I blew out a breath. "You really are good at what you do."

"I am," he confirmed. "By the way, there is no Shultz senior anymore. He's been dead for a while. The man that was dead in your house? He's all there was."

"Then why would he say—" It was Andrews's turn to pose an unfinished question.

"When a guy wants to buy a cow or a car or something important like that," Skidmore answered philosophically, "it's an advantage if he can say it's for someone else. 'I'm not asking for myself, you understand; this is for a friend.' Puts him in a better bargaining position."

"What are you saying?" Briarwood demanded. "Speak up. I can't hear you. These damned sirens. What are they? What did you say about Huyne?"

"This is— How did you—," I stuttered.

"You have to finish one of these sentences pretty soon," Skidmore told me, highly amused. "But as long as I have you confused, let me just tell you also that your family in the old country—the Briarwoods in Wales?—they're rich as all get-out. If Conner had stayed in touch with them, and you'd got your due, I expect you'd be telling your problems to the Rockefellers instead of me and June Cotage. Which, if you don't mind my saying, would probably have been an all-around good deal for everybody."

"That's how this maniac could afford to do everything he was doing," Andrews said.

"Bingo." Skidmore took ahold of Briarwood's elbow. "Let's get on up now. We got to put you in my police car."

"Wait," I said instantly, scrambling. "I have a thousand more questions to ask."

"Preston Taylor is your family lawyer?" Andrews asked Briarwood. He seemed a page or two behind.

"Brinsley Taylor, actually, started our dealings here in America. He was the founder of that firm. When Conner went to him for help, that Mr. Taylor did a bit of checking up, discovered the Briarwoods of Wales—and our money. He got in touch with us, never telling us about Conner, never telling Conner about us, as I have recently discovered. But his firm has handled many of our holdings in America since then, and it's been mutually beneficial, so Bob's your uncle at least in that regard. It seemed a nice nip of serendipity. But Preston Taylor's my man now. And I'm his client."

" 'Bob's your uncle,' " Andrews pointed out, grinning.

I ignored Andrews. "That's why Taylor lied about Shultz's phone call. He didn't know that Huyne was a fake?"

"What would that have got me?" Briarwood asked. "Huyne's a private investigator; he found Shultz for me, and then he found you, too. He didn't know that you were a Briarwood, though. That might have changed things a bit. Wish he'd dug that up. Doesn't seem as if it would have been so difficult to—"

"You and Shultz were in league?" Andrews couldn't believe it. "And there is no Mr. Shultz senior?"

"Well," Briarwood allowed as Skidmore pulled him to his feet, "obviously there was a Mr. Shultz senior at some time or other. I mean, he did buy the coin from someone here in Georgia, in these mountains. We still don't know who?"

I shook my head.

"Honestly?" he insisted.

"What would be the point of keeping it from you now?" I asked.

"No point, I suppose." He winced.

His shoulder was beginning to sting. The blood had dried a bit, and might have irritated the wound.

"And you hired Shultz just to—what? Get a good story?" Andrews pulled on his earlobe.

"There's a world of difference," Briarwood lectured, irritated, "between a *good story* and a complete history of the facts. But if the two are married, well, then you have a book that someone might publish, and that could get you noticed at your university. Could just put you on the old map."

I could hear people rushing up the hill toward us. Paramedics, I assumed.

"Why would that matter?" Andrews asked, absolutely amazed. "You can't have needed the money, can you?"

"Did you go to England to direct at the Globe," I asked Andrews quietly, "just to ensure the two percent annual raise at your university? There's more to this sort of thing than a little bit of money."

"Well." He looked away.

"Come on," Skidmore said softly, pulling on Briarwood's good elbow. "We'll ask a whole lot more questions after we've seen to your gunshot."

"I just—I still don't quite understand," Andrews said, coming to stand next to me.

Paramedics had topped the rise and now rushed toward Briarwood. One of them examined the wound, and the professor gave a low moan. There was a bit of discussion about the stretcher going down and up the hills, but it was determined that Briarwood should walk—better for everyone.

One of the men who had hauled the stretcher up looked over at Andrews and me. "Is one of you name of Fever?" he asked.

I blinked. "Yes."

"That man down there in the—whatever that is, the pond, I reckon—he's asking for you."

"Dan's alive?"

I shot toward the downhill path.

Dan was lying on a stretcher in the back of an ambulance. There was an access road behind the mansion that ended in a patch of dried leaves below the gazebo.

He saw me coming up the steps from the well house.

"Good," he called out strongly. "You didn't die. I didn't think you would."

"Okay." I was trying to catch my breath. "But I thought you were dead."

"Me? Not tonight. I have too many things to do this week. Maybe I could schedule it sometime in November—that's pretty free at the moment."

I made it to the ambulance and sat on the back, almost eye level with Dan.

"How's your head?" I leaned against the inside of the ambulance.

"Hurts," he grunted. "Last thing I remember is going down into the water face-first. I guess you turned me over and dragged me into the reeds. That's where I came to."

"Sorry I couldn't stay with you," I said between breaths. "I was trying to stay away from the man with the bat."

"Is that what he hit me with, a baseball bat?"

"Cricket bat."

"No kidding. Where'd he get a thing like that?"

"England."

"Yeah. They got that sort of thing over there."

"They do." I smiled. "I'm really glad you're all right."

"Look." He turned serious very suddenly. "They're about to cart me off to a hospital against my will, and I told them I had to talk to you before they could take me. They didn't like it, so I'd better make this quick. We did a good job, you and I, and the curse is gone. Nice work. I wanted you to know that we really did a great thing tonight, and it was important to me."

"I'm not sure why." I said it as gently as I could.

"Listen." He struggled up on one elbow and leaned closer to me. "You can say this thing with the Barnsley family is bad luck, or karma, or physics. It doesn't matter to me what you call it. Some people seem to have been dealt a strange hand, and that strangeness follows them wherever they go. I believe the Barnsley family was cursed because they used cursed water from a sacred spring when they shouldn't have, and I believe that you and I lifted that curse tonight. I also believe that our activity was a part of a larger pattern, a participation in the Divine Mind. My impression is that you believe it was just another strange event in a random array of happenings in your life, and that's okay by me. But I'm going to the hospital with a cracked head, and I'm very content because of what I believe. You're going home to your nice little house in relative health, and you don't seem all that content to me. So whose system is better, yours or mine?"

"Well, first," I said hesitantly, "I wouldn't call what I have a *system.* It's more along the lines of a *mess;* second, I'm not the sort of person who can just say, 'Oh, you're right, I do believe in magic.' I need evidence. And third, *your* system is better. Much better. And I'm sick with envy, wishing it could be mine."

"I see." He laid back down on the stretcher.

"It isn't that I don't—," I began.

"That's all right, Fever." Dan nodded gently. "It's your choice to suffer; be sick with envy. If that's what makes you happy, who am I to intrude?"

"If it makes me happy? It doesn't— Listen, if you think you're finally going to get away with dispensing the Cherokee philosophy—" I wanted to make light of what he'd been saying.

He was willing to oblige.

"I don't know why you always think that." He grinned. "What I just told you? That's from Krishnamurti."

The engine of the ambulance fired up. The paramedic who had

told me Dan wanted to speak with me came to the back and motioned for me to get out.

"I'll visit you in the hospital," I told Dan over the sound of the engine.

"Don't bother." He closed his eyes. "I'll be home tomorrow. Visit me there."

The ambulance doors slammed shut and the siren revved up; moments later the red taillights were lost around a corner of the haunted mansion, and Dan was gone.

Andrews came up beside me.

"Your friend's okay?" He stared at the spot where the ambulance had disappeared.

"Yes."

"Skidmore got Dr. Freakazoid into the police car. He was still raving about his *book.* Skid didn't want to let the man out of his sight, so he's following the ambulance to take Briarwood to the hospital. I'm riding back with you."

"Good." I looked at his profile. "Hey?"

"Mmm," he answered, obviously exhausted.

"You were like the cavalry tonight," I told him softly. "I'd be very unhappy or dead if your timing hadn't been so perfect."

"Those are the perimeters? Unhappy to dead?" He smiled. "I know you were on the ground and he was on top of you, but you can be pretty mean when you're backed into a corner. I didn't count you out when I saw that. I actually thought Skid overreacted. It's my belief that a single cricket bat hasn't got a chance in hell against that titanium cranium of yours. Besides, Skidmore's the cavalry. I'm the sidekick."

He yawned.

"I'm pretty tired, too," I admitted.

"I haven't slept in days." He looked around. "Where's your truck? I'm ready to go home."

"Up there." I raised my head in the direction of the business offices of Barnsley Gardens.

We started around the hill, skirting the edge of the mansion.

Inside the walls, moonlight played; somewhere white nicotiana was blooming, moonlight's perfect sensory metaphor, making each breath an ecstasy. Crickets and tree frogs rattled the air once more; the worst of the charcoal clouds had blown to the east, and the sky was clear. A crisp breeze rattled the first bare limbs of the season. I finally realized it had been cold all evening, and I thought that summer might be gone at long last.

When we wake up in the morning, I thought, autumn will surely have arrived.

Twenty-two

Our sky the next day was so hard and blue that it cracked the sun and light poured over everything. There didn't seem to be a shadow anywhere on the planet. The air outside my bedroom window was so clear in my first waking moments that I thought someone had come in during the night and taken out all the glass. When I tossed off the blankets, I shivered—and was delighted by it. The spine of Summer's book had been broken for the last time; that story was done, time to set it aside. Open the new one, turn the first page, white as frost, in the book of Autumn.

Out of bed, bare feet on the cold floor, every breath like a cracking apple, I went to the window and stared out. There it was: the first moment of fall.

"Andrews!" I called. "Are you awake?"

I glanced at the clock. It was nearly one o'clock. I'd slept in my clothes again and really wanted a shower.

A weak groan from the other room was my only answer at first, then: "I'm starved! Miss Etta's!"

Andrews was hungry: the dew of normalcy had refreshed the leaves of grass, and all was right with the world.

"What day is this?" I couldn't take my eyes off all the sunlight over the rims of the mountains.

"No idea." He yawned.

"It's just that if today is Monday—and I'm very afraid that it is—Miss Etta's might be closed."

"Tragedy strikes," he mumbled, coming to my doorway.

He had slept in his clothes, too, and he looked like he'd been in a hurricane.

"Not as badly as you might think." I rubbed my face. "If I call June right this second, she might have us over for dinner. Hek doesn't usually get home until about two o'clock from his services; we'll be right on time."

"He has services on Monday?"

"He has services *every* day." I rubbed my forehead. "And when he comes home, they have their big meal."

"Isn't it a bit—sounds rude: 'Oh, hello, can we come to dinner?' "

"The beauty of June's hospitality," I informed him, "is that she thinks it's rude when I *don't* come to dinner."

"But I mean, will she have made enough food?"

"She's a southern woman. She's cooked for ten."

"Go to the phone *now*." Andrews stepped aside.

June knew there was more to my call than a visit for dinner. I hadn't been to their house for a meal in months. She suspected that I had something to tell her, something to ask her; both. Andrews had wanted to leave right away, but I prevailed upon him to shower, shave, and attire himself in something other than a wrinkled Hawaiian shirt. When I explained to him that dinner would not begin until Hek arrived, he grumbled his way into cleanliness.

We were out the door by two o'clock, dressed as nicely as the likes of us ever did: I in the only pale blue stay-pressed dress shirt I owned and Andrews in a polo shirt the color of a pistachio nut. We climbed into the truck and were on our way.

The day, against any calendar evidence, did actually seem the first of fall. Overnight, the leaves had begun, just barely, to blush and bronze. It was unusual enough for Andrews to notice about halfway through the short drive.

"A little early for autumn in Georgia, isn't it?" He yawned, mesmerized by the long valleys he could see out his window.

"It is," I agreed. "But sometimes the weather conforms to a certain spirit abroad in the land."

"What the hell are you saying?" He turned from the scenic splendor to my profile. "You can't go around talking in metaphysical clichés just because a scary man from the Celtic side of your family hit you in the head."

"He didn't hit me in the head. I fell on a gravestone. And I only mean that it's time for summer to be over; it's time for a better season."

"All right." He wasn't convinced that I hadn't slipped a cog. "By the way, listen to what I came up with in the shower. I think Professor Briarwood may be to his little village in Wales what Fever Devilin is to Blue Mountain."

"Shut up."

"Seems clear to me."

As it happened, I struggled a bit with his comparison, but I thought I mustered a fine response—more than enough to invalidate his proposition.

"Except that I never traveled to another country," I responded, diction crisp as ice, "to kill a man."

"Point taken," he conceded, "but there he is, a nutty professor type, folkloring his way though the rye, and a bit obsessed with his family."

"Point in your favor," I acknowledged.

"Or several."

"*And,*" I said, topping him, "I realize that his psychosis is clear evidence that I come by my strangeness at least in part through the courtesy of genetics."

"Those little bastards," Andrews mumbled.

"What?"

"Genes," he said, mocking me. "You can't escape them. I myself am doomed by the demon of grand breeding—a damnable heritage of beauty. There is no escape."

"I'm thinking of pushing you out of the truck," I offered casually.

"Wouldn't do you any good," he chattered on. "I was also born lucky."

"Lucky someone hasn't thrown you from a speeding truck already."

"See?"

Hek and June's house swung into view around the long curve in the road, and I slowed me down.

Their stark white house was a beacon against the black bottom soil, backed by three mountains. Everything about the place, as I had often observed, had an angel's attention. Clear sunlight washed the tin roof. The air was new, lighter than summer air, and I imagined that I could smell the chicken roasting in June's oven as we pulled off the road and headed toward the front porch.

June appeared in the doorway before the truck engine was off, neck to knee in a flower-print apron, wooden spoon in hand. White hair haloed her head, and her eyes were like candlelight.

"Get on into this house," she demanded. "I'm so proud you could come for dinner.

"She's happy to see us," Andrews marveled.

"I told you."

I was on the porch in five steps. June moved aside. Even given the heartfelt joy she and I were both experiencing at the prospect of dining together, there was no maudlin physicalization, no outward and visible sign of an inward and spiritual feeling.

Andrews barged in, drawn by the delectable seduction of cornbread dressing and sweet onions.

"Your timing is perfect." June steered between us toward the kitchen. "Hek's home and washing up."

"I can't tell you how much I'm looking forward to this meal," Andrews intoned as if he were in church.

"Now," June demurred, "we don't have much to eat."

That disclaimer, I knew, was obligatory, a bizarre example of modest manners from a bygone era.

A single step past the threshold of the kitchen door revealed the truth: a table so laden with earthly delights that not a centimeter of surface was visible. A tablecloth made from exactly the same material as June's apron hung nearly to the floor, and June had set out her wedding china—a gift from her mother—which was certainly a hundred years old. Considering that I was capable of breaking at least a plate a week in my own home, I had always appreciated the fact that June had kept these dishes sparklingly clean her entire marriage without ever so much as scratching the delicate golden pattern around the edge. Four large dinner plates were stacked at the head of the table, where Hek would sit.

I thought Andrews might pass out.

"You said it was only chicken and dressing."

He couldn't take his eyes off the pork roast. It was covered with an arranged pattern of baked apples and looked more like a gallery piece than an item of food.

"June's eyes danced, though her mouth remained a straight line, "Well, I always cook a little extra, just in case."

She stepped to the oven, opened it, and drew out a long golden baking dish.

"Here's the dressing."

White steam rose up like the sigh of a sleeping child.

Andrews may have had tears in his eyes.

Hek sauntered into the room, rubbing his belly.

"My, don't all this look good," he said, staring at the table with the same abandon as Andrews.

Without ceremony, we all sat. Hek's grace was a single sentence.

"Lord, let us take from Junie's food all the love she put into it."

He immediately began to carve, first the roast, then the chicken. Everyone got equal portions of everything, and plates were passed around. For the rest of the bounty, we were on our own—field peas, boiled new potatoes with fresh parsley, baby pattypan squash that looked like white flying saucers, raw spinach mixed with quartered hard-boiled eggs and bacon, crisp sugar snap peas salted and buttered. I knew that everything on the table had come directly or very recently from Hek and June's garden, including the bird and roast.

For a while, there was no talking. It would have been unimaginably rude to try to wedge words between the diner and the dinner.

But just as Andrews began to reach for seconds of half the items on the table, I managed my first strategic shot.

"So, we found the person who killed that man Shultz in my house the other night."

Of course it was awkward and obvious, but they'd been expecting something, and I wanted to give them a sense of my own discomfort.

"You'll never guess who he was," I went on. "A family member. Distant. He was a Briarwood from Wales. Looking for that coin we talked about."

Hek nodded. June got up from the table under the pretense of fetching the pitcher of iced tea. Andrews stared at me as if I had strangled a kitten at the table, angry that I was wrecking the pristine beauty of the meal.

In the ensuing silence, I could hear the oven timer ticking. It meant that June's dessert was still cooking—blueberry cobbler was my guess. I waited a moment, taking in everyone's discomfort.

"He'd been hunting down that coin for decades," I went on, taking a bite of chicken, "because it was something of a family heirloom, as it turns out. Minted in the 1600s by our brood in Wales. It may well be the only one of its kind left in existence. He seemed to think it was priceless. So I was thinking, now that everything is over, you wouldn't mind telling me who sold that coin to Mr. Shultz's father all those years ago."

I was absolutely certain that they knew.

"Well . . ." June looked out her kitchen window.

Hek had stopped shoveling food onto his fork.

"A man was killed in my home because of it." It came out of my mouth with a much harsher sound than I thought it was going to.

Hek set down his fork; June nodded.

"You were off at college when your daddy died," June began. "I don't know what I expected from your mother—she was so strange.

Maybe I thought it wouldn't bother her. She didn't live with your daddy no more, and, you know, what with her ways—"

My mother had not been faithful to my father, perhaps, ever in their marriage—that's what June meant by "her ways" I should have known at that moment where the story was headed, but the truth was invisible to me, the way family truths often were. And I was slow-witted from a long night's sleep.

"Only she fell apart." June looked into the porcelain sink as if she might have lost something there. "I reckon she wasn't quite so hard a woman as . . . as some used to think."

June meant herself, of course.

"She come over here," Hek said, continuing the story while looking at his plate, "busted up. You know, your daddy just closed his eyes and went to sleep when he passed on. He give not a warning nor a word of farewell. Just left."

His final vanishing act, I thought.

"I can understand why you would have been surprised by her emotional response," I began.

"I don't need your help with this," Hek snapped. "Do you want to hear what was said, or not?"

Clearly Hek had something to say that was difficult for him, and he didn't want to be interrupted.

I nodded.

"She come over here busted up is what I'm saying." He tapped the tabletop for emphasis. "But a part of it was about money."

"She was worried about the funeral expense," June added.

"The short of it is this: She'd heard Conner talk about the things he'd bought at the auction and—"

"At the Barnsley estate," I said, interrupting pointedly.

Hek drew in a breath.

"So you know about that's where the auction was," June pronounced. "Good."

"I spent last night at the Barnsley estate," I explained, "trying to keep the man who killed Shultz from killing me, too."

"So there's more to the story." Hek was impatient with me.

"Sorry." I didn't sound it.

"Your mother knew from Conner that the things he'd bought at auction were worth something. The picture painting had already been sold, you know, for your schooling; the other thing, the Cherokee cross, she was scared of that."

"Made my father bury it in the backyard, as it turns out," I said.

"If you keep interrupting me," he warned.

I nodded, held a finger to my lips.

"Only thing left was the coin."

Stupidly, it was not until then that I realized where he was going. I had a sudden catch in my throat, like a hand choking my neck.

"Wait."

But Hek ignored me.

"She found it in that old trunk of your great-grandfather's, put advertisements in some of these newspapers, and sold it to that man from Atlanta."

"Jesus Christ!" Andrews exploded. "Your *mother* sold the coin?"

It seemed obvious now that it was out in the open.

"Son!" Hek rose out of his seat. "You blaspheme in this house and I get my shotgun on you!"

"Oh." Andrews was stunned by Hek's vehemence. "Right. You're a preacher. Sorry a thousand times. I—I have absolutely no manners and ought not to be allowed to roam freely."

"Hek," June said soothingly, "it most likely come as a shock, your news." She lowered her voice. "And you know that boy's from over there in England," she added, as if that were the perfect excuse for all of the patented Andrews foibles.

But it worked on Hek. He sat back down, even if his face was a little flushed.

"Your mother sold the coin," he concluded, as if no one else had yet thought of it.

"She only thought she'd get funeral money," June concluded. "But that man give her five thousand dollars, she said."

"That was about the last time we seen her, your mother." Hek nodded once, his benediction, and went back to work on the field peas.

"Her final words at the funeral were words of anger," June said softly. "Some people are that way about death—mad at the one who's gone. Last thing I heard her to say was to call your father a bad name."

"A curse," Andrews said softly to himself.

"And of course at that point," I murmured, looking directly at Andrews, "she was a widow."

Skid called not long after Andrews and I got home from Hek and June's. Professor Briarwood was being held in the hospital's psychiatric ward. Apparently, his Mr. Hyde persona had interfered with an emergency room doctor's care. Burly orderlies were dispensed; Briarwood was sedated.

The man calling himself Detective Huyne, along with his friend, had checked out of the Mountain Vista Hotel in Pine City and had disappeared. Skid was pursuing the issue, but he held little hope of finding the false policemen, given the limited resources of a small-town sheriff's office.

I asked if he knew anything more about lawyer Taylor. Skid told me that Taylor had filed half a dozen legal documents to block anyone, myself included, from ever looking at Briarwood or Devilin files in his office. If I wanted to fight him, of course, I could. I would eventually prevail, but it would be a considerable battle. The primary ingredient in a successful legal war of that sort, Skid reminded me, was always funding. Taylor had it; I didn't. And Taylor's bid for governor was proceeding very nicely, so he had every reason to keep me from exposing his foibles. Skid concluded by suggesting I let it rest, then telling me to fix my living room window.

So Andrews and I spent a bit of time covering said broken window with plywood and also looking at the damaged lock on my door. They both would be properly repaired later in the week; our stopgap measures would hold for a day or two.

As the sun was going down, we sat in the kitchen, deliberately talking about nothing—bad movies we loved, good books we hated, people we thought were funny. Anything to avoid a reexamination of recent events.

I knew Andrews wanted to go home, but I was glad he was going to stay one more night.

Just as I was about to tell him so, I noticed a strange shift in the shadows behind my house—a pattern of light like a giant swan in the pine trees. I squinted into the woods, and the image came clearer. I only saw her for a moment, through a hard slant of white from the setting sun, but there she was: the woman from the Cotman portrait, Eloise Barnsley. She was wandering slowly around the perimeter of my house, so pale that she was nearly transparent. I instantly thought of the Welsh story of the Widow of the Swans, the enchanted woman who outlived everything she loved.

Before I could make my voice work to alert Andrews, she was swallowed by the darker leaves; gone into the first black of night. But he could see my face, and noticed the odd expression there.

"Fever?" Andrews stared into my eyes, then over his shoulder out the kitchen window. "What is it?"

"I saw Eloise Barnsley." I could barely form the words.

"Oh." He relaxed, turning back toward me. "Jesus. The way you looked, I thought maybe Professor Bizarro had escaped from the hospital and was out there in your yard. Gave me a bit of a startle. Your imagination is going to be the death of you *and* me."

"I saw her."

"Which, you realize, is completely impossible, right?"

I looked down at my fingers. They were shaking.

"Right," I admitted.

"What you saw, boy-o," he intoned, "was an echo of the past few days. And I guess I can't fault you for that."

"Maybe."

"Look," he said, trying to explain, "it's all part of a kind of pattern, the way the mind— no, wait, you're the one who doesn't believe in patterns."

"Please shut up."

"What's your take, then? What *did* you just see? And please don't feed me a ghost story. I'm already full."

"I don't know."

"All right, I'll give it another go." He rubbed his face with both hands. "I think you were quite taken with the tale of your ancestor and Lady Barnsley, and then you fell in love with the portrait you saw in Atlanta. I watched it happen on your face while you were looking at it. That image is wandering around in your *brain,* not your yard."

"Maybe."

For some reason, I had a fleeting thought of the coin hidden upstairs in my mother's room, a silver ghost of the moon, just waiting there. I wondered when someone would ask me about it and want to know where it was. Maybe, I thought, I could use it to buy the portrait of Lady Barnsley; hang it in my living room. Maybe that was all she wanted: for her portrait to be back among family.

Andrews mistook my musing.

"Okay, then." He sighed, exasperated beyond measure. "What do you think it is? You're obviously dying to tell me."

I rallied, sipped a quick breath.

"Something much more frightening than a ghost story."

"Oh for God's sake."

"What if a curse actually has its own kind of energy field? And what if we take quantum physics seriously?"

"What if we do?" He was irritated because he couldn't see where I was going.

"Suppose a curse is like all other energy: It can't be created or destroyed; it can only change form. Suppose the curse that Dan and I lifted last night isn't really gone— or what if the rage Lady Barnsley let loose is still floating somewhere in the air? They've only changed form and are wandering now, looking for somewhere else to land."

I thought of where I'd been when the events of the previous few days had begun: engaged in useless pursuit, moving rocks up a hill and sweating in September heat.

"You mean you think that the form of some curse has found its way to your house," Andrews asked, "and is wandering in those woods? God, but you're a hopeless wretch. I give up. You can believe all that—if it makes you happy."

He shook his head. It was the face of Dr. Andrews but the voice of Dan Battle.

And the voice may have caused me to have a small epiphany. I was forced to consider that although it was clearly possible to see the events of this world as a series of chaotic, unrelated moments, maybe there was another possibility.

What if I *did* take new physics seriously? In Einstein's universe, the reality of an event depends entirely on the person who sees it happen. The observer *makes* the observation.

And if that were true, I thought, then it might be possible for me to see the events of this world the way Dan might, as a completely interdependent web of relationships, where everything relied on a kind of miracle of perfect connection.

"Maybe," I began slowly, as if conceding some long-battled game, "if I'm the observer of my own life, I have a choice. I can see my existence as a meaningless mess, or I can see it as a constant miracle."

"Right," Andrews responded hesitantly, staring into my eyes, still not certain where I was going.

"So I suppose I have to ask myself this: If it is up to me how I see everything, then what kind of world do I want to live in—a rocky place that's empty of significance, or a green place filled with wonder?"

But before I could finish the thought, my eyes widened and I blinked back what I was seeing in the woods outside my kitchen window.

Thank God Andrews turned around just in time to see it, too: a huge white swan bursting from the shadows and rowing upward toward the autumn sky.